FOR K... AND COUNTRY

SAS
OPERATION

For King and Country

DAVID MONNERY

HARPER

Harper
An imprint of HarperCollins*Publishers*
1 London Bridge Street,
London SE1 9GF
www.harpercollins.co.uk

This paperback edition 2016
1

First published by 22 Books/Bloomsbury Publishing plc 1997

A catalogue record for this book
is available from the British Library

ISBN: 978 0 00 815554 4

Set in Sabon by Born Group using Atomik ePublisher from Easypress

Printed and bound in Great Britain

MIX
Paper from
responsible sources
www.fsc.org **FSC C007454**

1

Italy, January 1944

The SAS men sat in two rows, facing each other across the empty belly of the rumbling Halifax. It was almost eleven o'clock on the night of 19 January 1944, and these eight soldiers had been entrusted with Operation Jacaranda, the destruction of a railway bridge across the River Potenza just outside the small town of San Severino in eastern central Italy. In just over fifty-five hours 50,000 Allied troops would be attempting a landing on the Anzio peninsula just south of Rome, and this was one of several SAS parties that were being parachuted in to disrupt the inevitable German attempts at reinforcement. There were only a few rail routes across the ridge of mountains which formed Italy's backbone, and cutting any or all of these would hinder any shift of German forces from the east coast to the west.

The eight men were dressed in camouflage Denison smocks, khaki trousers and heavy boots. The 1937-pattern webbing pouches around their waists held ammunition for the holstered Webley .455 revolvers and directional compasses. Jump helmets and silenced models of the Sten sub-machine-gun sat in each lap. Variety could only be found in bodily posture, facial expression and the colours of the berets stuffed through the epaulettes of the smocks. Five of these were beige, reflecting a preponderance of SAS veterans, the other three the newly adopted maroon.

Ten minutes earlier the air had been full of shouted jokes, but the proximity of the drop zone had reduced them all to silence.

Captain Julian Morgan, 'Jools' as he'd been known since prep school, looked the most relaxed. He seemed to be grinning at some private joke as he pushed back the flop of blond hair which was forever falling over his left eye, but he was just tracing his own progress from service in India through the excitements of North Africa and Sicily to this imminent descent on the Italian mainland. There had been moments of terror and moments of sadness – enough SAS pioneers had died in the desert – but deep down he knew he was having the time of his life.

On the seat beside him was Sergeant Morrie Beckwith, his dark face as stern as ever. He was thinking, as he always did at such moments, of his wife Margie back in Wolverhampton, and worrying over what would become of her and the children if something happened to him. He told himself, as he'd frequently told her, that he was much safer in the SAS than he would have been catching artillery in the infantry, torpedoes in the Navy or flak in the Air Force, but he didn't believe it any more than she had.

On his left, Trevor Corrigan was finding it hard to sit still. His body was telling him he needed a crap, but since he'd had one just before setting off he was inclined to think that his body was having him on. He tried to concentrate on the girl he'd met in the Salerno café two nights ago, but conjuring up a picture of her was easier than holding on to it, and in the end he just let her go and sat there farting quietly, willing the journey to be over.

Last in line on that side of the Halifax, Roger Imrie was also contemplating his first drop behind enemy lines with dry mouth and whirring brain. He was worried he would let the others down, worried about how his mother would cope on the farm if something happened to both him and his bomber-pilot brother, worried that his parachute would fail to open. He'd always thought that that would be the worst kind of death, just falling and falling, with all that time to think about it, until you were splattered all over the ground.

Sitting opposite Imrie, Lieutenant Robert Farnham noticed the spasm of fear which leapt across the younger man's face, and knew that he was imagining the worst in one form or another. He could remember doing the same himself, but these days his quiet and watchful countenance reflected a genuine calmness within. Since Catherine's death in 1940 – she had been killed in their country cottage when a London-bound German pilot had decided to dump his bombs and run rather than look for a real target – his own life had become almost a matter of indifference to him. He wanted to kill Germans and he wanted to win the war, but the edge of caution which came with having someone else to live for had been dulled. His sister, Eileen, would no doubt miss him, but probably not for long. Another couple of years and she'd meet and marry some nice young survivor.

The man next to Farnham looked equally unperturbed by the prospect of imminent action, but then not much ever seemed to worry Corporal Neil Rafferty. If his face wasn't sporting its habitual innocent smile, it would be wearing its current air of good-natured puzzlement. At this moment he was thinking about the two officers and how different they were, and wondering whether he felt more comfortable with Farnham's cool serious-ness or the more popular Morgan's dashing enthusiasm.

Such thoughts were far from Ian Tobin's mind. He was thinking, as usual, about sex. When he wasn't thinking about it he was worrying that he thought about it too much, and when he did think about it he found it disturbing that he could think about it with anyone, and not just with Megan, even though he was sure he really loved her. At the moment he was most concerned at the thought that he might die a virgin, without having it off with anyone. He and Megan had agreed to wait until they were married, but at times like this he couldn't help thinking that the man sitting on his left had a surer handle on what was really important.

Mickie McCaigh was also thinking about sex, reliving the moment two nights earlier when Lucia had flicked aside the shoulder strap on her dress and revealed that she was wearing nothing underneath. Her breasts had been so damned perfect, and the way she had arched herself back over the end of the bed . . . He sighed and tried to think about something else, not wanting to leave the plane with a throbbing erection, and smiled as he remembered his father's last words of advice. 'You'll probably have to kill a few men,' the old man had told him, 'so make sure you make love to even more women. It's the only way to hang on to your marbles.'

McCaigh was doing his best – in fact, so far he was well ahead – and he had a sneaking suspicion the old man had been right. It was all completely crazy anyway – jumping out of a plane over Italy because some jumped-up little twerp in Germany had invaded Poland five years ago – but he was seeing the world and its women, and he felt as sane as he ever had.

* * *

The dispatcher opened the bomb bay, adding the howl of the wind to the rumble of the plane's engines, and the eight men got to their feet. With the padded helmets on and the Stens slung across their backs they fixed the static lines to the suggested points on the fuselage and double-checked that they were secure – in Africa, during the formative months of the SAS, several men had fallen to their deaths when chutes failed to open.

The wait for the word to go seemed endless, but finally the lights changed colour, the dispatcher mouthed 'good luck' to the lead jumper and almost shoved him through the hole. The other seven followed in quick succession, for even an extra second's delay could land someone out of sight of the man in front, and the moon had already disappeared behind a thickening layer of cloud. It was going to be dark on the ground.

The eight ghostly shapes drifted down, each man concentrating on keeping himself balanced as his eyes sought definition in the darkness below. The landing zone, according to the briefer back in Salerno, was mainly bare plateau, but the 'mainly' was worrying, and no one wanted to be the odd man out, landing in the only tree for miles around and breaking his neck.

In the lead position Morgan saw the ground suddenly rise up to meet him, and just about had time to appreciate the lack of trees – the intelligence gathered from an Italian restaurant-owning family in Soho had obviously been accurate – before his feet were touching down on a gently sloping section of the plateau. He went into the roll, and was on his feet again almost instantly, pulling in the billowing chute like a fisherman gathering a net.

As expected, the clouds were thick enough to render the moon almost irrelevant, and visibility was severely limited.

From where Morgan stood he couldn't see much more than a football pitch's worth of sloping grass, interspersed with outcrops of rock. He hoped no one would be landing on one of those.

No sooner had this thought flashed through his mind than a metallic crash echoed across the plateau.

Morgan started walking back down the line of descent, half dragging and half carrying the bundled chute, compass in hand. At least his sense of direction hadn't deserted him. He was walking south, as his instinct had told him he was. On a clear day, or even a clear night, he would have been able to see the Adriatic some thirty miles away to the left, the snow-covered peaks of the Monti Sibillini some fifteen miles in front of him, but at this particular moment the known world was about a hundred yards in diameter, and seemed to be shrinking.

The noise had been made by Corrigan, who had landed on grass but rolled into a clutch of rocks. He announced himself unhurt, but the biscuit-tin radio he was carrying – so named for the Huntley & Palmer tin in which it was packed – looked significantly the worse for wear.

'Good job we brought two,' Farnham said, examining it. By this time the whole team had converged on the site of Corrigan's fall to earth.

'Mickie, Ian – start digging,' Morgan ordered, tossing the jump helmet in their direction and fixing his beige beret at an appropriately rakish angle. He stared into the distance, imagining what lay ahead. If the Halifax navigator had done his sums right they should be about seven miles to the north of the Potenza valley town of San Severino. And about a thousand feet above it. According to the Soho restaurateurs the journey down from the plateau would offer all the tree cover they needed for the hours of daylight.

There were also several hill villages *en route*, and how their occupants would react to the appearance of British soldiers was harder to predict. According to the informants in London some villages were more hospitable than others, but they had disagreed violently as to which was which. The Oxford Italian history don subsequently consulted by Intelligence was not surprised. 'The villages around there are all walled,' he explained, 'and not because they've been worried about foreign invaders. Those villages have been fighting each other since the fall of the Roman Empire.'

Morgan grinned at the memory and turned to see how the excavation was going. It was almost complete. One last shovel full and the eight chutes were pressed into the hole, the sections of turf carefully relaid.

McCaigh straightened up and took a first real look at his surroundings. 'Hard to imagine Vera Lynn bursting into song in a place like this,' he muttered.

They set off in single file, Stens at the ready. Beckwith took the lead, with Morgan only a step behind him, clutching the map which had been drawn in the British Museum map room and further detailed – if the stains were any guide – during a spaghetti sauce-making competition. Not that it was needed for the moment, for all trace of the moon had now vanished and they could hardly see a yard in front of their faces. Bunching to keep in contact, the column of men was looking more like a conga line than an armed raiding party.

Progress, not surprisingly, was slow, and to make matters worse rain began to fall. Fitful at first, it soon became a steady downpour.

They continued south, hoping that their starting point had been where it was supposed to be, silently cursing the rain and whatever else came to mind. Hitler, army food and the Americans were high on most lists, though the pecking order varied.

About an hour after starting out, with everyone soaked to the skin, they finally reached the edge of the plateau and started downhill. Another ten minutes and they found themselves descending a wooded valley. It was too late for the trees to keep them dry, but Farnham thought it a good place to dig in for the rest of the night and following day. He suggested as much to Morgan, who overrode his instinctive desire to push on and reluctantly agreed.

By this time it was almost two in the morning, and much of the next hour was spent in excavating two cross-shaped hides. Both were about two feet deep, with an arm for each of the four occupants and a central well for their equipment. The men's groundsheets, supported by cut branches and covered in foliage, offered both concealment and shelter from the rain. 'We might be soaked to the skin, but we're not going to get any wetter,' Morrie Beckwith announced hopefully.

'Someone shoot the bugger,' came a voice from the other hide.

For the next sixteen hours six of the eight men only left their scrapes to relieve themselves in the surrounding trees. It was still raining when dawn came, though by this time the heavy downpour had subsided into a drifting mist. Visibility didn't improve much until around noon, when the mist suddenly grew thinner and wafted away, revealing brightening clouds in the branches above. These too soon broke apart, revealing not only the sun but an arc of mostly invisible rainbow in the eastern sky.

'That's a good omen,' Corrigan decided.

'Just about cancels out your diving into a rock with the radio,' Beckwith told him brutally.

The inhabitants of the other hide were still laughing when Morgan appeared in Farnham's observation slit. 'I'm going back up the hill to take a recce,' he announced. 'Get a decent fix on where we are. And Rafferty might as well come with me. I've heard he can read a map.'

Rafferty gave his companions an 'aren't I the lucky one' grin and crawled out of the hide to join the captain. They walked cautiously up through the still-dripping trees, whose branches seemed full of birds eager to make up for lost warbling time, and stood watching for a few moments on the uppermost edge of the wood before starting up the slope which they had descended the previous night. It was just as bare by daylight – there were no signs of human use, no buildings in the distance, no grazing animals, just rocks and rough mountain grass.

A couple of hundred yards up the slope there was more to see. Looking south, they could see the snowcapped peaks of the Monti Sibillini shining like a row of blazing torches in the afternoon sun; looking east, their eyes could follow the parallel valleys of the rivers Potenza and Chienti to the far-distant sea. About five miles from where they stood a dark line seemed to snake across the hills between the two valleys, and Morgan's binoculars confirmed that this was the railway they'd been sent to cripple.

San Severino was still hidden from view, but looking out across the wooded cleft in which they were camped the two men could see the land fall away into a much deeper and broader valley. The town was down there somewhere, and training his binoculars in its likely direction Morgan thought he could make out several diaphanous trails of rising smoke against the wall of hills beyond.

9

'Look,' Rafferty said suddenly, and following his arm Morgan could see another trail of smoke, this one moving towards him on the distant railway. Before the train vanished from view in the valley below them, he had counted twenty-three flat wagons, each carrying a Wehrmacht tank. He was probably only imagining it, but several minutes later he seemed to hear the train rattling across the bridge they had come to destroy.

Darkness fell soon after five, but there was another seven hours of boredom to be endured before the time came to leave the security of the hides. By then the clouds had returned and the temperature had plummeted, giving the damp air a distinctly raw edge, but at least it hadn't started to rain again. The eight men had changed into their only other set of under-garments, and the chances of getting the first set dry seemed remote. 'Another night like last night and we'll all come down with fucking pneumonia,' Trevor Corrigan observed as he disentangled a groundsheet from the wet foliage which had been laid across it.

'You know the flu epidemic after the last war killed more people than the war did?' Roger Imrie offered.

'A fountain of knowledge,' McCaigh said sardonically.

'A fountain of crap,' Beckwith snorted.

'It's true,' Imrie protested, as if they cared.

'So instead of dropping bombs on the Germans perhaps we should just parachute in people with runny noses,' McCaigh offered.

'OK, OK,' Morgan said, cutting through the laughter. 'Let's have a bit of hush. We might not be the only people in Italy.'

'I bet we're the only people this wet,' Corrigan said under his breath.

'You are,' Beckwith muttered back.

They set off on their night march, Morgan in the lead, Beckwith close behind him. It was almost as dark as it had been the previous night, but the CO had spent a considerable part of the day trying to memorize the map, and intended using his torch only as a last resort.

They had walked about three-quarters of a mile down the valley when it became apparent that the ground beneath their feet was now a fairly well-beaten path. A little further and they could see the gaunt silhouettes of buildings on the slope above them. 'Stigliano,' Morgan murmured to himself, just as the sound of a dog barking cut through the silence. His mental map confirmed, Morgan turned away from the village, heading up the slope to his right. The dog continued to bark, and eventually a human voice responded with what was presumably a string of Italian curses.

The team reached the top of the ridge and started down the other side. Another small village – Serripola on Morgan's map – became dimly visible, clinging precariously to the other side of the valley. They bypassed it by following the stream which tumbled along the bottom, then clambered up what they hoped was the last ridge before San Severino.

It was. The moon was now making an effort to shine through the clouds, and the roofs of the town below glowed in the pale light. It wasn't a big town, but Farnham guessed it would be a pretty one in daylight. It had apparently been founded about fifteen hundred years earlier by Romans on the run from Barbarians, and was said to have a lovely elliptical square and some nice churches. After the war, Farnham told himself. For now it was just a lot of buildings next door to a bridge.

The latter was still hidden from view by the curve of the ridge, but a faint yellow glow seemed to be emanating from its presumed position, suggesting a degree of illumination which reflected the enemy's understanding of its strategic importance. The thought crossed Farnham's mind that this was not going to be as easy as Morgan seemed to think.

'I think another recce's in order,' Morgan said softly, breaking Farnham's reverie. 'We need to find a spot for an OP with a decent view of the bridge,' he continued, 'and there's no sense in all of us stumbling around in the dark. I'll take Rafferty.'

Farnham nodded, his eyes still on the town below. It looked so peaceful.

It took Morgan and Rafferty twenty minutes to reach their destination, but the view was worth the trip. From the edge of the trees which covered the end of the snub-nosed ridge the land fell steeply away to the railway, which itself followed a narrow shelf between cliff and river. To their right, across the rushing waters of the Potenza, the town slept, cloaked in grey. About two hundred yards to their left, the single track swept across the river on a simple underslung truss bridge. It was about seventy-five feet long, and extremely well lit by search-lights at either end. At the far end, which alone seemed to offer easy access, a railwaymen's hut had been turned into a guard-house. There was a light in the window, and even at this distance the two SAS men could hear raised voices inside it. Another two armed soldiers were halfway across the bridge, and unlike many such sentries Morgan had seen in his military career, they seemed to be actually taking note of the world around them.

Beyond the bridge the railway completed an S-bend by turning into what was obviously the station and goods area. The single track divided into four, and long lines of goods wagons stood on the three to the left. The roof of a goods shed rose above them. On the other side of the through line, some thirty yards this side of the station itself, there was a small engine shed with a coaling platform and water-tower.

The wagons in the goods yard might offer some cover for the approach, Morgan thought. He turned his binoculars on the road bridge, which crossed the river another couple of hundred yards beyond the railway. It was unlit and apparently unguarded.

He smiled to himself. Blowing the bridge didn't look that difficult – the real trick would be surviving the aftermath. There were thirty miles of fairly open country between them and the scheduled Navy pickup, and the local Germans were likely to be distinctly miffed. 'Go and fetch the others,' he told Rafferty. 'We won't find a better spot for an OP than this.'

Daylight found all eight men well concealed in two rectangular trenches. One narrow end of each looked out across the bridge and station area, and it was here that the men took turns keeping watch through the narrow slit between ground and cover. The other ends were for sleeping, cooking on the tiny hexamine stoves, and, in the case of the eastern trench, manufacturing explosive devices. Morrie Beckwith was the resident expert, bringing together the ingredients they had carried with them – lumps of the new plastic explosive, thermite and lubricant – into his own variations on SAS pioneer Jock Lewes's famous Lewes bomb. Beckwith had an almost dreamy look on his face as he worked, which suggested both intense concentration and a strange joy in the process.

Those on watch had rather less to keep them interested. It soon became apparent that the day shift in the guardhouse below was remarkably similar to the night shift – a total of six guards, two of whom would be crossing and recrossing the bridge at roughly five-minute intervals. During the day a further pair of soldiers could be seen pacing up and down the distant station platform. There was presumably a local German garrison which supplied these guards, but where it was, and how many men it comprised, God only knew. The SAS men hoped it was a long way away.

A troop convoy comprising over twenty lorries passed through the town early in the afternoon, but trains were conspicuous by their absence. The Allied air forces no doubt discouraged the Germans from too much movement during the hours of daylight, but in any case this was a little-used line. If the SAS parties to the north did their jobs then the Germans would need it badly, but by that time, with any luck, it would be out of action.

Soon after dark Morgan called a conference in one of the hides, and all eight men squeezed in. Once the four visitors had made appropriate remarks about the décor and prevailing odours he went through the catalogue of their observations over the past sixteen hours, presented a possible plan of action and, in true SAS spirit, invited comments from all and sundry.

'Almost sounds too easy, boss,' McCaigh said.

It was close to one o'clock when the eight men slipped one by one across the road bridge, down the small embankment, and into the deeper shadow of the trees beside the river. The light was better than on the previous two nights, though still a long way short of what the moon could manage from a clear sky. It was probably about perfect, Morgan thought – bright enough for Beckwith to do his demolition work, dark enough to cloak their escape into the hills.

Three hundred yards upstream, the illuminated bridge looked more substantial than it had from their bird's-eye vantage-point.

They started working their way along the bank, crouching slightly as they walked, more from instinct than any real fear that they would silhouette themselves against the cliffs on the other side of the river. There was no need to worry about noise – the rush of the black water beside them was loud enough to drown out a male voice choir's rendition of 'God Save the King'.

Fifty yards or so from the guardhouse Morgan gestured everyone to the ground, and they all lay there waiting for the two-man patrol to reach the designated stage of their regular route. As they set foot on the near side of the bridge Morgan and Farnham rose to their feet and walked swiftly towards the windowless back wall of the railway hut turned guardhouse. Reaching it, they stood still for a moment, listening to the German voices inside. They sounded like they were having a good time.

At Morgan's signal the two men inched their way round the end of the hut furthest from the bridge, hoping the door was open, as it had been when they broke camp an hour and a half earlier.

It was.

The two men on patrol had almost reached the other end of the bridge. Morgan took one step inside the door and another to his left, allowing Farnham an equal angle of fire. The two men had a fleeting glimpse of bareheaded, greatcoated men sitting round a packing case, cards in hand, before the silent fusillade ripped the scene to pieces, shredding the back and head of the man who was facing away from the door, spurting blood and brains in a welter of collapsing bodies. There was a sound like furniture falling, a moment of utter silence, and then they could hear the river once more.

They pulled two of the bodies out of their greatcoats, grabbed a coal-scuttle helmet each, and waited by the door.

Glancing back at the four dead men, Farnham was struck by how young the faces looked. In a few days four homes in Germany would be getting letters from the Wehrmacht, and tears would be rolling down their mothers' cheeks.

A wave of cold anger ran through him, anger at the bastards who had set the whole bloody mess in motion.

Morgan was looking at his watch. It usually took the guards five minutes to complete their circuit, which meant there was one to go. Straining his ears, he thought he could hear the faint drumming of feet on the bridge, and seconds later he heard their voices. Thirty yards, he guessed. Twenty, fifteen . . .

The two SAS men exchanged nods, and walked calmly out through the door.

One of the approaching Germans shouted out a question in a cheerful voice, and in reply Morgan's Sten seemed to lift him off his feet. Farnham's target died less dramatically, dropping like a stone as the bullets stitched a line from belly button to forehead.

They walked quickly forward, grabbed the bodies by the ankles, and dragged them back across the cinders to the makeshift mass grave in the guardhouse. 'Call in the others,' Morgan told Farnham.

They were already on their way, squeezing into the hut one by one.

'Nice and warm in here,' Beckwith muttered, feigning not to notice the pile of corpses around the stove. The faces of both Tobin and Imrie, Farnham noticed, were decidedly pale.

'So far so . . .' Morgan started to say, but at that moment all eight heads turned in response to the unmistakable sound of approaching heavy vehicles. In a move worthy of the Marx Brothers all eight men moved towards the doorway, causing a general scrum, and tipping Imrie off his feet and into the lap of a German corpse. He froze for a second, took a deep breath and clambered back up.

Meanwhile Morgan had asserted rank and claimed the view from the door. Two large lorries had drawn up in the station forecourt about a hundred and fifty yards away. Their uniformed drivers had already climbed down and were lighting cigarettes. A man in an officer's cap was just disappearing into the station building.

'Maybe he's just stopped for a shit,' McCaigh suggested hopefully.

'It doesn't matter,' Morgan decided. 'Trev, Roger – get some coats and helmets on and start pretending to be guards. Robbie,' he went on, looking out through the doorway, 'form a line of defence. Two of you behind this hut, the other two behind the engine shed over there. If Jerry starts pouring out of those lorries and heading this way, start shooting.' He pushed a lock of unruly hair back inside the beret and turned to Beckwith. 'Come on, Morrie, we've got a bridge to blow.'

There was still no movement in the distant forecourt, though this time Morgan thought he could hear laughter from inside one of the lorries. The officer had not returned – if McCaigh had been right about his destination maybe the bastard was constipated.

As Corrigan and Imrie, suitably coated and helmeted, walked along the track towards the bridge, Morgan and Beckwith skirted round the pool of light, reached the bank of river some thirty yards downstream and then worked their way back along the water's edge. Climbing up into the under-slung girder was as easy as it had looked from the OP, and they encountered no difficulties crossing to the other side along the wide, L-shaped beams. The only real problem was a distinct lack of light, but then Beckwith had always claimed he could put together explosive charges in his sleep.

On the bridge above them Corrigan and Imrie had stopped to light cigarettes and were now leaning over the parapet, puffing away as contentedly as their German predecessors had done. Away to their right the lorries were still sitting in the forecourt.

The striking of a match betrayed the position of the missing officer. 'The bastard's standing on the platform,' Imrie suddenly realized.

'Maybe he's waiting for a train,' Corrigan said flippantly.

A few seconds later the two men were staring at each other, suddenly aware of what that might mean.

Thirty yards away, crouched behind a corner of the stone-built engine shed, Farnham was mentally sifting through the same implications. If the lorries were there to meet a train, then the chances of it arriving either just before or just after the bridge blew up were pretty good. But was there any way to take the train down with the bridge? He couldn't think of one. It was already too late – Beckwith would have the time pencils in place by now. They would have to trust to luck.

The mingled smell of coal, tar and oil was heavy in Farnham's nostrils, taking him back to his schooldays and the frequent illicit trips to Bishop's Stortford engine shed which he and Tubby Mayne had made. Fifteen years ago now. A lot had happened in that time. The Depression, the War, marriage, growing up. Tubby had been killed in the Battle of Britain.

He looked at his watch – Morgan and Beckwith had been under the bridge for almost fifteen minutes. And then he heard the train whistle in the distance. It was still a few miles away, he thought. Probably approaching one of the three tunnels that lay between San Severino and Tolentino.

Under the bridge Morgan had heard it too, and the same possibilities had occurred to him. But by this time Beckwith had placed all the charges and was now scurrying through the girders, squeezing the detonators on the black-coded time pencils. As the ampoules shattered, the acid began eating into the thin wire, and in roughly ten minutes – the 'roughly' was a sore point among users – the wires would break, releasing the springs and slamming firing pins into initiators, exploding the charges and hopefully, in this case, dropping the bridge into the river.

Morgan could hear the wheeze of the approaching locomotive. It couldn't be much more than a mile away.

Beckwith was only a few feet away now, breathing heavily as he reached for the final device. The last thing Morgan heard was his sergeant's mutter of frustration, and then the charge went off, tearing Beckwith limb from limb and hurling Morgan himself against an iron girder with the force of a hurricane. Both bodies dropped into the surging river.

Thirty yards away Farnham spun round to see the bridge still standing, the smoke clearing to reveal Corrigan on the far bank, pointing at something in the water. He just had time to notice that the German officer had vanished from the station platform when the man re-emerged in the forecourt barking orders at the standing lorries. There was a sound of boots hitting the ground.

Realizing he'd been holding his breath, Farnham took in a gulp of cold air and tried to think. As far as he could tell the best way out was the way they'd come in – the only alternative was to retreat across the bridge and then they'd be trapped between cliff and river.

'Get across to Neil,' he told Tobin, who was crouching wild-eyed beside him. 'Tell him to keep Jerry at a distance. I'm going to check the bridge.' Without waiting for an answer he launched himself across the space towards the river's edge, reaching it just in time to see what looked like a severed leg bobbing beyond the circle of illumination offered by the searchlights. On the far bank Corrigan and Imrie were gazing hopelessly at the water, and for a few seconds Farnham felt equally paralysed. The sound of the approaching train mingled with the clatter of boots in the forecourt and the guttural shouts of the German NCOs.

He forced himself to think. Morgan and Beckwith must have been under the bridge long enough to place and prime all the charges, but Farnham was certain that only one of them had exploded. The bridge would probably still go up, but when? There'd been no discussion of which time pencils would be used – making sure everyone was on the same page had never been one of Morgan's strengths. If they made a run for it now the Germans might have time to save the bridge, but could he ask the others to die holding them off when he wasn't even sure the bridge was going to blow?

He gulped in another lungful of air and decided he couldn't. 'Get back over here,' he shouted at Corrigan and Imrie, who both looked at him stupidly for a second and then started clambering back up from the water's edge.

A second later the Germans opened fire, presumably in response to the silent Stens of Rafferty, Tobin and McCaigh.

Farnham began zig-zagging his way back towards the shelter of the guardhouse. He was about halfway there when a second charge went off behind him, and then a third. He turned to see a huge cloud of smoke rising to obscure the cliffs beyond as the far end of the bridge, with what sounded eerily like a huge sigh, sank heavily into the river.

As the smoke cleared he could see Corrigan and Imrie climbing shakily to their feet on the far bank. The bad news was that they couldn't get back across; the good news was that neither could the Germans. Farnham gestured to them to escape along the tracks and after only a few seconds' hesitation Corrigan flashed a thumbs up and turned away, pulling Imrie after him.

Farnham resumed his run towards the guardhouse, just as a hail of bullets swept over his head. The train was now entering the station, pouring a dark plume of smoke at the sky and half drowning the sound of the German guns. With something akin to a leap of the heart Farnham realized that it was going to pull right through the station, effectively cutting them off from the German troops who were inching their way forward from the end of the platform.

Reaching the shelter of the guardhouse, he opened up with his own Sten and saw a German fall, though whether from his or Rafferty's fire he couldn't tell. The Italian locomotive was still coming forward, and at this rate it might even reach what remained of the bridge.

'The boss and Morrie are dead,' Farnham told the others. The edge of panic had disappeared and he now felt almost supernaturally calm and collected. 'Corrigan and Imrie were on the other side of the river when the bridge went down. They're making their own way home. We're going out the way we came in. OK?'

The others nodded at him.

The train was almost on top of them. 'So let's go,' Farnham said, leading off at a run towards the line of trees beside the river. To their left two more charges went off on the broken bridge, momentarily eclipsing the deafening hiss of the braking locomotive.

The train was composed entirely of closed and lightless wagons, and once away from the bridge area the four SAS

F/2382327

men found themselves cloaked once more in the relative safety of darkness. They raced towards the road, occasionally stumbling over rough pieces of ground, expecting to hear gunfire behind them at any moment, but the German troops were either very green or unusually disorganized, and none came. Reaching the road, Farnham resisted the temptation to seek the safety of the high ground they already knew, instead ploughing on through the orchard opposite. From this they emerged into an open field, which in the darkness seemed to stretch for miles.

This was the escape route they had decided on earlier that night in the OP. If anyone got separated from the party the plan was to rendezvous a quarter of a mile north of the tiny hill village of San Giuseppe, which was itself about six miles east of San Severino. The spot in question might be a swamp or a local trysting place – their map was somewhat limited, to say the least – but if Corrigan and Imrie escaped from the Germans then that would be where they'd expect to find their comrades waiting.

And then they could all cheerfully hike their way to the sea.

Farnham suddenly felt cold all over. The remaining radio had been in Corrigan's bergen, and that was still lying where Corrigan had left it, on the floor of the railway hut. They had no way of contacting the Navy, and if they missed the pick-up there would be no second chance. How could he have been so stupid?

As they tried to hurry across the wet field, slipping and sliding in the mud, he told himself it was done, and there was no point in dwelling on the fact. They still had forty-eight hours to go, or two whole nights. The Germans would be looking for them, but they couldn't have that many men in the area, and with any luck the Anzio landing – which would be starting in an hour or so – would give the enemy something more important to think about.

He became aware that Rafferty had stopped a few yards ahead of him. 'The railway's only just over there,' the younger man said, pointing to a dark line of bushes away to their right. 'Don't you think we'd be better off walking down the track than wading through all this muck? Just for a while, anyway. They can't follow us with their lorries, can they? And if they try backing up that train we'll hear it coming.'

It was a good idea, Farnham realized. Rafferty's brain seemed to be working better than his own. 'Let's do it,' he said.

The four men struggled across the last thirty yards of mud, bulldozed their way through the line of bushes and on to the track. Away to the right, they could see nothing of the station half a mile away – only the faint yellow glow which hung above it.

As they started walking in the opposite direction Farnham tried to think himself into the mind of the ranking German. He would know the intruders couldn't have got far, but he would have no idea of their direction, and the night was dark enough to hide an army. As regards the four of them, he would wait for daylight before casting a net. As regards the other two, Farnham realized with a sinking heart, he would immediately seek to slam the door on their escape route.

Maybe Corrigan and Imrie would find a way of crossing the river or scaling the cliffs, but their map hadn't suggested any. If it had, they would have made the initial approach from that direction.

He put the problem to the back of his mind and concentrated on adjusting his step to the evenly spaced wooden sleepers. Rafferty was about ten yards in front of him, Tobin about ten to his rear, McCaigh a similar number behind the Welshman. Their training was showing, Farnham thought, and about time too, because so far this operation had hardly covered the SAS with glory. Two dead men, the unit split up, one radio broken and another left behind, an over-hasty retreat from the scene of the action.

But at least the bridge was down.

They walked on, ears alert for the sounds of a train or motor traffic on the nearby road, but in half an hour only one motorcycle dispatch rider, also heading east, disturbed the dark silence. They had, by Rafferty's estimate, walked about three miles when the mouth of the tunnel suddenly emerged out of the gloom, and a few yards more when the rain started to fall. By the time they had reached the shelter of the portal it was coming down with a vengeance.

According to their map the tunnel was about three-quarters of a mile long.

'It'll keep us dry,' Rafferty argued.

'We're already wet through,' Tobin protested. Nor did he like the idea of a walk in the pitch dark. 'And we'd be like rats in a trap,' he added.

Farnham wasn't sure why, but he agreed with him. Taking the tunnel felt a bit too much like walking into the spider's parlour. He looked at his watch. It was almost three o'clock and they were probably about three miles from San Giuseppe. 'We'll go over the top,' he announced.

The next two hours were among the most miserable any of the four men could remember. In the teeth of a near-gale, with the cold rain whipping into their faces, they stumbled across two ranges of hills and climbed in and out of one deep valley. Wet through and freezing cold, their only consolation lay in their complete invisibility to the enemy. But then again, if the Germans were out searching for them in this weather, more than just Hitler needed his head examined.

At around five Farnham called a halt. They were crossing a small valley similar to the one they had camped in two nights before, and the low branches of the trees, once they were hung with groundsheets, could offer a temporary bivouac and the prospect of cooking up some soup to warm the blood. If they just pushed on, Farnham decided, there was every chance they'd blunder past San Giuseppe in the dark. They couldn't be far from the village, and if this weather kept up they wouldn't have much to fear from spotter planes, especially in the first hour of half-light.

It took McCaigh only a few minutes to get the hexamine stove set up and a couple of cans heating. 'I wonder where the stupid bastards have got to?' he muttered to no one in particular.

'What went wrong, do you think?' Tobin asked.

'Must have been a faulty time pencil,' Rafferty said. 'I can't see Morrie making a mistake.'

'Yeah,' McCaigh agreed. 'He was good.' He gave the soup a final stir. 'At least it was quick. The miserable bastard wouldn't have known what hit him.'

The others murmured agreement.

'He had a wife though, didn't he?' Tobin asked.

Rafferty frowned at him. 'Yeah,' he said curtly. The thought of getting killed wasn't so bad, but he found it hard to think about leaving Beth with no one to look after her and the baby.

Bending over the soup, McCaigh remembered his dad's line about 1918 – 'All those women in black, and not enough men left to satisfy half of them.' There was no woman praying for his return – well, maybe a few here and there were offering up the odd wishful thought – but his sixteen-year-old brother Patrick would probably go right off the rails if someone wasn't there to keep an eye on him.

Half an hour later, Farnham's claim that he could detect a lightening in the eastern sky was received with some scepticism, but a few minutes more and even McCaigh was willing to admit that the shade of darkness had slightly changed. Now the swirls of mist and rain were being painted in charcoal grey rather than black; the difference, he said, was 'like night and night'.

They pulled down their groundsheet roofing and started off once more. San Giuseppe turned out to be only a few hundred yards away, and they were almost on top of the village when the first cluster of buildings loomed alarmingly out of the gloom.

'Nice navigating, Neil,' Farnham murmured. He checked his compass, and pointed them north.

'Let's hope there's a Lyons Corner House where X marks the spot,' said McCaigh.

At first there seemed to be only a bare hillside, and that hardly seemed the ideal place to wait for their comrades, rain or no rain. But then fortune smiled on the four men, lifting a swirl of mist like a curtain to reveal a small chapel set amid a grove of oak trees. From the outside it looked ruined, but inside they found a simple altar set on a stone plinth in an otherwise bare chamber.

This was as good a place as anywhere to sit out the day, Farnham decided. There were no roads nearby, and the other two would have a good chance of finding them. Best of all, it was dry.

'Cup of tea for breakfast?' McCaigh suggested.

He was just pouring the first cup when the door opened and the two Italians walked in.

The newcomers looked almost reproachfully at the Sten gun that Rafferty was pointing in their direction. 'Friend,' the older of the two said economically, in Italian. He was probably in his forties, with greying hair, a weathered face and eyes that even at this moment seemed full of amusement. His companion was a young man barely out of his teens, still apparently struggling to grow a full moustache.

'Enzio,' the older man said, tapping himself on the chest. 'Giancarlo,' he added, pointing at the other. 'American?' he asked, offering two open palms to the four SAS men.

'We are English,' Farnham told him in reasonably adequate Italian. He'd been learning the language on and off since 1941, partly to fill in the periods of boredom endemic to army life, partly to maximize his chances of being selected for exactly this sort of mission. And he had to admit that during the last six months in Italy he had developed a definite hankering to return here when the war was over.

Enzio beamed at his linguistic proficiency, though Giancarlo seemed a bit disappointed that they were not Americans.

'You are the men who blew up the bridge in San Severino,' the older man half stated, half asked.

There didn't seem much point in denying it. 'We did,' Farnham agreed, wondering how the news had reached the middle of nowhere so fast.

'We are partisans,' Enzio said, as if in explanation. 'We have people in the town.'

'How did you find us here?' Farnham asked.

Enzio smiled. 'You were seen at San Giuseppe, and followed here,' he explained. 'By a six-year-old,' he added, his eyes almost dancing with amusement.

Farnham had the grace to laugh.

'But you cannot stay here,' Enzio went on. 'This is a holy place, and some people will not understand. You must come to the village, dry your clothes, have something good to eat, and then we can talk about your plans. You will be safe there,' he added, seeing the look of doubt on Farnham's face. 'The Germans are not likely to come, but if they do there will be warning. They cannot surprise us.'

Farnham smiled. 'This is very generous of you,' he told the Italian, 'but first I must talk to my men.'

'Of course,' Enzio said.

Farnham turned to the others. 'They say they're partisans. They're offering us shelter, food and somewhere to dry out. If they're who they say they are then they'll be able to help us get to the sea. And if the others don't turn up they'll probably have ways of finding out what's happened to them. What do you reckon?'

'Do you think they're the genuine article?' Rafferty asked.

'Yes,' Farnham said without hesitation.

'Then why not?'

'Sounds good to me,' McCaigh said. 'Especially the bit about drying out.'

'We shall be honoured,' Farnham told Enzio.

The two Italians escorted them back across the rainswept hillside to the village, and as they walked down the only street the doorways seemed full of curious eyes. Their destination was a large barn that had obviously been built to withstand the winter weather, for inside it was dry and relatively warm. Enzio left them for a few minutes, and then returned with a pile of dry clothes in varying sizes. Not long after that two oldish women arrived with a pot of steaming noodle soup and two loaves of freshly baked bread, all of which left the four men feeling truly warm for the first time since their departure from Salerno three nights before.

Every now and then the door would inch open to reveal one or more children staring in at them. One young girl, probably no more than six years old, with dark, saucer-like eyes seemed unable to drag herself away.

'But where are they keeping the older sisters?' McCaigh wondered out loud.

'They've probably been locked up for the duration of your visit,' Rafferty told him.

'Ah, fame,' McCaigh said dreamily.

'We should get some sleep,' Farnham said, interrupting the reverie. His instincts told him the Italians were trustworthy, but he wasn't about to lower their guard completely. 'I'll take first watch,' he added, and it seemed only seconds before the barn was echoing to satisfied snores. Farnham sat with his back against a stall, running through the events of the past twelve hours. He couldn't pretend he had liked Morgan – he'd always thought of him as one of those men who found it hard to imagine a world without them – but there was no doubting that the man had been tailor-made for the SAS.

Life was so easy to snuff out. One moment a whole person, in all his or her bewildering complexity, and the next – nothing. Unless of course you believed in an afterlife, and Farnham was pretty sure he didn't. It would have been nice to believe that a life in heaven had saved Catherine from extinction, but only for his own sake. She would have found it boring.

The morning went by. Farnham took a brief look around outside – he needed some idea of where they were – but otherwise kept to the safety of the barn. More food arrived early in the afternoon, this time accompanied by a jug of wine, from which he poured four conservative measures. This didn't seem the time or place for dulling their brains or motor skills.

Soon after dark Enzio returned, a stern look on his face. 'The Germans have captured them,' he said without preamble.

Farnham's heart sank but he wasn't surprised. 'Where are they?' he asked.

'They are being held in the town hall. They have been there most of the day – the story is that they walked straight into a German patrol in the darkness.'

'Are they being treated as prisoners of war?' Farnham asked anxiously. Late in 1942 Hitler had ordered the execution of all commandos captured behind enemy lines, regardless of whether or not they were in uniform. In Africa Rommel had ignored the order, but on at least two recent occasions German commanders in Italy had carried it out.

Enzio didn't know. 'The Army captured them, but the men in leather coats arrived this afternoon.' He shrugged.

Farnham's heart sank again. If they were being questioned by the Gestapo, then torture was a real possibility. That would be bad enough in itself, but both men knew the pick-up point at the mouth of the River Chienti. 'How many men are guarding them?' he asked Enzio. After all, a town hall was not a prison.

The Italian raised both eyebrows. 'You are thinking of a rescue?' he asked.

'If it is possible.'

Enzio blew a silent whistle with his lips. 'The town is full of Germans now. Your broken bridge – well, they are like flies around shit. But maybe the town hall . . . I don't know . . .'

'Could you get us into the town to take a look?' Farnham asked.

The Italian nodded. 'Two of you, perhaps. Early in the morning, when there are many carts on the road.'

'That would be wonderful. Now, I must tell the others what you have told me.'

Enzio nodded, turned away, and then turned back again. 'And I have other news for you. Better news. Your armies have landed this morning on the coast south of Rome.' He smiled. 'You were expecting this, I suppose.'

'It is why we came to blow the bridge, to make it harder for the Germans to reinforce their armies in the south.'

Enzio smiled again, and left.

Farnham turned to the others. Their grim faces told him they had guessed the gist, but he went through the conversation in detail. This was the SAS, not the regular army, and they needed to know everything he did before a decision could be taken on what to do next.

'So what do you think, boss?' McCaigh asked, once all the information had been shared.

Farnham chose his words carefully. 'If there's any chance of getting the two of them back without getting everyone – including them – killed, then I think we'll have to give it a shot. And if that means blowing the boat . . .'

'We can always steal a boat,' Rafferty said with a sniff. Both he and Tobin seemed to be developing colds. 'The Adriatic can't be that wide.'

'Yeah, but Yugoslavia's on the other side,' McCaigh said. 'And I seem to remember a German invasion.'

'So we sail south,' Rafferty said. 'We're bound to hit Africa sooner or later.'

Farnham did a round of the faces. They all knew that staying where they were was risky, let alone taking a trip back into the lion's den, but he could detect no real desire to cut and run. They'd rather head for the sea and home – who wouldn't? – but they wouldn't desert their mates without a damn good reason.

He felt proud of them. 'All right, then,' he said. 'I'll give Enzio the good news.'

* * *

31

The cart left the following morning as dawn was breaking, Farnham and Rafferty sharing the back with seven villagers, while Enzio, Giancarlo and a woman called Carmela sat in the front. Most of their fellow passengers seemed friendly, but Farnham couldn't help noticing the resentment in a few of the eyes. In their place, he thought, he might well have felt the same.

The rain and clouds had vanished overnight, giving the two Englishmen their first real view of the village and surrounding countryside. The twenty or so dwellings of San Giuseppe were perched high on a hillside, above the fields which its inhabitants worked, staring out across the mile-wide valley at a similar-sized village on the opposite slope. About six hundred feet below them the Chienti, exhausted after its precipitous descent from the mountains, was beginning its lazy meander to the sea.

Enzio had explained that by taking a roundabout route they could avoid the usual checkpoint at the eastern approach to the town, and it was almost two hours before the horses toiled across the brow of a bare hill and San Severino came into view below them. The descending road wound through a series of hairpin bends, and it was above the last of these, by the side of an apparently endless orchard, that Enzio pulled the animals to a halt and gave Farnham the bad news. 'There's a checkpoint ahead,' he said.

Looking over the Italian's shoulder, the SAS man could see the posse of helmeted guards and their motorcycles astride a small bridge at the southern entrance to the town.

'You'll have to wait for us here,' Enzio said. 'There's plenty of cover,' he added, indicating the orchard.

Farnham agreed reluctantly. There was no point in denying that neither he nor Rafferty looked like a local.

They climbed down and headed for the shelter of the trees as the horses resumed their downhill plod.

'We could try circling round,' Rafferty suggested, more in hope than expectation.

'We could,' Farnham agreed, 'but we wouldn't know where to look once we were in. How about up there?' he said, indicating a shelf of rock some fifty yards above them which looked out across both the orchard and the town.

They reached it just as their cart was drawing up at the checkpoint below. Enzio seemed to be talking to the German for a long time, and for a fleeting moment Farnham imagined the Italian suddenly pointing up the hillside to where they lay, but then the cart moved on into the town and he felt momentarily ashamed of his lack of trust.

Taking out his binoculars, he began to study the town below. Not surprisingly, his first point of call was the bridge they had brought down, and he was pleased to see that nothing much in the way of repair work seemed to have been done since their departure. The bridge sat in the rushing water, and there was as yet no sign of a crane to lift it out. The train which had come so fortuitously between them and the German troops was still standing where they'd left it, and on the track beyond it a later arrival could just be made out, stretching away into the distance.

Flies on shit, Enzio had said, and there was certainly no shortage of Germans in evidence. Troop carriers surrounded the station like a wagon train from a Western, two tanks were parked like book-ends either side of the road bridge over the river and several infantry patrols were visible on the town's already busy streets. The chances of rescuing Corrigan and Imrie seemed poised somewhere between slim and zero.

He trained the binoculars on the elliptical square he'd noticed two nights before, wondering if this was where the town hall would be. Perhaps it was the sunshine, but the square looked even more beautiful from this angle. The strange shape was pretty enough in its own right, but the colonnaded buildings which lined the perimeter would have looked lovely anywhere.

Farnham was just wondering why the square was so empty when a group of men suddenly walked into view. All but two were helmeted, and it didn't take Farnham many seconds to realize that the odd men out were Corrigan and Imrie. He couldn't actually see their faces, but Imrie's blond hair was a give-away. And in any case, who else could they be? The closest Allied op to Jacaranda was more than a hundred miles to the north.

'What is it?' Rafferty asked, sensing the other man's excitement.

'Corrigan and Imrie. In the square, but they're out of sight now.'

'Did they look OK?'

'They were walking all right,' Farnham said. He hoped Enzio would be able to find out where they'd been taken, and that it would be somewhere more accessible than the town hall of a town swarming with Germans. 'I didn't get . . .'

The volley of shots cut him off. A swarm of birds rose squawking into the air above the distant square and the rippling echo of gunfire seemed to bounce from one side of the valley to the other.

'Oh God,' Farnham murmured.

'The bastards!' Rafferty half cried out.

For the next few minutes they took turns with the binoculars, but there was no visual evidence of what they both knew to be true.

The wait for the villagers' return seemed endless, but eventually the familiar cart made its appearance on the road below.

They went to meet it, thinking that Enzio's news could hardly be worse than expected, but they were wrong.

'They have hung the bodies of your friends in the piazza,' he informed Farnham with a sigh. 'As an example of what happens to anyone who opposes them,' he added unnecessarily.

'What did he say?' Rafferty asked.

Farnham told him, and watched a single tear roll down the younger man's cheek. He closed his own eyes, but there in the darkness he could see Corrigan sitting by the broken radio with a silly grin on his face, the anxious smile on Imrie's face as he sat waiting in the belly of the Halifax. Thousands were dying every day, but a death was still a death.

By the time they arrived back in San Giuseppe early that afternoon Farnham had already decided on an immediate departure. He didn't want the four of them sitting around brooding over what had happened, and in any case there was precious little time to waste if they were to keep their rendezvous with the Navy at the mouth of the Chienti. They had thirty-plus miles to cover in fourteen hours, but that seemed possible now that the weather had improved. He wouldn't have fancied their chances in the previous day's rain.

When told of their plans Enzio offered an unexpected boost. He would take them part of the way, he said. After examining their intended route on Farnham's map he announced that he would take them down into the valley and up the other side. Then they could follow the small roads that clung to the distant ridge most of the way to the narrow coastal plain. 'And it is good that you are leaving now,' he added. 'A brother of one of the women in the village – he has suddenly disappeared. It may mean nothing, but . . .' He shrugged.

Ten minutes later they were on their way, perched on the same cart but pulled by fresh horses. Most of the villagers came out to give them goodbye waves and smiles of encouragement, and Farnham silently vowed that if he survived the war he'd return and thank them properly.

Enzio, it turned out, had more immediate gratification in mind. 'We need guns,' he told Farnham as the cart wound down the hill. 'The Germans think that things like they did today will scare people, and maybe they will scare a few, but things like that will also make more people willing to fight them. The people here never wanted to fight with them, but there's quite a few who can hardly wait to fight against them. But we must have guns. And explosives. And when they rebuild your bridge, we can blow it up again.'

Farnham promised to do what he could.

'You could drop them in the field where we found you in the rain,' Enzio added with a twinkle.

They reached the valley floor, and for the next ten minutes, as they drove along the dangerous stretch of main road beside the river, neither man spoke. But no enemy motorcycle or lorry hove into view before they turned off it once more, rattling across the Chienti on an old stone bridge and starting up another small road into the hills. As they climbed the winding track the sun was sinking swiftly towards the line of the Apennines, casting the valley behind them in a gorgeous warm glow, and Rafferty was taking one last look at this panoramic scene when he spotted the plume of smoke rising in the northern sky.

'Ask Enzio what that is,' he said to Farnham, hoping he was wrong.

The Italian looked back, and the change which came over his face in that moment would long remain in the Englishmen's memory. The eyes seemed to soften with sorrow as the features hardened with rage, as if the mind behind them was stretching to encompass the war.

'They are burning our winter feed,' Enzio said flatly.

'I'm sorry,' Farnham said, hoping that the Italian was right, and that feed was all the Germans were burning. 'You've brought us far enough,' he added. 'Get back to your people.'

Enzio shook his head, and jerked the horses back into motion. 'I will take you to Urbisaglia,' he said, and Farnham knew it would be useless to try to get him to change his mind.

An hour later, with the darkness almost complete, the Italian drove through the small village and brought the cart to a halt. 'Follow this road,' he told them, pointing to a track which led higher into the hills. 'And send us guns,' he told Farnham once more, after shaking hands with each man and climbing back on the cart.

The SAS men started walking. According to the map they now had only twenty-five miles to cover, but the roads were neither as straight as the map suggested nor as flat as the paper it was printed on, and Farnham reckoned they would need every minute of the hours remaining to make the rendezvous on time.

The track switched from side to side of the ridge, offering intermittent views of the valleys to north and south, and as the evening wore on the pinpoints of light in the distant villages flickered out and the glow of a waning half-moon flooded the winter fields. There was little traffic on the road – only a few solitary locals who gave them uncertain smiles and hurried on by – and not much more on the main roads which followed the valley bottoms. The railway line which paralleled the road to the north was definitely out of use, which at least offered some satisfaction to the four men.

Soon after midnight, with almost two-thirds of the journey behind them, they stopped in a convenient wood for food and a fifteen-minute rest. There had not been much conversation on the march and there wasn't much now. When not focused on the task in hand, each of the four men was prone to find himself wondering about the vagaries of fate.

It could so easily have been two of them who had been blown to pieces under the bridges, two of them who had been executed by the Germans in the town square. This war in Europe was not going to be like the war in North Africa, Rafferty thought to himself, and he supposed he'd been a fool to ever think it would. Armies fighting each other in deserts could afford to be chivalrous – in such circumstances war was a man's game in which only men got hurt. But Europe this time round . . . well, there were already enough rumours about what the Germans had done and were still doing to innocent civilians on the continent they had conquered, and now the RAF and USAF were doing to German civilians what the Luftwaffe had done to London and other English cities. The rules had broken down, and no one was safe.

In his mind's eye Rafferty could see Enzio's face as the Italian turned to see the smoke rising from his village.

Shortly after half past four they slipped across the empty coastal road and railway and walked the last half a mile across the empty dunes to the river's mouth. The moon was down, the sea dark and apparently empty, but at precisely five o'clock the hump of the submarine broke surface some three hundred yards from shore, and within minutes two dinghies was being lowered into the water.

Farnham flashed the light again to assist the vessel with its navigation, but there was no way of telling it that now only one dinghy was required.

2

The spring sunshine lay across the Dumfries railway yard. Staring through the grimy carriage window at the arched façade of the engine shed, Farnham found himself momentarily back in Italy, and almost expected a wave of Germans to materialize across the tracks.

Ten weeks had passed since Operation Jacaranda, the first four of them spent waiting in Salerno for new orders. Anzio had been a failure, the frontal assault on the Gustav Line had bogged down around Monte Cassino, and no one seemed to know what to do with those elements of the SAS still in Italy. At the end of February they had been shipped home to a cold and damp England, then sent north to the colder and damper Ayrshire hills, where the rest of the Regiment was already in training for the invasion of France. By now Farnham and his companions in the crowded compartment thought they knew every muddy trail in the Glentool Forest.

Neil Rafferty had the same ready smile as always, but Farnham was certain that the newly promoted sergeant had been more affected by the experience than any of them. He was more serious, less inclined to scoff at others' cynicism,

39

and occasionally seemed remarkably on edge for someone previously inclined to sail through life so blithely.

The change in Mickie McCaigh was not so noticeable. He had always been cynical in a witty sort of a way, but nowadays an edge of bitterness sometimes showed through.

Ian Tobin seemed the least affected. Maybe there was a lack of depth to the Welsh lad, but Farnham felt fond of him nevertheless. He had that sort of dogged desire to do the right thing which some found intensely irritating, but which Farnham's own family history had taught him to value.

As for himself, he had spent most of the past few weeks with the feeling that he was sleepwalking through the war. The days and nights in Italy had been intense, and the sense of anticlimax had been correspondingly profound. He couldn't wait for France. Though at this rate, he thought, as the train reluctantly dragged itself free of Dumfries station, they would be lucky to reach London this year. These days there were many stories of soldiers spending their entire leave on the seriously overcrowded trains, arriving home just in time to set off again.

Still, Farnham thought, if it wasn't for his sister he would just as soon spend the time on a train. He certainly had no wish to spend it with his father and stepmother.

A game of pontoon occupied the four of them until they reached Carlisle, where they had to change trains. The relevant platform was thronged with people waiting for the next London express, which was apparently already running half an hour late. This at least gave the SAS men a chance to stock up on food for the night ahead – the chances of a restaurant car were thin indeed – so, while Farnham and Tobin guarded their bags and a spot dangerously close to the platform edge, the other two purchased a mound of dubious-looking sandwiches from the station buffet. Chewing on an uniden-tifiable selection from the pile, Farnham gazed thoughtfully at the line of clapped-out locomotives stabled alongside a disused platform. Everything was wearing out, he thought. Germans or no Germans, this war was going to be around for a long time.

The train eventually arrived, and for the first two hours they had to make do with a crowded section of corridor, but at Preston a group of Engineers in the adjoining compartment got off. Night had now fallen on the outside world, and they had to read the names of the passing stations through the small diamond cut in the blackout screen. Inside the carriage visibility wasn't much better, thanks to the ever-thickening fug of cigarette smoke.

It was midnight when they reached Crewe. Tobin left them there, hoping his connection to Swansea was also running late. The others watched as he was swallowed by the unlit station, feeling more than a little envious. He might not find a train but at least the buffet would be open.

Their train continued south, stopping more and more frequently, or so it seemed to Farnham, who alone in the compartment seemed unable to sleep. He woke the snoring Rafferty at Bletchley, and watched him stumble off in search of a Cambridge train, hoping that a week with his wife and baby son would restore him to his old carefree self.

An hour or so later the train finally rolled into Euston, leaving him and McCaigh to emerge, somewhat bleary-eyed, into the pale grey light of a London dawn. They breakfasted together in a crowded greasy-spoon in Eversholt Street, and then went their separate ways, McCaigh heading down into the Underground while Farnham, suffering from too many claustrophobic hours on the train, waited for a bus.

From the upper deck of the bus which carried him to Hyde Park Corner it didn't look as if much had changed since his last brief sojourn in the capital, a couple of months before. The so-called 'Little Blitz' had tailed off during the past few weeks, and there were no startling new gaps in either the familiar terraces of Gower Street or the shops in Oxford Street.

He decided on impulse to walk from Hyde Park Corner, telling himself he was fed up with crowds of cheek-by-jowl humanity, but knowing in his heart that he simply wanted to delay his arrival at the house in Beaufort Gardens. Stepping through his father's front door meant stepping out of the war, and that meant having to confront the life and family he'd left behind when he joined the Army. It meant remembering that he loathed his father.

Randolph Farnham was a sixty-two-year-old insurance tycoon who worshipped wealth, power and breeding. He'd been an admirer of the Nazis before the war, and the outbreak of hostilities had not so much changed his mind as persuaded him that it wouldn't be wise to publicize such views. Over the past year Farnham Insurance had been more successful than most at using the small print to wriggle out of claims made by bomb-damage victims.

His wife Margaret – Farnham's stepmother – was just as selfish and not much more likeable, but her wanton disregard of convention could sometimes seem almost admirable. At a party before the war he had stumbled across her and one of her friends' husbands engaged in furiously silent sex in one of the guest rooms, and the look in her eyes when she noticed him had been one of pure amusement.

He had no desire to see her or his father, and in fact there were only two reasons why he ever came to Beaufort Gardens. One was that all his worldly goods – all that remained of them – had been brought here from the bombed-out cottage in Sussex; the other was the presence of his sixteen-year-old sister Eileen, on whom he doted. She was kind, interesting, lovely to look at and wise beyond her years, and quite how she had managed to become so under their father's roof was something that Farnham was at a loss to explain. But she had. Living proof, he thought, that children had a much bigger say in how they turned out than their parents liked to believe.

He covered the last few yards and rapped on the door with the heavy knocker. Norton answered, looking every one of his seventy-three years, and ushered him inside with the usual lack of friendliness. 'Your father has left for the office, Mr Robert,' he said stiffly. 'Mrs Farnham has not yet come down.'

Fuck them, Farnham thought. 'My sister?' he asked.

'She is at breakfast,' Norton said, but at that moment Eileen burst through the door at a run, a huge smile on her face.

'Robbie!' she cried happily, throwing her arms round his neck.

After a while they disengaged and he got a better look at her. She seemed older, he thought, though it had been only a couple of months since he last saw her. Her clothes seemed drabber than usual, but the eyes were as bright as ever.

'Let's go out,' she said. 'I've got two hours – we can go for a walk in the park.'

'All right,' he said, glad of the excuse to get out of the house before his stepmother appeared.

It took Eileen only a moment to grab a coat and they were out on the street, walking briskly across the Brompton Road and heading up Montpelier Street. 'What are you doing in two hours?' he asked. 'Shopping with one of your friends, I suppose,' he added with a grin.

'Shopping! Where have you been? There's nothing in the shops to buy. And I have to go to work,' she said triumphantly.

He was suitably astonished. 'You've got a holiday job?'

'In the East End. I'm a volunteer. Oh, Robbie, it's the most important thing I've ever done. I'm helping in this shelter for people who've been bombed out of their homes. It's run by a clergyman named Tim and two old ladies.'

'What do you do?'

'Everything. Cook, clean, visit people, help people sort out problems, try to trace missing relatives . . .' She giggled. 'I even helped Tim write his sermon last week.'

Farnham laughed. 'You were an atheist last time we talked.'

'I still am. But Tim says it doesn't matter as long as your heart's in the right place.'

'Right,' Farnham said drily. 'You're not sweet on this clergyman by any chance?'

'He's older than Father,' she said indignantly. 'And anyway I don't have time to be sweet on anyone. Oh, Robbie, I'm so glad you're here because I need a big favour.'

He sighed. 'And what might that be?'

She kept him waiting for an answer until they were safely across Knightsbridge. 'I don't want to go back to school until after the war's over,' she said as they entered Hyde Park. 'I'm much more useful where I am. And I'm learning so much more!'

'Yes?' Farnham asked, knowing full well what was coming.

'So will you talk to Father for me?' she pleaded.

'I'll try, but I doubt he'll listen.'

'Just soften him up for me, then I'll move in for the kill.'

'Don't get your hopes up too high, Eileen,' he warned her.

She turned her blue eyes on him. 'I won't. But I have to ask, don't I?'

'Yes, of course,' he agreed. Something in the way she said it set off an alarm bell in his mind, but she left him no time to think it through.

'So what are you doing?' she asked.

They had reached the edge of the Serpentine. 'Playing Cowboys and Indians in the Scottish hills,' he said wryly. 'Getting ready for the big day, like everyone else.'

'And when will it be?'

He grunted. 'You'd better ask Churchill that. Or Eisenhower.'

'It'll be soon though, won't it?'

'I should think so.'

'And you'll be part of it?' She sounded worried now.

'Me and a million others,' he said lightly, but she wasn't to be put off so easily.

'Robbie,' she said, 'I know it's been awfully hard for you. Since Catherine died, I mean. And I know you can't bear the thought of working for Father when all this is over, but there are lots of other things you could do.'

'I know,' he said. For some reason he felt close to tears.

'I suppose I'm being really selfish,' she went on, 'but I need my brother and I just want you to be careful.'

He put an arm round her shoulder and squeezed. 'I promise I will,' he said.

By the time McCaigh had taken the Circle Line to Liverpool Street and the LNER stopping service to Stoke Newington he felt as though he'd seen enough trains to last him several lifetimes. Three hundred and sixty miles in twenty-four hours, he told himself as he took the short cut through Abney Park cemetery. Fifteen miles an hour. He had always been good at arithmetic.

His mum's welcome more than made up for the rigours of the journey. She plied him with another breakfast – his

Uncle Derek had apparently been present when certain items fell off a lorry in nearby Dalston – and went through all the local gossip. One family they all knew in Kynaston Street had been killed by a direct hit only a couple of weeks before.

'Has it been bad?' he asked her. ·

She shook her head. 'Nothing like the real Blitz. And everything's much better organized these days. We quite enjoy it down the shelter these days, what with bingo and all that. Or at least your dad and I do. When the siren goes Patrick's usually nowhere to be found.'

'He's at school now, isn't he?'

She shrugged. 'Supposed to be, but I doubt it. He's been helping out with the fire wardens lately – real proud of himself, he is. He must have lied about his age – either that or your mate Terry took pity on him. At least it's stopped him moaning on and on about how the war's going to end before he has the chance to join up. Way he talks you'd think it was like being in the films. And I don't want you encouraging him, either,' she added with a threatening look.

'I won't,' he promised.

She believed him. 'When you came home last time I thought you were keeping something back, but I didn't like to pry.'

'Nah,' he said, 'not really. We were on this op in Italy – eight of us – and four got killed. Felt a bit close to home, I suppose.'

'Not surprised.' She got up to pour them both another cup of tea. 'Bloody Eyeties,' she muttered as she put the cosy back over the teapot.

He laughed. 'Matter of fact it was Eyeties who helped the rest of us escape from the bloody Krauts,' he told her.

She looked at him. 'But you're all right?'

'Yeah, you know me.' He changed the subject. 'How's Dad?'

'He's at work, if you can call gazing at trees work.' Donal McCaigh was the head park keeper at nearby Clissold Park. He'd been a trainee teacher just before the last war, but several exposures to mustard gas in the Ypres salient had left his lungs permanently impaired, and forced him into an outdoor career. 'He'll be home for lunch. So should Patrick, though I think he's got a game this afternoon.'

McCaigh's sixteen-year-old brother had been an above-average footballer since he could walk, and most of the family were hoping he'd get a chance to turn professional after the war. The exception was his mother, who wanted him to go for something with a future. 'If he hasn't,' she added, 'he'll just be bouncing that damn ball against the wall out the back all bloody afternoon.'

McCaigh grinned.

'You should be thinking about going to university when the war ends,' she told him, the bit now firmly between her teeth.

'I'll probably be past thirty!' he said.

'Won't matter,' she said emphatically. 'They'll be taking all ages after this. And you've got most of the family's brain rations – why waste them? I tell you, Mickie, there's a lot of things are going to be different after this war, and a lot of opportunities. You want to be prepared.'

'I'll give you another lecture tomorrow,' she said, laughing. 'Now why don't you catch up on your kip. I've made up the other bed for you, and I'll wake you for lunch.'

It seemed like a good idea, and his head had no sooner hit the fresh pillow than he was out for the count.

Neil Rafferty had been lucky with his connection at Bletchley, and the sun was just clambering above the houses beyond the sidings when his train drew into Cambridge. There were no buses in the station forecourt but the house he and Beth had rented for the past two years was only a twenty-minute walk away, and it felt good to be stretching his legs after such a long journey.

Even as a child he had loved this time of day, and the grandparents who had brought him up had never had any trouble getting him out of bed, or at least not when the sun was shining. He had never known his father, who had died on the Somme before he was born, and he had no memories of his mother, who had succumbed to the postwar flu epidemic. His father's parents had taken him in and he had grown up in their Cambridge house, surrounded by his professorial grandfather's books and the model cars and ships which his father had once laboured to construct.

He would visit them later that afternoon, after spending the morning with Beth and the baby.

The thought of his wife made him lengthen his stride. He hadn't seen her for more than a month, and there hadn't even been a letter for over a fortnight, but he was hoping that this visit would be special. It could hardly turn out as badly as the last one, which had coincided with her time of the month. In two days she'd hardly let him touch her.

This time they had a whole week, and he felt better already. The last couple of months hadn't been easy, but as he walked through the Cambridge streets in the early morning sunshine Italy seemed a long way away.

Rafferty was not a man given to introspection – his mind gravitated to the practical, to problem-solving – but he had spent quite a lot of time trying to understand why those few days in Italy had affected him so deeply. No simple explanation had occurred to him – it had, he decided, been a combination of factors. The brutality of the Germans had shaken him, and he supposed that the deaths of the four SAS men had brought home his own vulnerability. Jools Morgan had always seemed so indestructible, then bang, he was gone. Somehow it had all become real in that moment – not only the war and soldiering but the life he lived outside all that. Beth and the baby. England in the sun.

He passed the end of the road where his grandparents lived, resisting the temptation to drop in for just a few minutes. Another two turnings and he was approaching his own front door. The house was nothing special, just a two-up two-down, but the ivy they had started was already threatening to engulf the front room window. Too impatient to rummage through his bag for the key, he banged twice with the knocker.

Beth opened the door with a smile on her face, and he reached forward to take her in his arms. She backed away, the smile gone, replaced by surprise and something else. 'Neil,' she said instinctively. 'Don't . . .' And then she saw the expression on his face. 'What are you . . . didn't you get my letter?'

There was suddenly a hole where his stomach had been. 'What letter? What's happening?'

She just stared at him, as if she didn't know what to say.

'What letter?' he repeated.

She gulped. 'I've fallen in love with someone else,' she said, the words spilling out in a rush. 'I wrote and told you. I've been waiting for a letter. I didn't expect . . .'

'Who?' he asked, as if it mattered.

'An American. His name's Brad. I told you everything in the letter.'

'I never got a letter.'

She stood there in her dressing gown, a piteous look on her face. 'I'm sorry, Neil. I couldn't help it. It just happened.'

He stared at her, and in the silence heard someone move upstairs. 'He's here?' he said incredulously, anger rising in his voice.

'I had no idea you were coming. I was waiting for a letter,' she said again.

They both heard the feet on the stairs, and Rafferty felt his anger spread through his limbs like a hot flush. As the uniformed legs came into view he took a step forward, fist clenched, impervious to reason.

The American was built like a tank; but that wouldn't have stopped him. What did was the child in the man's arms, his own child, its tiny hand caressing the American's cheek. The child looked at him as if he was a stranger.

Beth's small voice broke the silence. 'Neil, this is Brad. Maybe we should all sit down and have a cup of tea.'

Rafferty looked at her as if she was mad, and she thought better of the idea.

'I think maybe you two need to talk,' Brad said, handing the baby to Beth. For one minute Rafferty thought he was going to be offered a handshake, but the American must have seen the look in his eye. 'I'll see you tonight,' he told Beth. They didn't kiss each other but they didn't need to. Brad nodded at Rafferty and walked out through the still-open front door.

Beth walked over and pushed it shut. 'Let's go into the kitchen,' she said quietly.

He followed her through in a daze, and sat down heavily on one of the chairs they'd found in a flea market just before their marriage.

She was putting on the kettle. 'I am really sorry, Neil,' she said, her back turned away from him, and for one mad moment he felt like leaping up and hitting her, hitting her till she changed her mind.

'I didn't want to put you through this,' she went on, turning to face him.

He tried to think. 'How long have you been . . . how long have you known him?' he asked, wishing he could think of something to ask which would make a difference.

'We met at Christmas, but nothing happened until March, after your last trip home. I didn't mean to fall in love with him,' she said. 'I tried not to, but . . . it just happened. And once it had happened . . .'

He understood the words, but he still couldn't take it in. 'Do Gran and Grandad know?' he asked. Another meaningless question.

'They may have guessed something was wrong, but I haven't told them. I thought you should.'

He looked at her, shaking his head. 'Why?' he asked, and she knew he wasn't talking about his grandparents.

She put a hand over his. 'I don't know,' she said. 'It just happened.'

He shrugged off the stranger's hand and got to his feet. His son, now ensconced in the high chair, was looking at him with an anxious expression. 'We've got to talk about Ben,' he said.

'I know . . .'

'But not now. I need . . .' He needed to get away, to run, to cover his head and howl. 'I'll see you later,' he told her.

'I'm sorry,' she said again.

He grabbed his bag, yanked open the door and stumbled out into the sunshine.

Ian Tobin walked through the door of the family shop in Landore, Swansea, soon after eleven, having spent half the night on the platform at Crewe and another frustrating couple of hours waiting for a replacement engine at Llandrindod Wells. In retrospect this journey would come to seem like practice for the week ahead, most of which he would spend hanging around waiting for people.

He had known that his parents would be busy in the shop, but he had not expected to find Megan with a job, much less one in an engineering factory, and his disappointment at not having her to himself during the days was tinged with a disapproval which he did his best to keep to himself. They spent every evening together, sitting in the pub on Monday and Tuesday as the rain came down, then cycling out to Three Cliffs Bay on the Gower Peninsula when the weather cleared up on Wednesday. There they walked hand in hand on the empty beach, interrupting her stories of the working world every now and then for a lingering kiss. After an hour of this she seemed to suddenly notice that the beach and the grassy valley above were still too wet for lying down, and the disappointment in her voice made him feel hot all over.

It seemed to him that she'd grown up a lot in the past few months. She was more assured, she dressed more daringly, she even argued with him. And her language had certainly grown more colourful. Her brother Barry, who had been in Ian's class at school, had always sworn like a trooper, but Megan's newly expanded vocabulary had more likely been learned from the women she now worked with.

Tobin told himself that he liked the changes, that she had always been a bit too worried about what other people thought, but a feeling of ambivalence persisted. And when, on the following night, in the back row of the cinema, she not only let him put his hand up her skirt but also stroked his cock through his taut trousers, he was almost as surprised as he was excited. Back home he jerked himself off and lay there panting, wondering if she really wanted to go all the way.

For his last night of leave they had planned another trip to the beach, but in her lunch-hour she called him and said they'd been invited to a party. He had been looking forward to having her to himself, but she was so obviously excited at the prospect that he found it impossible to object. 'It's in Danygraig,' she said. 'Barry'll take us in the car.'

They arrived soon after eight, having driven through the blacked-out streets in Barry's decrepit Austin Seven. She had told him not to wear his uniform – 'Let's pretend there isn't a war on for a few hours' – and he had been forced to wear a pre-war suit that still, despite his mother's best attentions, smelt of mothballs.

The party was being held in one of the few standing houses on a bombed-out street. Its owners had obviously long since vanished, taking their furniture with them, but the increase in dancing room more than made up for the lack of places to sit down. There were already about thirty people crammed into the two downstairs rooms, and more continued to arrive as the night wore on. There seemed no shortage of records to play on the precariously perched gramophone, but whoever was in control of the selection obviously liked Duke Ellington.

In the kitchen there was more food and alcohol, both in quantity and variety, than Tobin had seen since the beginning of the war, and later, while he was waiting for Megan to return from the toilet, he saw fresh supplies arrive in a plain Morris van. The deliverers all seemed close friends of Barry's, and Tobin thought he recognized a couple of them from schooldays. An hour or so later he found himself talking to one of them. 'What's your unit?' he asked, just to make conversation. The man gave him a surprised look, then burst out laughing.

Tobin watched him walk away, wondering what he'd said. He had to admit that he felt pretty drunk, but . . .

'Why don't we go outside for some fresh air?' Megan suggested, appearing at his shoulder. Her face was flushed, and he thought she looked very lovely.

They went out the back door, and she pulled him through the yard, where several couples were happily groping at each other, and into the alley which had once run along behind a lively street. Despite a clear, starry sky, the night seemed warm, and they walked arm in arm past the strange wilderness of broken houses to the edge of the docks. In the distance the black shapes of ships and the angular silhouettes of the serried cranes were clearly visible in the darkness.

Megan turned with her back to the wall, pulling him to her, and they kissed for a while, tongues entwining. He cupped her right breast and gently kneaded it, and after a while she undid the front buttons of her blouse, deftly loosened her bra, and let him get his hand inside. Her nipple grew nearly as hard as his cock, which she was rubbing up against as they kissed.

'I can take my knickers down,' she said breathlessly.

A sliver of panic cut through his drunken desire, and he searched for its source. He hadn't got a johnny, and in any case she was drunk. This was Megan – he shouldn't be taking advantage of her. 'I haven't got any protection,' he heard a voice say, and it was his own.

'Oh shit,' she said softly, and the delicious grinding of her stomach against his cock came to an end. 'You're right,' she said, 'but you do want me, don't you?'

'Oh God, yes,' he murmured. 'It's just . . .'

'That's why I love you,' she said, 'because you take care of me.' She kissed him lightly on the lips. 'I think we should be getting back. I don't want Barry to think we've left and go without us.'

They walked back to the party, which was now pumping Glenn Miller into the air. Quite a few people had left though, and Barry, who now had a redhead in tow, announced himself almost ready to join them. First though, he had some settling up to do, and Tobin saw a large wad of notes change hands.

Early the following morning, lying in bed and thinking about the long trip back to Ayrshire, his sober brain started making the connections his drunken one had missed. The booze and food had been black market – that went without saying – but Megan's brother was obviously one of the local kingpins. Tobin had always rather liked Barry, and had felt really sorry for him when he failed his physical back in 1940, but this was something else. And the man who had laughed when asked about his unit – he had to be a deserter. Which explained the 'no uniform' thing – probably half the men there had been deserters. Having a good time and making money while others died for them.

That made Tobin angry. Deserters were worse than conchies, who at least were willing to do dangerous jobs which didn't involve fighting.

But what could he do? He felt like reporting the whole business, but he couldn't do that without shopping Megan's brother.

He would talk to her about it, he decided, and later that morning, as they waited on the platform at Swansea Victoria for his train to be brought in from the sidings, he did.

'I don't like deserters, either,' she said, 'but Barry's not a deserter – he just gets people stuff they want. Most of it comes in from Ireland, so nobody goes short. And he's my brother.'

'I know he is . . .'

'So what can I do? If we report the deserters he'll probably get into trouble, and that'll break Mum's heart.' She looked up at him. 'Maybe you could talk to him. He likes you.'

'How can I? I'm leaving.'

'Next time you come. And let's stop talking about him. Let's just pretend we're the only two people in the world.'

He smiled at her, and a pang of desire shot through his groin as he remembered the night before.

Lieutenant-Colonel Hamish Donegan strolled down Pinner High Street towards the Metropolitan Line station, still savouring the breakfast which his landlady had miraculously put together. There was no doubting the woman could cook, and given the paucity of ingredients available these days, that was no small gift. Donegan could have had a much more sumptuous room at the SAS's HQ at the Moor Park Golf Club, but Mrs Bickerstaff's spam omelette was certainly worth a ten-minute train journey twice a day.

It was a fine spring morning, with fluffy white clouds sailing happily across a blue sky. In his home town, five hundred miles to the north, it would probably still be snowing, but it was harder to think of anywhere in the British Isles less like Inverness than Pinner. There was something so indelibly English about London's Metroland.

He crossed the road, nodded his usual greeting to the two old women who were seated on the same bench every morning, and wondered when he'd get back home again. The last time had been almost three months ago, and on that occasion his two boys could hardly have been more awkward with him if he'd been a complete stranger. And he knew Jean was feeling the strain of separation – he could hear it in her voice during their weekly telephone calls.

Well, he thought, showing his pass to the ticket collector and heading up the stairs to the platform, there was some way to go yet. These days everyone seemed to assume that the war was as good as won, but the Germans still held most of Europe, and getting a foothold in France was going to be neither easy nor cost-free. Donegan suddenly remembered one of the staff instructors at Sandhurst telling his class that any fool could win a battle if the odds were overwhelming enough – the sign of a great general was to do it without losing a man.

SAS casualties, in both Africa and Italy, had been horrendously high, and the reason, in Donegan's mind, was as clear as day. The SAS was not being used in the intended manner.

He knew. He had been involved from the beginning, had sat in the bar of Shepheard's Hotel in Cairo on more than one occasion, hammering out the new unit's *raison d'être* with David Stirling and Jock Lewes. Independent strategic missions were the name of the game, small groups of fast-moving, lightly armed men operating way behind enemy lines, disrupting communications, diverting supplies, keeping the enemy on the hop. There had been teething problems in Africa, but overall the theory had proved workable, and on the few occasions it had been applied in Italy the success rate had been high. But most of the powers that be seemed determined to use the SAS as either shock troops or reconnaissance forces operating just ahead of the main armies, and they were not equipped for either role, as a series of costly failures had amply demonstrated.

The strange thing was that the SAS had not only survived these débâcles of others' making but actually prospered. There were now five regiments which bore the SAS name, two British, two French and one Belgian. A group of 'Phantom' signallers had been permanently attached, and a whole raft of staff officers, supply units, clerks and sundry others had swollen the brigade into an empire-builder's paradise. The good news was that most of the surviving originals, like Donegan himself, were now in influential positions; the bad news was that the feeling of camaraderie which went with a small, tight-knit unit had virtually disappeared.

Which was probably inevitable, Donegan thought, as the Metropolitan Line train slid into the platform behind one of the company's elegant electric locomotives. 'Benjamin Disraeli' was this one's name. He'd have to tick it off the list which his elder son Alistair had copied from a train-spotter's book.

Donegan climbed into an empty compartment, thankful that his journeys each day went against the rush hour, and re-established his train of thought. The very fact that the SAS had been expanded following its poor record in Italy suggested that the top brass hadn't learnt much from the experience, and their plans for using the Brigade in France merely confirmed as much. Small parties would be dropped just ahead of an Allied bridgehead – and later the advancing Allied armies – for the purposes of tactical reconnaissance. Which meant dropping lightly armed groups into the area between the German front-line divisions and their armoured reserves. The SAS teams would either spend their whole time in hiding or suffer the sort of losses associated with medieval suicide squads.

One of the regimental COs had already resigned in protest, and there might well be more. Donegan sighed, stepped down on to the platform at Moor Park and walked through the sunlit spring foliage to his office. Once seated behind his desk he ordered two cups of tea, glanced briefly through his in-tray and summoned his number two, the unflappable Major Spenner, whose account of his weekend at home with the family filled Donegan with envy.

'Lieutenant Farnham will be here in twenty minutes,' Spenner said, looking at his watch.

'Captain Farnham,' Donegan corrected him, rummaging around in the in-tray for the relevant piece of paper. 'Now explain to me why he's being sent. This sounds like an SOE job to me. Or one for a Jedburgh team, come to that.' The Special Operations Executive had been sending agents into occupied France since 1941, initially to establish escape routes, then as a means of funnelling money and supplies to the rapidly blossoming French resistance groups. The Jedburgh teams, which comprised one French, one British and one American officer, were a more recent innovation; their task was to contact and help organize those resistance groups.

'Because the cupboard's bare,' was Spenner's answer to his question. 'Every man and woman they have seems to be accounted for. So they asked us if we had anyone fluent in French with experience of working behind enemy lines. Farnham seemed the best bet.'

'He did a good job in Italy,' Donegan agreed.

'And it won't hurt us to have someone with experience of working in France. Once the balloon goes up we'll probably be sending over most of the Brigade, and they won't just have the Germans to worry about. The French resistance groups are an awkward bunch of sods.'

'And then there's the Americans,' Donegan added facetiously.

In the ante-room down the corridor Farnham could find nothing else worth reading in the sadly shrunken *Times*. He sat back in the chair, thinking that whatever the reason for this summons to Moor Park it had been nice to have the extra time with Eileen. The previous day she had taken him to the

Shelter on the Isle of Dogs, and it had been abundantly clear how much she was appreciated, by both co-workers and those they were looking after. The East End itself had been more of a shock. He had known how much the area had suffered from German bombing, but the reality of so much desolation was still mind-numbing.

Remembering his promise to Eileen that he would talk to their father on her behalf, Farnham had been on his best behaviour with both the old man and his stepmother, studiously ignoring outrageous remarks about the Jews' responsibility for provoking the war. It had all been to no avail, of course: when he eventually broached the subject his father had claimed he already regretted letting Eileen work at the Shelter over the Easter holiday, and certainly wouldn't countenance the thought of her leaving school to work there permanently. Not because he was worried about her education, but because the East End was full of Jews, Chinks and communists, and he didn't want his daughter contaminated.

Eileen had taken this news calmly. Almost too calmly in fact, as if she already had Plan B up her sleeve. And then on Friday night the call had come from Moor Park, requesting his attendance in the CO's office at nine o'clock sharp on Monday morning. On Saturday morning, wondering if the others were involved, he had called Rafferty's home number in Cambridge. Getting no answer, he had tried the McCaigh household in Stoke Newington. Mickie, according to his mother, had left for Scotland that morning, and hadn't received any messages from anybody.

So it seemed to be just him. And indeed, there didn't seem to be anyone else waiting in the ante-room for an audience with the CO. Farnham had known Donegan since the summer of 1942, when the two men had been involved in the raid on the Sidi Haneish airfield in western Egypt, and had come to both like and respect the hulking great Scot.

'The CO's ready for you,' the adjutant almost bellowed in his ear, before leading him down the corridor and ushering him through a door. Donegan was looming like a minor mountain behind his desk, and Bill Spenner was grinning a welcome from one of the chairs opposite.

'Sit down, Robbie,' Donegan said. 'Want a cup of tea?'

'No thanks.' Farnham was eager to hear the reason for his summons.

Donegan seemed to realize as much. 'We've got a job for you, or at least the War Office has. I'm not sure exactly who's in charge of this particular caper. Anyway, it's France. The Vosges,' he added, swinging round in his chair and pointing a large finger at the line of mountains which separated Alsace and the Rhine from the rest of France.

'Alone?' Farnham asked.

'That's the idea. This is a fact-finding mission, and one man has a better chance of blending in. The local Maquis group will be expecting you, and Bill here will fill you in later on what we know about them.'

'What sort of facts am I looking for?' Farnham asked, though he already had a pretty good idea.

Donegan swung round to face the map again. 'Wherever we land in France,' he said, 'whether it's the Pas de Calais or Normandy or anywhere else, the German supply lines will stretch back across the Rhine into Germany itself. If they want to bring reinforcements from the Eastern Front – if they have any to spare, that is – they'll have to travel across Germany and the Rhine to get to France. So these roads and railways' – he tapped each with his finger, starting at the Channel coast and finishing at the Swiss border – 'are absolutely bloody vital to the buggers. And, as you can see' – the finger tapped twice more – 'several of the railway lines go through the Vosges. We want to know how good a job the locals are capable of doing when it comes to denying those lines to the Germans, both on specific occasions, like the day before the invasion, and on a week-by-week basis. We'd also like an assessment of whether this would be a suitable area for an SAS operation after the balloon goes up, and how the Maquis would feel about a bunch of our lads driving their jeeps with the usual care and consideration through their peaceful villages.'

Farnham smiled. 'How are we going to cooperate with the Maquis? I mean, are we going to form integrated battle groups, just team up on an *ad hoc* basis, or just leave each other to get on with it and hope we don't attack the same German column from different sides at the same time?'

Donegan grunted. 'That's another question we'd like an answer to. Some of the French resistance groups are getting a bit touchy about taking British or American orders.'

'The communists?'

'No, not particularly,' Spenner told them. 'In fact, De Gaulle's lot seem to spend just as much time worrying about slights to the honour of France, if not more. The communists tend to take their decisions on purely practical grounds. This particular group seems a mixed bag, by the way.'

'Make it more interesting for you,' Donegan said generously. 'They'll no doubt ply you with demands for equipment, and we'll do our best to get them whatever it is you think they need. After you've been on a few jaunts with them you'll probably have a pretty good idea of what they're made of.' He paused for a moment, then turned to the map for the last time. 'And there's one other thing. Just here, outside a village called Struthof, the Germans have built a concentration camp.

It's the only one on French soil as far as we know, and the government – our government – would like to know what's going on there. Presumably they think it might give them an idea of what's going on in all the others, in Germany and Poland and God only knows where else.' He looked straight at Farnham. 'Since this isn't strictly an SAS operation, and you won't be wearing uniform, I should . . .'

'I volunteer,' Farnham interjected, and immediately felt a slight pang of guilt. Such eagerness was a little hard to square with his promise to be careful.

3

France, May 1944
The Halifax droned on its east-south-easterly course across northern France. It had been airborne for about an hour, and was now, according to Farnham's calculations, somewhere above Champagne. He and Catherine had spent the second half of their honeymoon there, driving round the beautiful countryside by day, making love in gorgeous inns by night. All of which seemed several lifetimes away.

Feeling cramped, he stretched first one leg and then the other. On the other side of the bomb bay doors the H-type container was waiting, its static line already hooked to the plane's fuselage. The container's five separate cylinders were held together by metal rods in the shape suggested by the name; once on the ground they would be separated for easier portage. Inside the various compartments were a dazzling array of gifts for the local Maquis – Sten guns, ammunition, money, some plastic explosive with the necessary detonators – and the means by which they could order and accept delivery of more, namely a radio set with spares, an S-phone and a Eureka-Rebecca set.

Or at least, this was what Farnham hoped had been packed inside the container. One agent of recent memory had been parachuted into central France with a canister full of lamp-shades, and his hosts had not been particularly impressed.

There couldn't be much more than twenty minutes to go. The Vosges, though certainly tall enough to qualify as mountains, were a range of rounded summits, and for centuries many of these had been cleared for pasture, shaved of their growth like the crowns of monks. The weathermen had forecast clear skies in the area, favouring an accurate drop, and for that Farnham was grateful, for his one great fear as a parachutist was landing in a tree and breaking his neck.

Thinking about that reminded him of a story he had heard at Moor Park only a couple of days before. An SOE agent had fallen into a tree, ending up suspended in thin air. It had been too dark to see the ground, and the things he had dropped from his pockets had soundlessly disappeared, so he had hung there until dawn arrived and revealed the humiliating truth – a thick bed of moss lay not three inches below his toes.

Farnham was still smiling when the dispatcher put his head round the door and told him 'fifteen minutes'.

He used the time for a mental run-through of the new identity inscribed in the bewildering array of papers with which he had been presented, courtesy of the Free French office in London. His name was Jacques Messier, and he worked for a Paris construction firm which turned out tank traps for the Germans. His family still lived in St Dié, a small railway town in the western foothills of the Vosges. As proof of all this he carried an identity card, a draft card, a trade union card, demobilization papers, all seven kinds of ration cards – which, being French, naturally included one for wine – and a marriage certificate. Since Farnham wasn't circumcised, he didn't need a baptismal certificate to prove he wasn't a Jew.

As he clipped his own static line to the fuselage he wondered about the people who were hopefully waiting in the pasture below. In England the French Resistance was acquiring almost legendary status. The cities were supposed to be full of beautiful young girls in berets on sabotage missions, the forests full of outlaws doing Robin Hood impersonations, with the local Gestapo chief filling in for the evil Sheriff of Nottingham. That was the myth, but what was the reality? What sort of men was he going to find down there?

Farnham tried imagining what might have happened in England had the Germans successfully invaded the island. Who would have taken to the mountains and the woods? Ex-soldiers? Students? Ordinary workers? He could imagine his sister doing so. And he could certainly imagine his father as a collaborator.

The dispatcher opened the bomb bay, revealing a landscape of heavily forested slopes, and only moments later the green light was on, a hand was slapping him on the back and he was falling into the void. A pull on the rip-cord and the chute billowed open above him, jerking him upright.

Now he could see the triangle of bonfires below. The pilot had done his calculations perfectly, and there was no need to realign his angle of drop. The parachute carrying the H-type container was above and behind him, also on target. Farnham had a brief picture of dark figures racing across the meadow to meet him, and then he was touching down, rolling through the sweet-smelling grass and gathering in the chute. 'You won't be burying this one,' the dispatcher had told him. 'French women like their silk.'

There were about a dozen of them. Some were returning across the grass after extinguishing the fires, some were gathering in the chute from the H-container, some seemed to be standing guard on the perimeter. Two were approaching Farnham at a brisk walk.

'Robert?' the first asked, pronouncing it 'Robair' in the French fashion. He was a big man in his thirties, with dark hair, bushy eyebrows and moustache, wearing a ragged-looking coat and a crumpled but official-looking peaked cap. 'I am Jules,' he said, offering a hand.

'And I am Yves,' the other man said. He was older, probably in his early forties, thin and bespectacled, with short hair and eyes that seemed piercing in the gloom. He was wearing a thick jacket, baggy trousers and a beret. 'And these are Henri and Pierre,' he added, indicating the two men who were now rolling up Farnham's chute, presumably with girl-friends in mind. They looked like brothers, and the younger of the two was not that far removed from adolescence. Both had pugnacious faces and dark, curly hair.

In the distance Farnham could see other Maquisards bending over the H-type container – they were probably trying to work out how it came apart. 'I will show your men how to break it up,' he told Jules and Yves in French, and was gratified to realize that they understood his accent.

Two minutes later the five canisters had been separated and assigned to their porters, and Farnham had been cursorily introduced to another ten or so men of varying ages. Tomorrow he would probably need to be told their names again, but for the moment he was left with an impression of serious Gallic faces, of smiling mouths and wary eyes.

The other thing he noticed was the paucity of weaponry on display. Jules had a German sub-machine-gun slung across his back, and two of the other men were carrying rifles, but that was all. The Stens were going to come in handy.

They left the open pasture to the stars, funnelling into single file as they entered the surrounding forest and started down a winding path through densely packed trees. There was no wind to stir the branches and the only sounds were those of their passage, the rustle of leaves underfoot and the heavier breathing of the men carrying the canisters. Within minutes it was hard to imagine the open space beneath the vast sky which they had left behind, and even harder to imagine life before the drop. The plane, the Kentish airfield, the packed train from London – all suddenly seemed light-years away.

The walk to the Maquis camp took about an hour. It was mostly downhill and mostly by path, though for about two hundred yards they followed a wider track through the forest. At no time did they have to leave the cover of the trees, which suggested to Farnham that both drop zone and camp-site had been carefully chosen.

The latter was hard to make much sense of in the darkness, and his first impression went no deeper than a scattering of tents beneath the trees. He was escorted to one of these, which had apparently been set aside for his exclusive use. There were blankets waiting on a dry oilskin groundsheet, and while he was still staring at this new home from home a cup of hot chocolate was pressed into his palm by a grinning young Maquisard.

'We will talk in the morning,' Yves was telling him, and Farnham had no sooner agreed than he found himself alone. Resistance fighters obviously needed their beauty sleep, and he had to admit to feeling pretty tired himself.

He woke to the sound of birds singing in the trees. There were voices in the distance, and as he lay looking up at the filtered sunlight on the ceiling of his tent two or more men walked by, giving each other updates on their latest bowel movements. Farnham smiled to himself, shook himself out of his sleeping bag and reached for his clothes. All were well worn, and had been made in France.

Once dressed, he squeezed out through the tent opening and stood beside it for a moment, examining the view. The trees stretched away in all directions, either on a level or sloping downhill. They were mostly oak and beech, rising to a high canopy through which the sun shone fitfully down. The camp-site seemed to be draped across the flat brow of a hill, which would account for the relative dryness of the ground.

The camouflaged bell-tents had been erected at roughly ten-yard intervals, and Farnham reckoned that a spotter plane pilot would need the eyes of several hawks to see them.

He walked down through the trees to where two men were sitting on adjoining stumps, cleaning and oiling their vintage French Army rifles, and asked them where he could find their leader, Jules. They pointed him further in the same direction. 'But the leader's name is Yves,' they added with a grin.

Farnham walked thoughtfully on, feeling stupid. Why had he assumed that Jules was the leader? Because Yves wore glasses and looked like a schoolteacher?

He found both men leaning across a trestle table in what was obviously the command tent, examining a map. The five canisters were also there, laid out in a line on the floor, opened but not emptied.

Yves noticed the look on Farnham's face. 'We have waited for your blessing before distributing the guns,' the Maquisard said with a smile.

'You have it,' Farnham told him, which brought a grin to Jules' face. 'Good,' the Frenchman said. 'I was hoping to use them in the morning's exercises.' He grinned again and disappeared through the tent flap.

'Would you like some coffee?' Yves asked. 'And something to eat?'

Farnham nodded, and found himself alone again. The map, not surprisingly, was of the surrounding area, and someone had been at work with a soft pencil, marking in various approaches to the nearby town of St Dié.

Jules returned with a Maquisard whose name Farnham had already forgotten and carted away the two canisters containing the Stens and ammo, and then Yves reappeared with a cup of bitter-tasting chicory coffee and two hunks of stalish bread wrapped around a piece of cold and extremely fatty bacon. Farnham tried consoling himself with the thought that in a few days' time this would probably seem like a feast.

'It was a long winter,' Yves said apologetically, 'and the moment spring came more and more men decided it was time to join us. Feeding them has been just as difficult as finding weapons for them.'

'Why so many?' Farnham asked, hoping that the answer would tell him something about the answerer.

Yves shrugged like an Englishman's idea of a Frenchman. 'They all have their reasons. Some want to make sure they're on the right side now that the Germans seem to be on the run, but that's understandable. Last year most of the new recruits were avoiding the German labour drive – life in the forest seemed a better bet than working in a factory on the wrong side of the Rhine. And I'm sure some of them thought they'd made a mistake when winter came,' he added with a thin smile. 'People like to think that wars are fought by idealists, but most of the time they're fought by people who would have stayed at home if only the situation had allowed them to.'

'That's a depressing thought,' Farnham said, risking another mouthful of chicory.

'I don't find it so,' Yves said. 'There's something so much nobler about a reluctant soldier.'

It seemed early in the day for philosophy. 'What sort of exercises was Jules talking about?' Farnham asked.

'In the mornings we have physical training, followed by study sessions in guerrilla tactics and the enemy's anti-guerrilla tactics, and finally a field exercise which embodies the lessons which have hopefully been learned. In the afternoon there are more sessions on camp organization and leadership techniques in this sort of warfare.'

Farnham was impressed, and said so.

'Have you finished your coffee?' Yves asked. 'Or at least as much of it as you can swallow? Come, I will show you the lie of the land.' He plucked a pair of worn-looking field glasses from a hook, ducked out of the tent and led Farnham further into the camp. In a large space beneath a spreading oak about twenty men were doing press-ups, their grunts of exertion mingling with the birdsong above their heads. Most of them were naked to the waist, beneath which some wore trousers, some long johns and some just shorts.

'Are there no women in this outfit?' Farnham asked as they began walking again.

'Not living out here,' Yves said. 'We had a couple two years ago, and they were both great fighters, but their presence caused too many problems. It wasn't their fault, but . . .' He shrugged. 'We have women in the towns, and they often do much more dangerous jobs than those we do up here.'

They were through the camp now, and the screen of foliage in front of them was thinning, which suggested that they were coming to the end of the forest. The north-western side of the hill, it soon became clear, was bare of the trees which covered the other sides and crown, and from the edge of the latter they could see out across the wide valley of the River Meurthe. A mile or so to the west, and some five hundred feet beneath them, was the small village of Le Chipal. Several other villages could also be seen strung out at intervals along the winding road which ran through the foothills of the Vosges. More interesting to Farnham, about six or seven miles to the north a steam train was visible on the main St Dié to Strasbourg line, puffing small clouds of white smoke against the blue hills beyond. Following the line to the west he found St Dié itself, a red and brown smudge in the gap between heavily forested hills.

'What's the enemy strength in this area?' he asked Yves.

'It varies from week to week. There are small garrisons in St Dié and Gérardmer, much larger ones in Épinal and Colmar. The Gestapo's main regional centre is in Nancy, but they have branch centres in Épinal and St Dié. The Milice, of course, are everywhere, and now that they're beginning to realize they've picked the wrong side some of them have abandoned all restraint. It hurts me to say it, but they're worse than the Germans.'

'What do you need to step up operations in advance of the invasion?' Farnham asked.

'We would like more of everything,' Yves said promptly, 'but we need more guns, more food and more clothes. The guns you brought will make a big difference; another shipment and we will have as many as we need. As for food, the farmers nearby have always been generous, but there are just too many of us now. We have started sending scrounging parties further afield, with orders not to take no for an answer. Of course we leave requisition receipts, which will

73

be redeemable once the war is over, but the farmers don't like it and I can't say I blame them. If there were any other choice . . .' He grimaced. 'And as for clothes . . .' He held up a threadbare sleeve. 'You have seen what we are all wearing, and at this rate most of us will be in rags by the summer. But I hope you have arrived just in time to see us solve that particular problem. In Ste Marguerite, which is just outside St Dié, there is an old army storehouse, and it's full of clothing. There are uniforms, shoes, knapsacks, even cooking stuff, just waiting for a new army to claim them. And tomorrow night we intend to do just that.'

A little under forty hours later Farnham was one of eighteen men waiting in a small clearing on a hill, about one and a half miles south of Ste Marguerite. The Maquis camp in the foothills was only about five miles to the south-east as the crow flew, but in following a route that avoided settlements and made the most of tree cover they had walked almost twice that far.

The waiting faces were nervous, but Farnham would have been more concerned if they hadn't been, for the military experience of most was limited to their surrender in 1940. Yves had apparently served through the final months of the last war, but that hardly qualified him for guerrilla warfare. Nevertheless, the plan which he and Jules had concocted for this operation seemed, in outline at least, professional enough.

Farnham wasn't sure why they were waiting on this hill. The new moon was still casting its gossamer light across the clearing, and perhaps they were waiting for it to set, which wouldn't be for at least half an hour. He supposed he could walk over and ask, but Yves had made it very clear that, for the moment at least, he was to do as he was told and nothing more. After the last few years it was a strange feeling, having no responsibility, no decisions to take. Restful perhaps, but also frustrating.

The silence was suddenly broken by a bird call which seemed to come from further down the hill. One of the Maquisards answered in kind, and a few moments later two people walked into the clearing. One was a man in his thirties, dressed for the town rather than the country, with shirt and tie visible through the open neck of his coat.

The other was a woman, and from the moment of her entrance Farnham found it hard to take his eyes off her. She was probably in her twenties, and the wisps of blonde hair which had escaped from under her hat glowed in the faint moonlight. It was impossible to tell the colour of her eyes, but the face was drawn in shadow relief, emphasizing, perhaps even exaggerating, its beauty.

Her companion was doing most of the talking with Yves and Jules, leaving her to glance around at the rest of the unit. She gave smiles of recognition to some, but when her eyes briefly met Farnham's there was only a polite neutrality. He wondered what her name was, but knew he couldn't ask anyone. In the Resistance names were not shared without a very good reason.

Their report delivered, she and her companion disappeared back into the trees, taking two of the Maquisards with them. These two, Farnham remembered, had been allotted the task of cutting the telephone line between St Dié and Ste Marguerite, just in case something went wrong and someone at the storehouse tried to call for reinforcements. He wondered what her role might be.

The clearing seemed emptier without her, but at least the next period of waiting was shorter. It was two minutes past one by Farnham's watch when Jules gave the signal for their departure, and the band started down through the trees towards the wide valley below. Ten minutes later they were emerging on to the small road which skirted the flood plain of the braided Meurthe and walking north towards Ste Marguerite. A few darkened cottages loomed in front of them, but only a barking dog noticed their passage, and soon they could see the railway bridge which carried the St Dié to Strasbourg line across the road.

Near the rear of the column, Farnham was thinking that this unit showed excellent discipline. They were out on an open road, far from likely listeners, but there was no conversation at all, not even a whispered murmur. And either French boots and roads were softer than English, or these Maquisards could have given the SAS some lessons in marching quietly.

The crescent moon had now set behind the hills to the south of St Dié, leaving only the light of the stars in the clear sky above. They reached the bridge, and Jules led the way up the embankment to where the four lines of gleaming rail stretched away in either direction. The column followed them west, across the low bridge which carried trains across the Meurthe, and then clambered down another embankment to the path which followed the river. The buildings of Ste Marguerite were clearly visible now, a long line of shadowy rectangles straddling the road about half a mile to the north. On the left of the path, just before the bridge which carried the distant road across the river, Farnham could make out the complex of buildings which made up the storehouse.

A few minutes more and they were gathered beneath the surrounding wall, eight feet of brick topped with glass-encrusted concrete. An old mattress was lying innocently in the weeds beneath the wall – Farnham assumed it had not been dumped there accidentally – and two of the Maquisards quickly manhandled it across the top of the wall. The first man was hoisted up on to the mattress, from which he scanned the yard on the other side of the wall and grinned an all-clear.

The others followed him over and down into the yard on the far side, where they waited, ears straining for the sound of the lorry. They heard it arrive right on time, the driver sounding an insolent toot on his horn as he reached the gates.

Yves gestured the Maquisards forward, leaving Farnham, who had been politely ordered to sit out these next few minutes, to follow the planned sequence of events in his head. At this moment Henri and Jacques would be staring down from the cab of the stolen lorry in their stolen gendarmerie uniforms, demanding entrance. The local gendarme on duty might or might not be fooled, but in either instance he would be cut off from the communications in the guardhouse behind him, which would now be under the control of the first Maquisard team. The second would be looking after the off-duty shift in the barracks, reinforcing a good night's sleep with rags soaked in chloroform.

The minutes went by, and no shots echoed through the town to signal failure. Instead one of the Maquisards came to collect Farnham, leading him past the guardhouse, with its prone gendarmes, to the storehouse proper, where the loading was already underway. He joined in willingly, carting clothing, footwear and an unexpected haul of blankets out to the waiting lorry. On his last trip he noticed a pair of Maquisards busy at work disabling the lorry and two cars which were parked in the storehouse yard. Inside the guardhouse the phone had already been ripped from the wall.

After about five minutes Yves signalled enough, and all but Henri and Jacques climbed into the back of the vehicle.

Henri reversed it out into the road, Jacques pulled the gates shut and climbed back into the cab, and the lorry rumbled off through the sleeping village. A few minutes later they stopped again, this time to pick up the two men who had left the hill ahead of them, but Farnham could see no sign of the woman or her companion.

They were still on a main road, and the faces of the men around him reflected the dangers that represented, but no unexpected road-block appeared in front of them, and there was no sign of pursuit behind. A few minutes later they turned off into a winding lane, and now at last the Maquisards began to relax. There were grins on the faces, the first murmurs of conversation, even a joke or two.

The lorry rattled along the uneven roads for about half an hour, finally coming to a halt in a virtual tunnel of trees. Each man loaded himself up with all he could carry, and the long column started up the hill, reminding Farnham of Hope and Crosby's line of African porters in *Road to Zanzibar*, which he'd seen in London the previous summer with Eileen. The sounds of the lorry – which Henri had instructions to abandon as far from their camp-site as seemed safe – faded into the distance, leaving him to concentrate on keeping his footing and not losing sight of the man in front. Every now and then, though, an image of the woman on the hilltop would come unbidden to his mind, and he would smile to himself in the darkness.

For the next few days the mood in the Maquis camp was little short of triumphant. There were smiles everywhere, and even the blisters which came with the new boots seemed a source of enjoyment. The fact that the Germans had taken no reprisals for the raid on the storehouse was a great relief, and the news that they had mounted a full-scale sweep of the heavily wooded hill beneath which Henri had abandoned the lorry produced great amusement.

With each day that went by Farnham felt less of a stranger, and with only a few exceptions the Maquisards responded warmly to his overtures of friendship. They enjoyed listening to his accent, enjoyed his tales of the war in Africa and Italy, and were interested to hear how England was coping with the war in general, and the influx of Americans in particular. In north-eastern France there were many who still remembered the last Yankee onslaught in 1918.

Mindful of London's directives, Farnham cautiously probed the political allegiances of his new comrades. Noticing a certain tension between Yves and Jules, who seemed to function almost as joint leaders of the unit, he theorized that it might have a political source. The cynical Yves would be the communist, the patriotic Jules the Gaullist.

As it turned out, both were happy to talk politics with him, and happy to admit that they were socialist in their leanings, by which they seemed to mean nothing more precise than that they expected a better world to emerge from the war. The tension between them, such as it was, stemmed from temperament rather than politics. Yves, who had been a schoolteacher in St Dié, had an analytical brain and a tendency to take things to extremes, whereas Jules, who had worked on the railways all his life, tended towards wishful thinking and overcautiousness. They made a good team.

There were communists in the unit – three of them – but they made no attempt to either hide their political convictions or make them an issue. They seemed just as keen, but no keener than anyone else, to fight the Germans. They didn't huddle together and whisper secrets to each other, or kneel on the grass and salaam towards Moscow five times a day. In fact, all three seemed perfectly sensible, perfectly ordinary, young Frenchmen.

Farnham had never been very good with names, but by the end of his first week in France he reckoned he could put one to each of the faces in camp. Some, of course, he knew better than others: Charles, the chemist's son, and Jean-Paul, the farmer's son, who shared the tent next to his; the cheeky-faced François, who couldn't be more than seventeen, and his constant companion Paul, who looked even younger; Henri and Pierre, who were brothers, and as nice a pair of lads as Farnham could remember meeting anywhere.

He also got to know the area better, taking himself off on long walks at all times of the day and night. At first he had been escorted, but it didn't take Yves long to realize that their English guest was unlikely to either get himself lost or stand on the ridge above St Dié waving a Union Jack, and he was soon given licence to roam wherever the mood took him. Above their camp the tree cover was so extensive that views were hard to come by, but every now and then he would come upon one, and find himself entranced by the receding lines of forested slopes fading into misty horizons, the strange outcrops of red sandstone which occasionally broke those slopes, the ruins of medieval fortifications which hung above them. Everywhere he went there were birds to see and hear, from the smallest songbird to the hawk-like creatures hanging on the thermals above the valleys. He added 'find out which birds are which' to his list of things to do after the war.

Back in the camp he helped out with the training, offering insights from his SAS experience in Africa to the guerrilla warfare sessions, teaching small groups how best to deal with the Sten gun's tendency to jam and how to use the time pencils with the plastic explosive. One group of four was chosen for instruction in the use of the S-phone and Eureka-Rebecca sets, so that once he was back in England there would be no shortage of men to guide in supplies or reinforcements. In his mind, Farnham was already rehearsing his pitch for a full SAS team to operate in this area once the Allied invasion was a reality.

It was after returning from one of these classes – he had taken his students up to the drop zone for a real-life simulation – that Farnham was invited to the command tent for a discussion of the unit's next operation. This, he now heard, would be directed against the locomotive shed in St Dié, where Jules had once been an apprentice mechanic. The specific target was the shed turntable.

Studying the carefully drawn diagram, Farnham realized that the shed was of a type common on the continent but rare in Britain – he could only think of St Blazey in Cornwall, though there were probably a couple of others. It was constructed like a semicircular stable around the turntable, which could be aligned to feed a locomotive into any of the eighteen stalls. Put the turntable out of commission, and up to eighteen engines would be trapped until it could be repaired. And if they destroyed the actual turning plate, then Jules thought it might well be out of operation for months.

He had the know-how, and Farnham had brought the explosive.

The two of them spent most of the next night moving across country to the forested hill which lay south of St Dié, and which afforded a panoramic view of the town. The station lay directly below them, the junction to its right, the locomotive shed nestling between the diverging tracks. In this hour before dawn the whole area was fiercely lit, and the guards patrolling the area were not from the local gendarmerie – they were regular troops of the Wehrmacht. More than fifty of them, by Farnham's reckoning.

He had only just finished counting when the air-raid sirens began to howl, and the lights started going out section by section, drawing darkness across the valley like a blackout curtain. Farnham listened for the drone of approaching planes, and after a few minutes thought he could hear some in the distance, but the faint sound swiftly faded. On that particular night the Allied bombers were obviously heading elsewhere.

In the valley below the switches were flicked back on as the Germans drew the same conclusion, and the Wehrmacht guards climbed out of their shelters into the bright artificial light. It occurred to Farnham that an air raid would be a good time to set their charges on the turntable, always assuming that they weren't hit by an English or American bomb.

The day dawned, and the town beyond the tracks slowly came to life. The two men stayed on watch through the hours of daylight, counting and making notes on each of the trains which steamed through the station. Most were heading west, carrying men and war *matériel* to the Germans' Atlantic coast defences, and the few non-military trains which had managed to find a place in the timetable seemed almost empty. These days the Allied air forces were obviously something of a deterrent to travel.

One train which steamed majestically through an hour or so before dusk couldn't help but capture Farnham's imagination. The engine, a huge 4-8-2, was encased from end to end in camouflage-painted, streamline-style armoured plating. A real challenge to a modeller, he thought, remembering his own obsession as a young teenager. The planning of that first model railway had been the last time he had truly shared anything with his father, and not long afterwards he came to realize that the man was incapable of dealing with any situation in which he didn't have complete control. Farnham thought about his sister, and wondered how she was coping with their father. Better than he had, probably.

Alongside him, Jules was becoming fidgety. The Frenchman had been friendly enough, but he was clearly a man of few words at the best of times. He was by no means stupid, but he preferred to express himself through his hands, and he seemed to stare down at the railway as if it were a long-lost lover.

Around seven it was dark enough for them to start back, and three hours of steady walking through the forest brought them home. After a late supper and a long conversation with Yves, Farnham called London on the radio and explained what they needed.

Four days later, as Sunday gave way to Monday, Farnham, Jules and two other Maquisards crouched in the shadows of the fence which separated the road at the bottom of the hill from the tracks. Beyond the latter lay the brilliantly illuminated railway yard and locomotive shed. A few minutes earlier they had heard the voices of patrolling German guards not twenty yards from where they squatted, faces blacked, Stens at the ready.

The team's number had been kept to four on the grounds that any more would simply have increased the odds on their being spotted, without significantly adding to their chances of escape. They had chosen Sunday because the locomotive shed was more likely to be full, and in that at least they had been right, for sixteen of the eighteen stalls were occupied.

Farnham looked at his watch for what seemed the twentieth time, inwardly praying that London and the RAF weren't going to let them down, and this time he received his due reward. The sirens began to wail, and one by one the blocks of lights were doused until only one remained. This section lingered for almost half a minute, as if either fate or the Germans were trying to tease them, before its extinction plunged the yards into darkness.

'Let's go,' Jules ordered tersely.

The four men scrambled across the rickety fence and across the tracks, splashing through the ballast and on to the compacted cinders of the yard, barely visible even to each other in the gloom. At that moment two searchlights were turned on, one after the other, on the hills to the west of the town, and as their beams swayed in the night sky the drone of approaching bombers seeped out of the silence.

Jules led them across the confusion of tracks at the mouth of the depot and ducked between a signal box and a plate-layers' hut. The serrated silhouette of the engine shed loomed about a hundred yards ahead; and they ran alongside the access line before skirting round the turntable and slipping inside the first stall. This contained only a tank engine, but the second was playing host to a heavy goods engine, which offered all they could hope for in the way of shelter. One by one the four of them slid themselves down into what Jules claimed was the safest spot in the yard – an inspection pit beneath a locomotive.

The bombers were now loud in the sky, and the crouching men didn't have long to wait before the first stick of bombs fell. About half a mile to the west, Farnham thought, but it was hard to judge. The German anti-aircraft batteries boomed in response, and another rain of explosives crashed to earth, nearer this time. Farnham had not really expected a direct hit on the railway yard – precision bombing, as everyone but

Bomber Command seemed to know, was one of the war's great oxymorons – but the next detonations proved him wrong. A blinding yellow flash and a thunderous roar left him with ears ringing and the pattern of their sheltering locomotive's wheels imprinted on his retina.

The bomb had fallen not more than thirty yards away. It would be ironic, Farnham found himself thinking, if it had seriously disabled the turntable, something which Jules claimed would require a detonation within inches of the turning plate mechanism.

The fourth and final stick of bombs landed further east, somewhere in the vicinity of the station, and the four men scrambled out of the inspection pit. They had ten minutes.

Jules and Farnham dropped into the turntable well, leaving the other two crouching at either end of the track bridge, Stens at the ready, eyes scouring the dark yard for premature movement. The searchlights on the hills were still sweeping across the sky but the drone of the bombers was rapidly fading into the east. The second wave was supposed to be about forty miles, or ten minutes, behind the first, and the news of its approach should be keeping the Germans in their shelters.

In the dark well Farnham was moulding the plastic explosive into the area Jules indicated. Satisfied, he pushed home the time pencil and squeezed the detonator. 'OK,' he whispered.

As the two men climbed back out of the well a swelling roar in the western sky was announcing the second wave of bombers. This lot were early, Farnham thought angrily, as the four men raced back across the yard and the main-line tracks, flattening themselves behind the fence as the first bombs fell. They weren't very accurate either – most of the bombs were falling well to the north of the railway, on to the sleeping town. Looking back as they climbed up through the trees, he could see a couple of buildings burning in the distance, and at that moment there was a small yellow flash in the railway yard, followed by a dull booming sound.

Too late, Farnham thought. They had hoped to hide the sabotage within the bombing raid, but the last bombs had fallen several minutes before, and they would be lucky indeed if no one had seen that tell-tale flash.

The following evening a messenger reached camp with the news that it had indeed been seen. The turntable would be out of commission for weeks, maybe months, and the consequent trapping of the sixteen locomotives would cost the Germans several hundred trains in the lead-up to the invasion. They had not greeted this development with the hoped-for stoicism, but had rounded up ten prominent townspeople and hung them from lampposts in the main street. Another ten low-level railway workers had been held hostage for the good behaviour of their more vital superiors. Seven other residents of St Dié had been killed in the bombing, but no Allied planes had been shot down.

Summoned from his tent to hear the news, Farnham had to work hard to keep his attention from wandering. The messenger was the woman whom he had seen on the hill above Ste Marguerite ten days before. Her head was bare this time, the honey-blonde hair tumbling past her shoulders. Her overcoat was open, revealing a pale blue dress with a V-shaped neck and pearl buttons down the front.

'This is Madeleine,' Yves introduced her. 'She'll be taking you to meet our contact in Schirmeck, who should be able to help you with the concentration camp at Struthof.'

She offered her hand and smiled at Farnham, who smiled back, feeling like a schoolboy. Her eyes were grey, he noticed.

'Either he'll have the information you need, or he'll find someone to take you up the valley for a look,' Yves was saying.

'Sounds perfect,' Farnham said. 'And how will we get to Schirmeck?' he asked her.

'The train would have been the safest – it's only an hour from St Dié – but all civil journeys have been cancelled for at least the next week.' She smiled wryly. 'There seems to be a locomotive shortage, so we must take the bus. Which reminds me,' she continued, businesslike again. 'I need to see your papers.'

Farnham handed them over, and watched as she went through them.

'They are good,' she said at last, 'but not good enough. The problem is, they are false.' She smiled at the expression on his face. 'They would pass a casual inspection, but the moment anyone tries to check them you will be in trouble. These days we use only real identities, ones which can be checked.' She put the papers into her bag. 'I will get you a new set for the trip.'

'Thanks.'

'Now, there is a bus that leaves St Dié at two o'clock, and it stops at the crossroads near Raves about twenty minutes later. I will be on that bus on Wednesday, with your new papers. OK?'

Farnham nodded.

Madeleine turned to Yves, and Farnham half listened as she told the Maquis leader about Hans-Magnus Ziegler, the new Gestapo chief in St Dié, who had been responsible for the reprisal executions that morning. Her face was even lovelier in profile, and Farnham's eyes were drawn to the gentle curve of her breasts beneath the pale blue dress. He looked up to find Yves eyeing him with some amusement, and hoped that the light was poor enough to hide his subsequent blush.

He spent the next couple of days telling himself that it was absurd, that he didn't know anything about her, that his behaving like a lovesick idiot could get them both killed, that this was just four years of celibacy catching up with him. But he could hardly wait to see her again.

The bus was about half an hour late reaching the Raves crossroads and not surprisingly, given the withdrawal of trains, close to full. Equally astonishing, given the number of healthy young males on board, she had managed to keep the seat beside her vacant. He sat down, feigning surprise at meeting an old friend unexpectedly, and they kissed cheeks. She was wearing the same pale blue dress as before, and a perfume redolent of spring flowers – lily of the valley, he thought, without knowing why.

As agreed beforehand, they didn't talk. She looked out of the window, and he did the same, though often his eyes would flicker back to her face, or the way her blonde hair seemed to float on her shoulders.

It was a bright and sunny day, warm enough to qualify for summer. For the first five miles the bus climbed an increasingly tortuous road up a narrowing valley, finally reaching the watershed in the small town of Saale. From there road and railway slowly descended the valley of the Bruche in a north-easterly direction, crossing and recrossing both each other and the river with a dizzying regularity. Farnham started taking mental notes of sabotage-friendly locations, but soon abandoned the task – there were just too many. An efficient raiding group operating in the forested hills above would have little trouble shutting down both road and rail traffic for weeks on end.

As this thought was taking root in his mind, a long troop train steamed past in the opposite direction. Bareheaded Wehrmacht soldiers were leaning out of the windows smoking cigarettes, and no doubt wondering whether they'd ever see Germany and their families again.

Fifteen miles more and they were entering Schirmeck, a small town built in the space where two valleys converged. They had not passed a single German vehicle on the road but here they seemed to be everywhere – a troop lorry and two staff cars drove past as they walked the fifty yards from the bus stop to the small square at the centre of the town. Farnham wasn't sure whether or not he was imagining it, but the streets seemed unusually empty for a weekday afternoon, and those people that were out seemed almost uniformly eager to avoid eye contact.

Madeleine took his arm and guided him up a steep and narrow street of old two-storey houses. The sixth or seventh was a solicitor's office, and after one quick look back down the street she ushered him inside.

A small, balding man with bright eyes and a bushy moustache greeted them with a smile. 'Ah, you are here. Good. I was half afraid you would go straight to the inn, but I didn't want to risk waiting at the bus stop . . .'

'It was arranged that we should come here first,' Madeleine said, as he shook hands with Farnham.

'I know. I was just worried. The Germans have taken to checking all the local inns lately, sometimes more than once on the same day. So I think it would be wiser if you stayed here with me. There's a small attic room which you can sleep in,' he told Madeleine, 'while our friend here is roaming the hills.'

'This will not be safe for you,' she objected.

He shrugged. 'You're here now, and they might see you leave. There's no telling, so you might as well stay. Come,' he said. 'And don't let any signed photographs of De Gaulle slip out of your pockets,' he added with a grin. 'My name is Marcel, by the way,' he told Farnham, as they started up the narrow staircase.

The attic room was reached by a ladder, and had obviously been used for guests before. Two camp-beds faced each other across a threadbare carpet, which looked even more faded than it was in the sunlight pouring through the dormer window. The house faced west, Farnham noted, his eyes straying to the well-thumbed books which sat on the window-sill.

'I shall have to leave you for a while,' Marcel was telling Madeleine, 'to check on our friend's guide for the night. It should be dark in a couple of hours, and I think it would be wise to pull the curtains if you wish to turn on the light.'

'Of course,' she said.

He waved them both goodbye and disappeared down the stairs.

Madeleine took off her jacket, sat down on one of the camp-beds and slipped off her brogues. After massaging her toes for a moment she drew her legs together and encircled them with her arms.

She looked worried, Farnham thought, and said as much.

'No more than usual,' she said with a faint smile. 'I never liked this town,' she added. 'Even before the war.'

'Why not?'

She shrugged, and pushed her hair back behind her ears. 'I don't know.' She grinned suddenly. 'My first boyfriend went off with a girl from here, so maybe that was it.'

He found it hard to imagine anyone leaving her willingly. 'When was that?'

'I was fourteen. Half my life ago.' She shook her head. 'Let's talk about you. Were you a soldier before the war?'

'Yes. Just. I was commissioned in the summer of '39.'

'Why?' she asked with disarming frankness. 'You don't look the sort, though perhaps that's because I don't know much about Englishmen.'

'Maybe. I didn't join up because I was aching to fight anyone, I'm afraid.' He looked at her, and decided there was no point in anything but the simple truth. 'Looking back now, I think I was probably just trying to make my father understand that I didn't want anything to do with his world. There were probably other ways of doing that, but . . . well, then the war came along, and everything else went out the window.'

'You don't like your father?'

'No.'

'And your mother?'

'My mother died when I was young. I have a stepmother, but I can't pretend I like her any better than my father.'

'That is sad.'

He shrugged. 'I have a sister – she's sixteen, almost seventeen, and she's wonderful. She keeps me on my toes though.' He told Madeleine about their last meeting, and about the work Eileen was doing in the East End.

'It sounds like you love her very much,' the Frenchwoman said.

'I do,' Farnham said simply, and for a few moments they were both silent.

'Are you married?' Madeleine asked eventually.

'I was. She was killed in a bombing raid. In 1940. A long time ago.'

'The look in your eyes says it was only yesterday,' she said softly.

'I . . .'

'I'm sorry,' she said. 'People are always telling me I am too plain-spoken.'

'No, no . . . are you married?' he asked.

'I am a widow. My husband was killed in the same year as your wife.' She smiled sadly. 'Now there's a coincidence. One that we share with about a million others.'

'Was he killed in the fighting?'

'Yes, somewhere near Sedan. But I'm sure he didn't die with the "Marseillaise" on his lips. He was a communist, and he had no more time for this country than he had for any other. That was all before the attack on the Soviet Union, of course. He would have been happy in the Resistance after that.'

'Why did you join?' Farnham asked.

She considered the question, as if it was a strange one. 'Not to avenge anyone,' she said at last. 'And not for France. All countries have things to be proud of and things to be ashamed of. At first I persuaded myself that what I most hated about the Nazis, and what gave me a reason to fight, was that their only idea of the future was to drag everyone back into the past. You only have to look at their rallies, their architecture – it's Rome and Greece, not the twentieth century. And the way they insist on women being good housewives and mothers and nothing else, and the way they hate jazz . . . I love jazz.' She looked at him. 'I still believe all these things, but I know that this is not why I am involved in the fight. I am involved because that's what life should be – involvement. I can't just sit and watch. I have to be part of it.'

'That sounds a better reason than most.'

'I think it is. Just sometimes I wonder how many Germans there are feeling the same way, and I remember how Jacques – my husband – always had to know what was *right*.'

He smiled wryly. 'Maybe we've struck lucky with this war, and found ourselves on the right side through no fault of our own.'

She liked that. 'Tell me,' she said, 'as a soldier, do you think the Germans can still win the war?'

'No,' he replied.

'So how long will it last? I listen to your BBC, but I never know whether to believe everything I hear.'

'It's impossible to tell. If the invasion is a success, then . . .' He shrugged. 'The Germans will have three fronts to fight on, and they must be running low on war *matériel*. I can remember someone forecasting that they'd run out of oil in 1942. And the bombing must be doing a hell of a lot of damage. But there's just too many imponderables. What the Russians are going to do, the Japanese, these secret weapons we keep hearing rumours of . . .?'

'What are they?'

'Pilotless planes are the favourite. Flying bombs. But who knows? The war could be over by Christmas, or it could last another five years.'

It was getting dark now, and they could hardly see each other's face. 'I don't think we should turn on the light, even with the curtains drawn,' she said. 'Not until Marcel comes back, anyway.'

He was about to agree when they heard the door open downstairs, followed by the sound of footsteps. 'It's me,' Marcel shouted, and they breathed out in unison. Their host had another man with him, one not long out of his teens, whom he introduced as Lucien. As far as Farnham could tell Madeleine hadn't met him before.

'We should leave soon,' the young man said. Ordinary farm clothes adorned his thin frame and a soft, peaked cap sat on his head. 'In another hour or so there will only be Germans left on the streets.'

'I'm ready,' Farnham said, reaching for his jacket.

'Take this,' Marcel told him, handing over an ancient but formidable-looking handgun. 'It was my father's pistol in the last war,' he added. 'It still works.'

'I have food for two,' Lucien said, reminding Farnham he hadn't eaten since morning.

Madeleine wished him good luck, offering him her hand. He shook it gravely. 'You'll be here when I get back?'

'Yes.'

He turned and followed Lucien down the stairs. The street outside was in darkness, the main road below not much brighter, but the young Frenchman led him up the hill, and within a couple of minutes the houses were coming to an end, the road turning into a dirt track which wound up through a couple of steeply sloping fields before plunging into the forest.

Once they were among the trees Lucien slowed his pace and allowed himself the luxury of conversation. It was only about two and a half miles on the road from Schirmeck to the Struthof camp, he explained, but Farnham's need for a lengthy period of observation had been explained to him, and for this they would have to climb around and above the site, which would more than double the distance they needed to travel. And since they would have to stay well away from the German-patrolled paths the going was not likely to be easy. If they arrived at the chosen spot before midnight, Lucien concluded, then he would be much gratified.

Five hours of struggle followed, most of it across dark and densely wooded slopes, and as he trudged after his nimble guide Farnham found himself feeling nostalgic for a life lived in daylight. He imagined himself strolling round the Serpentine in the summer sunshine, preferably with Madeleine on his arm.

It was soon after ten when they heard dogs barking in the distance, and Lucien immediately signalled a halt. The two men crouched beneath the trees for a quarter of an hour, half expecting to hear another bout of barking or even the sudden sound of men running towards them through the forest, but nothing else disturbed the silence, and they cautiously resumed their journey.

Just before midnight they reached the spot Lucien had in mind, and after so many hours of walking blindly through the thick forest, Farnham was gratified to see just how well the young Frenchman had chosen. The hill they were on, like the one on which Yves' Maquis camp was pitched, had a bald spot, and from the shelter of trees they could look out across a wide swathe of countryside below. Almost directly in front of them, about a mile to the west and some six hundred feet below, the camp sat astride a humpback ridge. On either side of this ridge narrow valleys ran down to join the Bruche above and below the town of Schirmeck, which was itself hidden by the lie of the land.

The camp was as brightly lit as a beacon, and Farnham remembered Madeleine's assertion that the Nazis' most heart-felt desire was to create the future in the image of the past. Looking at the searchlights lazily sweeping from the watchtowers, the dark blocks of buildings in their geometrically shaped enclosure, he had the feeling that time had somehow been kaleidoscoped. If H.G. Wells could have brought the Barbarians forward in his time machine, then this would have been the sort of encampment they would have built.

'This is all right?' Lucien was asking.

'Perfect,' Farnham agreed. 'But we'll need to dig a scrape, because you can bet your life someone down there will have a pair of binoculars.'

This was easier said than done, given that their only digging implements were broken branches and their hands, but after an hour or so they had excavated and covered a shallow trench large enough to accommodate them both. And if Lucien was impressed with Farnham's branch and foliage roof, he found even more to admire in the miniature camera which the Englishman removed from the false compartment in his boot heel. Farnham wished the men in London could have seen the look on the Frenchman's face – it would have made their war.

Personally, he had his doubts as to whether it would work, but there would be no harm in trying to take some pictures once the sun came up.

'You should get some sleep now,' Lucien told him. 'I can sleep during the day, while you are on watch.'

This made sense, and Farnham tried to oblige, but it was some time before his body would cooperate. He was just beginning to think it was hopeless when Lucien's hand on his shoulder woke him up. Through the roof of the scrape a faint grey light was seeping. 'It will soon be dawn,' the Frenchman said.

They divided the bread and cheese that remained into four, and took a share each for breakfast, washing it down with some cold coffee. The sky to the west was still clear, and when the sun alighted on the crest of the hills beyond the Bruche valley it became obvious that another fine day was in prospect. Slowly but surely the shadows were stripped from the land in between, revealing the camp on the ridge and the twisting road which ran down from its gates to the valley on the left. The wire fencing, which was now glistening in the sunlight, enclosed an area about a quarter of a mile square.

There were, by Farnham's count, twenty-two buildings in the camp, and twelve of these, arranged in four rows of three, looked a good bet for the prisoners' quarters. Another four, set on the other side of an open space, were probably for administration and the guards, which left six unaccounted for. Some were presumably for cooking and washing, others might be set aside for prison work. The one with the tall chimney had to be a boiler house, though Farnham could see no heating pipes running from it.

He wished he had more to look through than just his naked eyes, but Yves, with good reason, had forbidden him to travel with his binoculars. One routine search and he would have been answering questions at the Gestapo HQ in St Dié.

He reached for the camera, thinking that the angle of the sun wouldn't get any better. The men in London could probably interpret a photograph far better than he could the reality.

'That is the crematorium,' Lucien said quietly at his shoulder. 'The one with the smoke.'

'The what?'

'Perhaps you call it something else in England. The place where they burn the bodies.'

He was not joking. Farnham thought back to the meeting in London, and his conviction that the men from Intelligence had not been telling him all they knew. 'Which bodies?' he asked quietly.

Lucien looked at him in wonderment. 'The bodies of the people they kill. That building in the far right-hand corner – that is the room where they are gassed. About thirty at a time.'

'How do you know?'

'There are people in the villages who work in the camp, doing the Germans' laundry, some cooking, other jobs. They see and hear things. And the Germans talk to women, especially when they are drunk.'

Farnham paused to let it all sink in. 'And who are they killing?' he asked eventually.

'Jews mostly, but communists and queers too. I guess they'd kill a queer Jewish communist three times over if they could.' Lucien still had the look of surprise on his face. 'I thought this was why you wanted to see . . . because you knew what was happening here.'

'I didn't,' Farnham said wearily. 'I think someone in London knows, and they sent me to make sure.'

'Ah, I understand now,' Lucien said. He yawned. 'Wake me when it gets dark,' he said, and sank back on to the floor of the scrape.

Farnham took his pictures, keeping one negative in reserve, just in case something unusual transpired in the course of the day. But nothing did, and he lay there for hours, his eyes mostly transfixed by the smoke which rose from the crematorium. Not that long ago he would have found it hard to believe that down there, in that camp, people were being systematically killed just because of who they were. He had never managed to swallow his father's theory that the British and Germans offered civilization's defence against the Latin races to the south and the Slavs to the east, but neither had he ever thought of the Germans as being particularly cruel. Unfeeling perhaps, but not vicious.

The smoke carried on drifting into the blue sky. How many more of these camps were there? If Jews were being killed simply because they were Jews, then what defence could any Jew have?

* * *

As they walked back down the hill that evening, the distant lights of Schirmeck evoked in Farnham a momentary spasm of anger. He had no doubt that everyone knew – the moment he had stepped off the bus on the previous day he had felt something in the air, seen it in the faces. Those people at home eating their supper, or drinking and chatting in one of the bars, were doing their best to pretend that life went on as normal, knowing all the time that in the hills above them a terrible evil was afoot. They knew, but they did nothing.

His anger faded as the town grew nearer. What could they do? Charge up the hill and end up being gassed themselves?

They were nearing the point where the dirt track metamorphosed into the road, some two hundred yards above Marcel's house, which was still hidden from view around a bend. The road was unlit, which made it easy to see the headlight beams suddenly sweeping across the houses ahead. Almost at once these moving circles of light came to a halt, without the car itself coming into view.

It seemed probable to Farnham that it had stopped outside Marcel's house, and he found himself walking faster. One bright-yellow headlight came into view, then the other. In the darkness behind them he saw at least two figures moving towards the house, then heard the sharp rap on the door.

There didn't seem much doubt about who the visitors were – no Resistance people would drive up in such a car, lights blazing. But what should he do? Wait to see if Marcel could talk his way out of trouble? No, Farnham thought instinctively. They might drag the Frenchman out at any moment – him and Madeleine – and then it would be too late. He pulled Lucien to one side, and announced that he was going down to investigate.

'I'll come with you,' Lucien said, 'but I don't have a weapon.'

'No,' Farnham told him. 'If we're all taken you'll have to warn the others. So get going.'

The young Maquisard's mouth flirted with obstinacy before the sense of what Farnham was saying took hold. He touched the Englishman briefly on the shoulder, wished him luck and started back up the road.

Farnham took a deep breath and set off, walking swiftly towards the illuminated area ahead. The headlights were soon shining directly at him, and at any moment he expected a guttural shout to emerge from behind them, but none came. In the right-hand pocket of his trousers the butt of the pistol felt cold against his hand.

And then the shot came from the house – a loud crack, like wood splintering in a fire. He walked faster, wanting to run but knowing that a running man would be instantly recognized as an enemy.

He was about fifty feet away when they emerged on to the pavement. Two of them, both in long leather coats, each holding one of Madeleine's arms. They didn't notice him for a couple of seconds, which gave him ten more feet, and then one of them snarled something in German, giving him the chance to feign incomprehension as he kept walking.

The nearest German let go of Madeleine's right arm and turned towards him, still snarling, his hand reaching into his coat pocket.

Farnham was now about twenty-five feet away, which was still quite a distance with a strange gun, shooting into the light. He slid it from his pocket, straightened his arm at eye level, braced his legs and pulled the trigger, hoping to God the gun didn't explode in his hand.

The German jerked backwards and a thunderous roar echoed down the street. His partner made the mistake of trying to pull Madeleine closer to him as he reached for his own gun. When that got caught in his coat pocket he needed the hand that was holding her, and she half fell, half threw herself to one side, giving Farnham a clear target. The pistol boomed again, and the second German collapsed with a groan.

Farnham strode forward. The first man was dead, the second looked like he might survive. But he had seen Madeleine. Farnham hesitated for only a second before putting the barrel of the pistol against the side of the man's head and pulling the trigger.

Madeleine was back on her feet. 'Are you all right?' he asked.

'Yes.'

'Where's Marcel?'

'He's dead.'

'Then let's go,' he said, looking round. Which way should they go? He could hear feet and voices on the main road below, and the dark road stretching up into the hills looked inviting, but something told him that was not the way to run. 'Get in the car,' he told her.

She gave him an enquiring glance, apparently decided that this wasn't the time for a discussion, and got in.

In the driver's seat Farnham was struggling with the controls. The engine was already running, but there was no space to turn the car, and for several long seconds he couldn't find reverse. When he did the car leapt backwards like a metal gazelle, and as they careered downhill towards the main street he thought for one dreadful moment that he was going to crash it. The left-hand wheels jumped up on to the pavement on the corner, and there was a loud thumping noise as someone ran into the back of the moving car. On the other side a man in uniform had leapt out of their way, his rifle clattering on the street.

More by luck than judgement, Farnham had spun the car round so that its bonnet was facing west. But in the distance they could see more headlights, a whole stream of them. A Wehrmacht convoy was headed their way. Then another gunshot sounded, and they heard the sound of breaking glass behind them.

Farnham rammed the gear-stick into first and took off, shifting gears upwards as he spun round the town square and shot out along the road which led east. As they reached the last of the buildings the valley narrowed before them, and the road was joined on either side by the river and railway. 'Where does this road go?' he asked her, scanning the mirror for signs of pursuit.

'Germany,' she said quietly.

He glanced across at her. 'Are you sure you're OK?' he asked.

'Yes,' she said. 'I'm sorry.'

'Can we double back somewhere, find another road which will take us west?'

'I don't think so. I don't know this . . .'

'Don't worry about it,' Farnham interjected, having just noticed that the fuel gauge showed close to empty. 'We haven't got enough petrol for more than a few miles.' They were turning a bend in the valley when he thought he glimpsed lights in the distance behind them. 'And we've got company,' he added.

'We'll have to get into the forest,' she said.

'Yes, but where?'

'Turn off the lights,' she said, and after a moment's hesitation he did so. She was right. The moon must be lurking somewhere behind the mountains, because the natural light was good enough to drive by, and without the headlights shining in front of them they could make out more of the valley's topography.

Both road and railway had crossed over the river about half a mile back, leaving them on the left-hand side of the valley, the tracks in the centre, the rushing water on the right. To their left the walls of the valley rose steeply, and finding a suitable place to climb would be a hit-and-miss affair, but the river lay between them and the gentler slopes to the right.

'Up ahead,' she said excitedly, pointing through the windscreen at a bridge which carried the railway across the river.

It looked as good a bet as any. And the Germans would have to follow them on foot. Farnham pulled the car up, just as the engine misfired again. It was the bridge or nothing.

They scrambled out and over the wooden fence which separated the road from the railway, half tumbled down a low bank to the tracks and started running between the rails towards the bridge. Farnham could hear no sign of pursuit, but the river was loud enough to drown it. As they neared the entrance to the bridge he prayed they wouldn't meet a train halfway across.

The black waters swirled beneath the girders, and they had to slow their progress to avoid falling through the gaps in the plating, but the road behind them was still empty when they reached the other side. Once over the bridge, the tracks swung left, running along an embankment between the river and a series of bare rock-faces. Farnham was reminded of San Severino and the fate which had befallen Corrigan and Imrie, but there was nowhere else to go.

'Look!' she said. Three pairs of headlights had appeared on the road, and as the beams from the first pair encompassed the car they had abandoned the sound of screeching brakes was audible above the river.

'Come on!' Farnham urged, and they took off again, haring as fast as they could across the irregularly spaced sleepers. As he ran, it occurred to Farnham that if the Germans had the sense to drive one of their vehicles forward a couple of hundred yards and angle it so the headlights shone across the river he and Madeleine would be sitting ducks.

A couple of seconds later the sound of a motor revving produced a sinking sensation in his stomach. And then he heard the howling of dogs, and pictured them straining at the leash.

Ahead of him, Madeleine seemed to be losing speed, which was hardly surprising. They had to get off the tracks, and quickly. Farnham was reluctantly coming to the conclusion that even the river offered a better chance of escape when he noticed the stream which plunged under the tracks from a gap in the cliffs. Looking back, he could see figures racing across the bridge behind them. 'We'll have to jump,' he told her, staring down into the gloom where the stream entered the culvert. It looked about six feet, but there was no way of knowing what sort of surface they'd land on.

He half expected her to argue, but she was already judging her jump, and a second later she launched herself into space. He followed, landing beside her with a splash, jarring an ankle on a stone. But it wasn't sprained, and she was already starting up the fast-running stream, brogues in hand. He struggled after her, feeling the cold water biting at his feet, and listening for sounds of pursuit. After a couple of minutes he heard the dogs again, but this time their barking was swallowed by the louder noise of an approaching train. 'That should slow the bastards down,' he murmured to himself.

They kept climbing, concentrating on keeping their feet on the uneven stream bed, and heard the train go clanking past in the valley below. Once it had rumbled across the bridge the sound of its passage slowly faded, and in the ensuing silence they could hear nothing else. When, after another ten minutes, there was still no sign of their pursuers they climbed gratefully out of the stream and let the vastness of the forest close around them like a cloak.

It was another two hours before Farnham would let them stop, even for a short rest, and in the meantime they headed vaguely southwards, using the stars and newly risen moon as guides. They made use of those paths and dirt tracks which seemed to point in roughly the right direction, but sometimes there was no choice but to burrow through the virgin forest. Here the difficulties of forcing a passage often put a stop to conversation, but on the paths and tracks, once they began to feel safe from pursuit, the two of them talked.

The first thing Farnham wanted to know was what had happened in Schirmeck.

'I'm not sure,' she said. 'I was in the attic, keeping quiet. What I think happened was that Marcel realized they were going to find me up there, and after taking them up the first flight of stairs he made a run for it. I think he hoped that if they had to follow him out into the street then I would have time to get away, but they just shot him. When they brought me down from the attic he was lying at the bottom of the stairs with a bullet in his back.'

'How did they know about him?'

'I don't know, but these things happen all the time. It might have just been a lucky guess, or someone in the street saw us going in and reported it, or someone in the local Maquis betrayed him.'

'Do you think they expected to find you there?'

'Not me in particular.'

'We'll, you'll be safe with Yves' group.'

'Perhaps, but my work is in St Dié.'

He had been afraid she was going to say that.

'Those two Germans didn't know who I was, and they were the only ones who saw me.'

Which was true enough, he thought.

'Thank you for what you did,' she said, stopping for a moment and turning her face to his.

'You're welcome,' he replied, not sure whether she was referring to the rescue as a whole or his execution of the wounded German.

She turned away, and resumed walking. 'What happened to Lucien?' she asked over her shoulder.

'He wanted to come with me, but I told him someone would have to warn the others if I failed.'

'Did you find what you were looking for at Struthof?' she asked, as if he'd been out on a shopping expedition.

'More or less,' he said, hoping that the film had survived his walk up the stream. 'They're killing people in droves in that camp.'

'That's what Marcel told me.'

'You don't seem surprised.'

'I'm not. Nothing really surprises me about the Germans any more. I've known of too many people that they've tortured to death.'

There was no answer to that. 'How far do you think we are from Yves' camp?' he asked.

'About twenty-five miles perhaps. In a straight line, that is. Many more by paths like this. If we could keep walking through the day I think we would be lucky to reach it before midnight.'

'We should sleep through the day. Or at least for a few hours. And we need to find some food somewhere.'

'We can stop at a farm,' she said, 'but not during the day. There's no way of knowing which farmers can be trusted, and we don't want the Germans on our trail while it's still light.'

They walked on, their limbs growing heavier with each mile. The way south seemed mostly uphill, and by the early hours they knew they had climbed quite high into the mountains. Soon after three o'clock they came to a surprisingly good road, which followed the back of a long ridge, offering occasional glimpses of the distant lands to east and west through breaks in the trees. It had been built by the military, Madeleine guessed out loud, and probably in the past twenty years.

They followed this road south for another two hours, but as the first glimmer of light appeared in the eastern sky Farnham started looking for an alternative. Almost immediately the road took a convenient turn to the west, leaving them to plunge once more into the forest. Another half-hour and they were looking down at a wide valley which cut across the direction of their march. The sun was still behind the mountains to the east, the valley still in shadows, but they knew there wasn't enough time for a safe crossing of the open fields below.

'I reckon this is where we rest,' Farnham said. The wind seemed to be blowing both stronger and colder, but perhaps it was just that they had stopped moving. That and the lack of food. The thought of a hot, sweet cup of tea crossed his mind, and almost made him dizzy with desire.

'I think I know where we are,' Madeleine said beside him. 'That's the road to Sélestat,' she said, indicating the faint grey line which wound through the valley below. 'Ville is a few miles up that way. I remember cycling down this road before the war.' She crossed her arms over her breasts and hugged herself. 'We still have a long way to go.'

He could see she was shivering. 'I think I remember a small hollow back in the trees,' he said. 'It should be a bit warmer, and maybe we can get some sleep.'

She followed him dutifully, but the hollow turned out to be not much more than a grassy dent in the ground, and in the trees above the birds were making such a racket that sleep seemed unlikely.

At least the ground was dry. They both lay down, keeping a modest distance between them, and after a while she burst out laughing. 'This is absurd,' she said. 'We could at least help keep each other warm.' She crawled across to him. 'This is no time for being too English,' she said, and snuggled up next to him. 'I need an arm,' she complained.

He obligingly wound one around her shoulder and pulled her head on to his chest. He had to admit he felt warmer, in more ways than one. The faintest trace of lily of the valley was in his nostrils, and the temptation to stroke her hair was almost irresistible. A few moments later he realized he was stroking it, and she hadn't leapt to her feet in outrage.

Her right hand, which had been clasping her left, was now moving across his waist, encircling him. 'Your back's frozen,' she said suddenly, and jerking herself upright, she pulled off her coat. 'Put your left arm in here,' she said, holding up the right sleeve of the coat, 'and I'll put mine in here and . . .'

Suddenly they were kissing, all thought of the cold forgotten, lying side by side, legs wonderfully entangled, stomachs pressing together. As the dawn light brightened he could see her nipples pressing against the thin cotton dress, and as he gently caressed one with his fingers her hand ran down across his stomach to stroke his throbbing cock. 'I haven't done this for a long time,' she said softly.

'Neither have I,' he said.

His hands fumbled with the buttons on the front of her dress, until all were undone and he could draw it apart. Her brassière was fastened at the front, and he slipped the clasp and drew the cups aside to reveal pale and beautiful breasts, their tawny nipples quivering to the touch of his fingers and his tongue. He kissed each breast, kissed her stomach and her belly button, and as she arched her back he slipped off her knickers and kissed the triangle of moist golden hair.

She watched as he unbuttoned his trousers and pulled down his pants, then reached both hands forward to stroke him gently with both palms. 'Come inside me,' she said, guiding him in and crossing her ankles behind his back.

He came almost at once, but it didn't seem to matter, for after what seemed only minutes he was as hard as before, and this time they swayed to and fro, moving first urgently and then languidly, finally stopping altogether and letting passion alone push them into a shared climax.

And after that they slept, their bodies entwined, with the birds singing overhead. One of them should have been on guard while the other slept, but they were lucky, and neither friend nor foe came upon them. Around noon he woke up to find her looking at him, and this time she came down upon him, enclosing him and swaying above him as he caressed her naked breasts and flanks.

They slept again, finally waking as the sun went down, and lay for a while in each other's arms before succumbing to passion once more. Afterwards, lying on the grass with her head in the crook of his arm, Farnham watched the clouds scudding across the darkening sky, thinking that never in his life had he felt so good as he did at that moment. He felt reborn, felt like laughing out loud for joy.

Instead his stomach rumbled, loud and long.

'You sound as hungry as I feel,' she said.

With the light almost gone they made their way down into the valley, heading for the nearest farm. Barking dogs heralded their approach, and a man with a shotgun stood silhouetted in the farmhouse door, but a few words from Madeleine were enough to win them a hastily prepared package of bread and cheese, together with a half-full bottle of white wine. They began consuming this feast as they climbed the other side of the valley, savouring each mouthful as the energy seeped back into their limbs.

After a couple of hours of working their way across country they found another military road to take them south along the back of a major ridge. The moon had not yet risen, but the sky was as clear as the night before, the vast armada of stars twinkling above the endless slopes of dark and silent trees. Farnham learned that Madeleine's brother worked for the PTT – the French Post, Telegraph and Telephone Ministry – in St Dié, and that she had become, almost by accident, the liaison between this hotbed of urban resistance and the Maquis in the hills. Her home was in the town, but an aunt who lived in Le Chipal, just below the Maquis camp, provided her with a legitimate reason to travel between the two.

She asked him what he wanted to do after the war, and he realized that he had no real plans, just odd desires, like the one to visit Italy again. He asked her what she was hoping for. 'A family,' she said simply.

The moon came up, the miles went by. They reached another wide valley – the town of Ste Marie aux Mines, Madeleine said, was just out of sight to their left. After watching the road below for the time it took to eat the rest of their food, they cautiously made their way down, crossed the empty ribbon of tarmac and scaled the other side. They now had less than ten miles to travel, and as they marched down yet another winding track through the trees Farnham tried to shake off the sense that it would soon be over, that he would lose her. This was just the beginning, he told himself, but it didn't feel that way.

They were skirting a small, moonlit clearing not much more than a mile from the camp when she reached out to take his arm and bring him to a halt. 'I shall have to leave again soon after we get there,' she told him, 'so that I can be at my aunt's house before dawn.' Her arms were around his neck now. 'And this seems like a good place to say our goodbyes,' she murmured between kisses.

They arrived at the camp two hours later, and Yves was woken with the news of their arrival. 'I was just wondering what to tell London,' the Maquis leader told Farnham. 'A plane is coming to collect you on Saturday night, and I didn't know whether you'd be here to take it.'

'Well, I suppose I am,' Farnham said. Inside his head a voice was shouting: 'Fuck the plane! Fuck London! Fuck the war!'

'I must be getting down the hill,' Madeleine told Yves. 'Will you walk some of the way with me?' she asked Farnham.

'Of course.'

'We've become friends,' she told Yves with a smile.

Farnham accompanied her to within a stone's throw of the sleeping village, and after a passionate goodbye kiss watched as she walked away down the path, hair dancing on her shoulders. He had wanted to tell her that he loved her, but some deep fear had held him back.

For Farnham, the next three days passed by in a whirl. Jules accompanied him on a two-night trip to explore the railway between St Dié and Saale, and they came back with a plan for the simultaneous destruction of five railway and two road bridges, which they thought would effectively halt all military transport on that route for at least a week. It would be put into effect in the days immediately preceding the Allied invasion of the Continent, whenever that might be.

Arriving back at camp early on the day of his planned departure, he half hoped to find her there waiting, but there wasn't even a message. He spent the day filling in any last gaps in the training, talking with Yves and saying his goodbyes. Returning to his tent to pack, he found her waiting for him.

'It is against the rules of the unit for a man to have a woman in the camp,' she told him after they stopped kissing, 'so we must be quiet.' And after that there was only the rustle of clothes being removed, the faint swish of their naked bodies on the groundsheet, the whispers of endearment and the low groans of pleasure given and taken.

All too soon they were getting dressed again, and Henri was outside waiting for him. 'I love you,' she whispered as they kissed goodbye, and the words seemed to explode with joy inside him. 'And I you,' he told her, and there was a smile in her eyes which he couldn't help but believe.

All the way up the hill he could see her in his mind's eye, standing there saying goodbye, or naked above him in the forest, or her eyes searching his as they had reached climax in the tent not half an hour before. And a mixture of elation and sadness and panic whirled round his brain, and he wanted to insist on staying here in France, but he knew that neither of them knew how to let passion take precedence over duty.

They reached the meadow on the hilltop. Yves, Farnham and young François stayed beside light A, where the Lysander was supposed to touch down, while Jules, Henri and Jean-Paul carried lights B and C, which would mark the plane's turning circle, to their positions some six hundred yards away across the grass. The meadow hardly seemed flat enough to Farnham, but the RAF had told him it fell within the specifications.

François had laid the Eureka-Rebecca beacon beside light A, and was now wearing the S-phone apparatus, the two webbed straps around the neck supporting the set itself, the T-shaped aerial protruding out in front of the young Frenchman's chest like a stationary propeller. Earphones were clamped around his skull, and while his left hand held the microphone his right jiggled the frequency knob in search of the best reception.

As they waited Farnham mused that though it was only three weeks since he had landed in this meadow, it felt like months. War distorted time, he decided – days in Italy had seemed like weeks, and the weeks in Ayrshire, in retrospect, seemed like days. Nothing of importance had happened in those weeks, but here his life had changed for ever.

They heard the plane before they saw it. The homing device in the Eureka-Rebecca set had already told the pilot that this was the right place to land, and François now confirmed on the S-phone that it was safe for him to do so. A few seconds later the Lysander came into view, a dark wedge against the moonlit sky, and then it was bumping safely down about fifty feet past them, before being swallowed in the dark background of the distant trees. A couple of minutes later and it was taxiing back towards them. The pilot turned the plane into the wind and stopped alongside light A, cheerily shouting, 'All aboard for Blighty.'

First they had to unload the boxes of new Stens and explosives which Yves had ordered from London, but once this was done Farnham clambered up the metal ladder and into one of the passenger seats behind the pilot. He had a last glimpse of grinning Frenchmen, their arms upraised in farewell, and

4

The newspaper which McCaigh had found on the bench at Oxford had a blow-by-blow account of the battle for Caen, which Monty's 2nd Army had brought to a successful conclusion a couple of days before. Each of the four men read it in turn, and not surprisingly the same thoughts crossed all their minds. Nearly five weeks had now passed since the Allied landings on the Normandy beaches, and the Germans had made them fight for every bloody yard. Maybe this was the battle that heralded a general break-out. And maybe then their time would come.

Playing silly buggers in the Cotswolds had been bad enough when everyone else was chafing at the bit, but now that the fucking country seemed almost empty of soldiers it seemed like purgatory. Four parties of the British 1 SAS and 2 SAS, and a similar number of the French 3 SAS and 4 SAS, had been dropped into France in the days immediately before and after D-Day, and another half-dozen parties were scheduled to leave in the next week or so, but Farnham's squadron was not among them. The word from above was that their time would come, but that didn't make it any easier to answer the

115

question that they seemed to see in everyone's eyes – what the fuck were they still doing on this side of the bloody Channel?

For Rafferty, McCaigh and Tobin it was doubtless a lot worse than it was for Farnham. If the promotion to Major was anything to go by, he'd already done one good job in France, while they'd been deafening each other on the firing range, cleaning weapons, cross-country running, and occasionally breaking glasses in the local pub. The announcement, soon after Farnham's departure, that they were leaving Ayrshire had been greeted with whoops of exultation, but their new home in deepest Gloucestershire didn't seem much of an improvement. Nearer to France, maybe, but then so was Switzerland.

All three of them were approaching their weekend leave with feelings of anxiety, though in Ian Tobin's case the context was likely to be pleasurable. Megan's letters over the last three months had become increasingly racy, and his thoughts had often returned to the night of the party and the way she had squirmed against him. This time he was prepared, a chemist in Cirencester having obliged. Buying the condoms had been a deeply embarrassing experience – he still blushed whenever he thought about it – but the thought of having to enter a similar shop in Swansea had been incentive enough.

He had thought long and hard about Megan's brother and his deserter friends in the black market, and had shared his qualms with both McCaigh and Rafferty. The Londoner had told him it wasn't worth risking a breach with his girlfriend – 'There'll always be shits like that in wars, just like there'll always be maggots in a rotten apple. If you shop one bunch of the bastards another bunch'll just pick up the business. It's not worth it.' Rafferty, on the other hand, had been full of righteous anger when he heard the story, but then Rafferty seemed to be angry most of the time these days, and Tobin had decided to take McCaigh's advice.

Unlike Tobin, McCaigh knew why Rafferty was walking round like a man with multiple toothaches. A couple of weeks after their last leave the two men had got happily drunk together in a Fairford pub, and Rafferty had spilled the whole sad story of his wife's American boyfriend. It was a plot-line McCaigh had heard more than once over the past couple of years, but that didn't make it any less sad, and Rafferty obviously had no idea how to deal with the catastrophe which had befallen him. He'd always been such a contented sort of bloke, the kind that things like this weren't supposed to happen to, and he just couldn't understand why it had. Time and distance were what he needed, but the fact of the kid put paid to any notion of a complete break, and Rafferty seemed in for a rough ride this coming weekend. He had even asked McCaigh to come to Cambridge with him, but the Londoner had guiltily declined – he had family troubles of his own to sort out.

He had received three letters from his mother during the last month, which had just about doubled her tally for the war. The SAS men in Gloucestershire were apparently not the only people getting their knickers in a twist at the thought of sitting out the rest of the war. McCaigh's brother Patrick had apparently been searching high and low for someone to supply him with the false papers he needed to enlist. 'I've never seen him so worked up about something,' Susan McCaigh had written, adding that she was occasionally tempted to put a bullet through her younger son's foot with his grandfather's old Webley, but was frightened of the consequences for the boy's football career.

McCaigh smiled to himself and opened his eyes. He looked across at Farnham, who was sitting, eyes closed, with a faint smile playing on his lips. His disposition had changed as radically as Rafferty's over the last few months, only in the opposite direction. McCaigh didn't know why, but his best guess was a piece of French skirt. One of those Resistance women from the films, with the beret and the delicious accent and the last-resort Derringer in the garter belt. Ah, France, he thought, come and get me.

Tobin's train pulled into Swansea High Street soon after dark, and after eating a quick supper with his parents he walked across town to Megan's home. Her family were still at the table when he got there, and the food on display looked fit for royalty. 'It's our wedding anniversary,' Megan's mum explained, 'and Barry managed to get us something special.' Their elder son grinned knowingly, just as the younger – seven-year-old Cliff – tipped his dish of custard on to the floor.

Barry soon made his exit, and Megan's parents, it soon transpired, were going out for a celebratory drink together. 'I'm sorry we can't go out,' Megan told Tobin once they'd been left holding the baby, 'but it is their anniversary, and you didn't give me enough warning you were coming . . .'

'I couldn't . . .'

'I know. And anyway,' she said, putting her arms round his neck and giving him a kiss, 'we can have a nice time here, listening to the radio and cuddling on the sofa. Barry left us some beer.'

'Black-market beer, I suppose.'

'It tastes the same. You're not still upset about that, are you?'

'I just think it's wrong.'

She sighed. 'OK, but can we just enjoy ourselves tonight? Please.'

He couldn't resist the fingers massaging the back of his neck. 'Yeah, of course.'

And they did, exploring the limits of what was possible given that her mum and dad might arrive back at any moment. Between bouts of 'canoodling' – as she liked to call it – they talked about their lives without each other, and it seemed to Tobin that she was getting a lot more out of hers than he was out of his. She taught him a new dance she had learnt – from who, he wondered, but didn't ask – and they dutifully listened to the nine o'clock news on the radio. 'The war'll be over soon,' she said afterwards, but there didn't seem much joy in the way she said it.

At ten-thirty her parents arrived back and Tobin got up to go. 'I'm working tomorrow,' Megan told him at the door, 'but there's another party in the evening.' She gently rubbed herself up against him. 'And maybe we can carry on where we left off at the last one.'

Tobin walked home through the dark streets torn between desire and a feeling of discontent which he couldn't quite put his finger on. Why wouldn't she be happy that the war was ending? They'd known each other since they weren't much more than kids but sometimes lately she seemed a complete mystery to him. Sometimes he wasn't even sure he liked her. But one thing he did know – he wanted her more than ever. Walking up his own street he patted the pocket with the packet of johnnies as if it contained a lucky talisman.

The next morning he helped in the shop for a while, chatting with all the regulars, and then took the bus down to Rhossili and walked along the cliffs above Worm's Head. A stiff wind was blowing in from the Atlantic, hurrying the clouds across the blue sky, and he felt invigorated, almost purified, as he made his way back to wait for the return bus.

Back at home he spent an hour bathing and getting himself smartened up. Megan hadn't told him not to wear his uniform, but he assumed as much, and made the best of what else he had. At ten to seven he left the house and started walking. The johnnies were now sharing his inside jacket pocket with his wallet, and he had to be careful not to pull them out by accident.

There had been a short shower late in the afternoon and the trees were glistening in the evening sun. Tobin repressed a desire to skip.

It was one minute past seven when he knocked on the Allchurches' front door. It opened almost immediately, but not to reveal a dolled-up Megan. Instead, Tobin found himself face to face with a surprised-looking Mr Allchurch. Surprised, and almost hostile. 'What are you doing here?' Megan's father asked.

'We're going to a party. Is Megan ready?'

'I doubt that,' Mr Allchurch said, and turned his head. 'Megan!' he shouted. 'He's here.'

Somewhere inside the house Tobin could hear a woman crying, but it wasn't Megan. She was now standing in front of him, arms folded across the overall bib she wore for work. 'What are you doing here?' she snapped. The words echoed her father's, but the tone took no prisoners.

'What do you mean?' he asked. 'What's going on?'

'Couldn't you have climbed down off your high horse just this once?'

'What are you talking about?' he asked, bewildered.

'Are you going to try telling me that you had nothing to do with Barry being arrested?'

'He's been arrested,' Tobin repeated stupidly. And then he understood.

'You should be in the films,' she said angrily.

'Don't be stupid!' he shouted back, feeling his own anger rising to match hers. 'Of course I didn't!'

'I'm stupid, am I? You told me you wanted to turn him in last time you were here, and the day after you get back they arrest him. Well, it doesn't take a brainbox to work that one out.'

He looked at her helplessly. 'Megan, why would I come to take you to a party if I'd done that?'

'Probably because you think I'm too stupid to make the connection. Well, I've got news for you, Ian Tobin. I did!' And with that she slammed the door so hard that it rattled on its hinges.

He looked at it blankly, anger welling inside him. He wanted to crash his fist against it, kick it down. He wanted to hit something. Or someone.

Instead he turned away, striding faster and faster down the still-wet street. A small voice inside him told him he was getting it all out of proportion, that she was upset and had reasons for making such a mistake, but it was drowned in the roar of his anger. She had found him guilty without any evidence, refused to believe his denial. There had been no trust, none at all, and no love. She was in the wrong, and that was all there was to it. He walked down to the bay and watched the sun go down behind the Gower, the same angry thoughts churning through his mind.

In the public bar of the Leaning Bishop in Stoke Newington High Street Mickie McCaigh was half listening to Jimmy Cullen and Tel Rosenberg reminisce about the Test Match they'd seen at Lord's just before D-Day. These days, whenever anyone talked about cricket it reminded him of the story a bomber pilot had told him in Italy about a game which had taken place in Essex a few years back. The man's squadron had arranged to play the village near their airfield, but on the morning of the game four of the team had been shot down and killed. The game had gone on regardless, and the teller of the story had stood there at slip, one minute remembering a joke he had shared that morning with a man whose body was now floating in the North Sea, the next sharing in the jubilation of a brilliant catch at mid-off.

'Another pint?' his brother was asking him.

'You need to ask?' McCaigh said, handing him the empty and looking round at his fellow-customers. The pub was crowded, but there weren't many others in uniform.

'Lot of women in here tonight,' Jimmy said, managing to sound both lustful and disapproving at the same time. He had been wounded at Dunkirk, and still walked with a pronounced limp.

'Women should do their drinking at home, then?' McCaigh encouraged him.

'Decent women, anyway.'

McCaigh smiled. 'I get it – then we'd know that any woman in a pub was just asking for it?'

'Most of them are,' Tel said happily.

'No more than you are.'

'Yeah, but they're actually getting it,' Jimmy said triumphantly, just as Patrick returned with their pints.

'Getting what?' he asked.

'You're too young to know,' Tel told him, and turned to McCaigh. 'Did I tell you that Arsenal are going to be sharing White Hart Lane again this season?' he asked.

'About six times. Look on the bright side – their fans'll have further to travel.'

'Hey, look at this pair that just came in,' Jimmy said, and McCaigh had to admit he had a point. The two Wrens looked almost like twins with their bobbed blonde hair, amply filled tunics and gorgeous legs.

'I think I'm seeing double,' Tel murmured.

'I wish I was fucking double,' Jimmy said, and they all laughed. The scrum at the bar seemed to open up and engulf the two young women.

'How's Dad these days?' McCaigh asked his brother.

'Same as ever. When he's not at work he's down at the allotment. Except when that Middleton bloke is on the radio with his gardening tips.' Patrick's face broke into a grin. 'Did you know Mum listens to the Brains Trust these days. Last Sunday lunchtime she started going on about life on Mars! Dad just looked at her like she was someone he'd never seen before.'

McCaigh smiled, and was still wondering how to move the conversation in the direction he wanted when Patrick came to his rescue.

'Dad still doesn't get it about the war,' he said. 'That this one's different to his, I mean.'

A month ago McCaigh would probably have agreed with his father, and even after what Farnham had told them about the concentration camp he was far from certain, but this wasn't the moment for a moral debate. 'Yeah, well, the old man went through a lot,' he said.

Patrick had apparently been expecting an argument. 'So you agree this one is different, that's it's worth fighting?'

'Probably. But it'll all be over before you get a chance to cover yourself in blood and shit.'

'Maybe,' Patrick said, sounding more like fourteen than sixteen.

'Meaning?'

Patrick leant over conspiratorially. 'Billy Sangster's getting me another birth certificate.'

McCaigh kept his voice calm. 'What's he want in return?'

'Nothing. Not now anyway. He just wants me to sign an IOU for when the war's over, see?'

'For how much?'

'Only fifty quid.'

'Fifty quid! And what happens if you get blown to pieces? Does he collect from Mum and Dad?'

Patrick gave his brother a reproachful look. 'I wouldn't sign anything like that. If I get killed he tears up the IOU.'

'Nice of him. And I suppose he also sells phoney birth certificates to men who'd like to be younger than they really are, so that they don't get called up.'

'So where's the harm?' Patrick said triumphantly. 'All he's doing is seeing that the people who really want to go are the ones who get there.' He grinned happily at McCaigh. 'We might end up on the same battlefield.'

'I doubt it,' McCaigh said sharply.

'Why not?' Patrick asked, looking crestfallen.

'Because his lot don't get their uniforms mucky on real battlefields,' Jimmy interrupted maliciously. 'They're too busy swanning around the rear areas, if you know what I mean.'

'Oh right,' Patrick agreed, his smile back again. 'You remember that story Dad used to tell about us and the Jerries playing football in no man's land at Christmas?' he asked his brother. 'Well, I reckon on getting a hat trick in this year's game.'

Farnham had been allowed only a few hours in London on his return from France at the end of May, and most of those had been spent in a bitter argument with his father. Refused permission to suspend her schooling, Eileen had apparently disappeared, and Randolph Farnham was convinced that his son had encouraged her to do so. Since she had never discussed her work with her parents – helping others was not one of their interests – they had no idea where to look for her, and Farnham's refusal to reveal what he knew had turned his father's face a dangerous shade of purple. Back at Fairford he had found a letter waiting for him, begging him not to give her away, and he had written back with the assurance that he wouldn't.

In London once more, he had no desire to advertise his presence to his parents, and had accordingly sacrificed the dubious comforts of home in favour of a cheap Bayswater hotel room. He slept well enough on the first night, and on the Saturday morning set out to visit Eileen at the Shelter. It was a bright summer day, and the sharpness of the light seemed to magnify the changes which had come over the capital. Shabbiness and decay seemed everywhere – like the mud-coloured buses the whole city needed a new coat of paint – but it was more than that. With the passage of the troops overseas the life seemed to have drained out of London, and the spirit of adventure which had marked the war's early years seemed extinguished. 'Just get it over with,' the faces seemed to say.

As the bus threaded its way through the City towards the East End Farnham could see increasing evidence of Hitler's latest brainchild. V-1s, the Germans called them, the 'V' standing for *Vergeltungswaffe*, which Lord Haw-Haw had obligingly translated during one of his broadcasts from Berlin as 'retaliation weapon'. Londoners called them buzz-bombs, robot bombs or doodlebugs, and Eileen's last letter to her brother had been full of them. Seventy-three had apparently got through to London in the first mid-June attack, and over the next couple of weeks some parts of the capital had suffered as badly as they had during the Blitz. 'We had twelve alerts yesterday,' Eileen had written, 'and each time I either crouched on all fours under a table or sat in a convenient cupboard with my chin on my knees. You can hear the wretched thing coming, and if the engine's still going as it passes overhead you know it's missed you. The trouble is, that usually means it's hit some other poor blighter. The people round here are getting really depressed by it all. I think they've just about had enough. It's funny, they've moved all the AA guns to the south coast, presumably so they can shoot them down over open country, which makes a lot of sense, but some people are really angry about it. If they can't actually hear the AA guns firing, they think the government's stopped trying to protect them.'

Farnham couldn't help smiling at the thought of Eileen hiding under a table, but it wasn't really funny. A fellow SAS officer had arrived on the scene soon after a V-1 landed outside Bush House in the Aldwych. The leaves on the trees had all been blown away, the bare branches adorned with pieces of human flesh.

He changed buses at Mile End and soon the cranes of the India and Millwall Docks were looming above the lines of terraced houses. At the local police station he got precise directions, and after walking for about ten minutes found himself standing in front of an old Victorian building with a newly painted sign. The front doors were open, so he just walked into the empty hall, and through an open doorway he caught sight of Eileen kneeling on the floor with her back to him, talking to an old lady in a wheelchair.

He just stood there watching for a moment, but the old lady looked up at him, and Eileen turned her head. 'Robbie!'

she cried out happily, leaping to her feet. They hugged, and then she dragged him over to meet not only the old lady, whose name was Martha, but all the other elderly people in the room. 'I'm glad you're her brother,' Martha said, 'because she's too young for a boyfriend.'

'Oh no I'm not,' Eileen told her. 'But who needs one?'

Martha liked that, and told Eileen to take her brother for a cup of tea. She was going to practise her chat-up lines on some of the old men.

Instead of the kitchen, Eileen took Farnham up to see her room. It was about a tenth the size of the one she had at home in Knightsbridge, but he couldn't remember that one ever looking as neat or cared for. And she looked so grown-up, he thought. It had only been a few months, but they'd been months that mattered. 'So how it's going?' he asked, sitting down on the bed.

She sat down beside him and filled him in on the latest developments. He recognized some of the names from her letters, but it didn't seem important one way or the other – the details were all swept aside by the fire of her enthusiasm. She was convinced that after the war Shelters like this one would be just as useful; only then they would be helping all those people who got 'wounded in the struggle to survive'. They couldn't let the world return to the way it had been before the war. What would be the point of it all if people like their father inherited the peace?

'So you're planning to stay on here, and not finish at school?' he asked.

She grimaced. 'Oh, I don't know. I want to go to university and learn more about the world. And I want to travel everywhere when the war's over – not just Europe but Asia and Africa and everywhere. And I want to keep working here.'

He laughed.

'And what about you?' she said. 'Come on, tell me the good news.'

'What good news?'

'Oh come on, Robbie. It was positively bubbling up between the lines in your letters, and I can see it in your face now. You've met someone, haven't you?'

He smiled sheepishly. 'I think so. In France.'

'What do you mean, you think so?'

'All right. I've met someone.'

'This is like dragging blood out of a stone. What's she like?'

'She's . . . wonderful. She's beautiful. Her name's Madeleine, or at least I think it is.'

'You think it is?'

'That's how she was introduced to me. It was only after I got back here that I realized it might not be her real name. Lots of people in the Resistance keep their real names to themselves, and with good reason.'

'All right,' Eileen conceded, 'but what's she like?'

'She's . . . this is hard. We only really spent two days together. She was my local escort on one trip, and she was nearly captured by the Germans, and we had to get away together. We had to walk about thirty miles through the mountains.'

Eileen was enthralled. 'And she just fell into your arms?'

He grinned. 'Something like that.'

'A lot must have happened in those two days.'

'I think it did.'

She looked at him. 'I bet you thought it would never happen,' she said.

'You're right there, but . . .' He sighed. 'It only happened six weeks ago but already it's beginning to feel like it happened in another life.'

'The war can't go on for ever.'

'No, but she lives in a town with a railway junction which we'll be bombing at regular intervals.'

'But she doesn't live in a signal box, does she?'

'No, but I watched the RAF bomb that junction and half the bombs fell on the town.'

'That's terrible.'

'Yeah.'

'I'll pray for her each night when I pray for you. I don't suppose God will care if we've got her name wrong.'

Neil Rafferty repositioned his sore backside in the cinema seat and tried to concentrate on the film. It was the latest Hitchcock, something he'd been looking forward to seeing since he'd read about it in an American magazine, but his heart just wasn't in it.

In the seat next to his Mary Slater was sitting transfixed by the story, and looking not a little like the on-screen heroine. Her brother Tommy – Rafferty's oldest friend – was sitting on her other side, obviously torn between the film and Daphne, the rather stunning-looking brunette he had brought along for the evening. Tommy had known that Rafferty was seeing Beth that afternoon, and had obviously hoped to cheer him up with this evening out, or at least make sure he wasn't drowning his sorrows in private.

It wasn't working, Rafferty thought. And he could always throw himself in the river after everyone else had gone home.

He had dreaded seeing Beth again, but he couldn't just abandon his son, so he had arrived at the specified time, and for nearly an hour had managed to keep up the pretence that he no longer loved or hated her. Beth had kept up a relentless flow of small talk, little David had looked at him as if he was an interesting stranger, and Brad had not been there, at least in body. Going upstairs to use the toilet, Rafferty had impulsively put his head round the corner of their old bedroom door, and though it had all looked so familiar there was a different smell in the air. He had just stood there for a moment, weighed down by the sadness of it all.

Back downstairs he had tried to make contact with his son, but after a while he began to feel that all he was doing was sitting there asserting ownership. It would be different when the child began to talk, he told himself, but he didn't really believe it, and Beth delivered the killing blow just as he was about to leave. 'I think it's only fair to tell you now,' she had begun, 'before you get attached to him, I mean . . . but after the war's over, well, we'll probably be moving to America.'

He had just looked at her, astonished by the fact that such a possibility had never occurred to him.

'It's not as if you really know him,' she said defensively.

'He's my son,' Rafferty had said, feeling his eyes begin to water.

There had been nothing else to say, and he had walked away feeling as lost as ever. Could he stop her taking their son to America? Did he want to? She was right in a way – he did hardly know the boy. But . . .

In the adjoining seat Mary Slater jumped, and a little squeal escaped her lips. On the screen Uncle Charlie's face was looking anything but avuncular, and Teresa Wright was wearing the expression of someone who'd just made a potentially fatal discovery. Ten minutes later she was living happily ever after, the houselights were on and they were threading their way back to the lobby.

'I'm going to take Deirdre home,' Tommy told Rafferty, once the girls had gone off to the Ladies.

'Already?'

'Well, we may pull off the road somewhere. You'll look after Mary, yeah?'

'Tommy!'

'If I let her walk home alone in the blackout Mum and Dad'll kill me.'

Rafferty rolled his eyes at the ceiling. 'OK.'

'Thanks, mate. Just think of her as your little sister. Though she did have a crush on you years ago.' He grinned. 'And she's a nice kid,' he added.

'I know she is.' Rafferty had always liked her, but had certainly never thought of her as anything other than his friend's little sister. Now, watching her walk back across the lobby with the more flamboyant Deirdre, he realized she had grown up. How old was she – seventeen? No, eighteen more like.

'Do you want to go straight home?' he asked after the others had disappeared, hoping she'd say yes. 'Or would you like a drink or something?' he added dutifully.

'I don't really want a drink,' she said. 'Could we just take a walk? Along the river perhaps?'

'OK,' he said noncommittally, and they started off down the blacked-out streets in the direction of the Cam. After walking for about a minute in silence she suddenly said how sorry she was to hear about what had happened between him and his wife. She made it sound like he had been bereaved, and that was so exactly the way he felt that he felt a huge surge of gratitude. But the only thing he could think of to say in return was 'thank you', and another minute of silence ensued.

'Tommy says you and he may set up a car business after the war,' she said, trying again.

'Yeah, we've talked about it. There'll be no new cars for a couple of years, so everyone will want their old ones fixed up, and a lot of them have just been gathering rust for the last five years. It won't be hard to find work.'

They crossed the bridge over the Cam, and as they turned to walk down the path she slipped an arm through one of his. 'Tommy still looks up to you, you know,' she said.

'It's mutual,' he said. 'We've been friends a long time.'

'I know. I remember how horrible you were when you were about fourteen.'

'You can't have been more than four?'

'I'd have been six. You're both eight years older than me.' Trinity College loomed to their left, as the water rippled softly against the footbridge they were passing. 'I hope we can be friends, too,' she said.

'I don't see why not,' he replied casually.

'Could I write to you?' she asked.

'I suppose so. I don't have much time for writing letters,' he lied.

'That's all right. I won't expect any replies. But you will have to take me out for a meal when the war's over.'

He laughed for the first time that day. 'It's a deal,' he said.

McCaigh scanned the crowded Hackney billiard hall, his eyes lighting up when he saw the man with the familiar face and greased-back hair. It had taken him most of Saturday evening to find Billy Sangster, time which he could otherwise have used in more pleasurable pursuits, but at least his search had finally been rewarded. He threaded his way through the tables towards his quarry.

McCaigh had been a couple of years behind Sangster at their Stoke Newington school, and the black marketeer had no trouble recognizing him. 'You're looking fit, Mickie,' he said.

'So are you,' McCaigh said, though in fact Sangster's skin had the unhealthy tinge of someone who rarely saw daylight. 'I'd like a quiet word, Billy. About some business, if that's OK?'

'I'm always open. Let's go into the office.'

'You own this place?' McCaigh asked as they walked across the hall.

'The owner got himself killed in Africa, and I took it off the widow's hands.'

They entered the office and Sangster walked round behind his desk and sat down, waving McCaigh into the other chair.

The SAS man closed the door behind him but ignored the invitation to sit. 'I just wanted a little chat about my brother,' he began.

'He'll have his certificate in a couple of days,' Sangster said irritably.

'No, he won't,' McCaigh contradicted him. 'Or at least, if he does, there'll be consequences.'

Sangster smiled, but there was uncertainty in his eyes. 'You're not threatening me, Mickie?'

'I'm afraid so, Billy. Not with the law, of course, because that wouldn't be very sporting. And since I'll be back with my unit this time tomorrow night there's no way I can stop you giving him a fake certificate. So I'm just going to tell you this, Billy: if my brother goes to war then everything that happens to him is going to happen to you. If someone shoots off his cock then when I come home I'm going to shoot yours off. If he gets his face burnt off by a flame-thrower then so will you. If he's blown up by a mine then you'll probably go up with your car. Do you understand what I'm telling you, Billy? Of course, you might be lucky and he comes home all in one piece, or maybe he'll get killed and so will I, but is it worth fifty quid to find out?'

Sangster stared back at him, rage warring with fear in his face.

'And make up a good story as to why you can't do it,' McCaigh added, his hand on the office doorknob, 'or I'll just come back and maim you for the hell of it.' He opened the door and walked back across the billiard hall, a grin spreading on his face.

All through Sunday Tobin waited in vain for Megan to call and apologize. There was no phone in the Allchurch house so he couldn't ring her, but he wouldn't have done so anyway. And he certainly wasn't going round to have the door slammed in his face for a second time. Sooner or later she would find out who had shopped her stupid brother and then she'd come crying for forgiveness, and when she did then maybe, just maybe, he'd forgive her.

On the train back to Fairford, somewhere between Neath and Port Talbot, he tossed the unopened packet of johnnies out of the corridor window and into the night.

Farnham didn't return to the Fairford base on the Sunday evening, and in the briefing room on Tuesday morning Rafferty, McCaigh, Tobin and the others found out why. All the squadron commanders had been summoned to Moor Park on the Monday, to be filled in on what the immediate future held for them and their men. In the short term, as Farnham now explained to the fifty or so men gathered before him, they would continue to wait, train and wait some more. In the medium term, he said, raising his voice above the groans and frustration, the plan was to insert them *en masse* behind enemy lines in France. Since the average life expectancy of such a unit – in terms of mental and physical wear and tear

– wasn't thought to be much more than a month, the date of their insertion would need to be carefully calculated. The first prerequisite, though, was that the Allied armies break their way out of the defensive ring which the Germans still held around the expanded Normandy bridgehead.

This explanation, while not exactly what they wanted to hear, at least gave them all something to hang their hopes on, and for the next couple of weeks the endless retraining was endured with no more than the usual litany of complaints. In the evenings they crowded round the radio hoping to hear about the promised break-out, and any available newspaper was scoured for news of the military situation.

The post brought different kinds of news. McCaigh got a letter from his mum telling him that Patrick had been in a foul mood for about a week, but that he was now getting excited about the new football season. Both West Ham and Charlton had offered him trials, and he was still hoping that Spurs would do the same. Reading between the lines, McCaigh reckoned that Billy Sangster had heeded his threats, and with any luck Patrick wouldn't think about anything other than football for the next six months. And by then the war might even be over.

Rafferty got two letters from Cambridge on the same day, one from Beth, the other from Tommy's sister. The first was to tell him that his wife had packed up all his personal stuff and had it taken round to his grandparents' house. After reading this he found it hard to concentrate on Mary Slater's chatty epistle, which meandered along through Tommy's love life, the film they'd seen together, a book she was reading. Reading it again later that day it seemed to Rafferty so innocent, so divorced from the realities which Beth's betrayal had forced to the front of his mind.

Tobin got no letter from Megan, let alone the humble apology he was hoping for, but his mum did write with the news that Barry Allchurch had been remanded for trial on various black-marketeering charges, and was still in Gowerton prison. Which bloody well served him right, Tobin thought. He was still angry with the whole damn Allchurch family, and particularly her. If it was over then it was over, though the thought that it might be engendered a sense of emptiness which only sleep or violent activity could banish.

On the first day of August the military news took a turn for the better – the Americans had punched a hole in the German ring at Avranches – and in the succeeding days, as Patton's tanks flooded through the gap, the whole German defensive position began to crumble. The SAS men were given detailed maps of eastern France to study, which also seemed a good sign, and finally, on Thursday 10 August, the three squadrons were summoned once more to the Fairford briefing room, where they were addressed by Lieutenant-Colonel Donegan.

He gave them an outline of top brass thinking on how the current Allied advance would develop over the next few weeks, and how their intended activities in the Vosges region fitted into the overall strategy. 'Whether they're pushing in troops or supplies to bolster their position in France, or just trying to pull themselves back over the Rhine in good order, they'll need every east-west road and railway line they have running at full capacity. Cut those roads and railways and they'll be like puppets without strings.'

Farnham was then invited to give an appreciation of the local geography and the local Resistance, with whom it was assumed the SAS unit would be reaching some sort of arrangement. It was thought unlikely that the Maquis would agree to serve under a British commander, but there were hopes that they could be persuaded to fight alongside the SAS as allies, with at least some level of tactical coordination between the two forces.

Donegan then took the stage once again with a more detailed breakdown of how they were getting there, what they would be taking with them and what exactly it was hoped they would achieve on French soil. They would be leaving, he concluded, in three days' time, late on the Sunday evening. For those who wanted them, thirty-six-hour passes would be available, commencing at eight o'clock the following morning.

It was early afternoon before their train reached Paddington. McCaigh had invited Rafferty and Tobin over to Stoke Newington for the night, but Tobin had declined. He had been through London a few times, he told them, but he'd never really seen it, and this seemed like a good opportunity.

A Circle Line train took him to Westminster, where he walked round the outsides of Westminster Abbey and the Houses of Parliament, marvelling at their size and grandeur. Next he walked up to Downing Street, and stood at the end of the cordoned-off little road, wondering whether Winnie was in until a police constable moved him on. Retracing his steps, he walked across Westminster Bridge and sat by the river, gazing up at the Houses of Parliament and trying not to wish that Megan was there with him.

On the river itself several barges were working their way upstream, heavily laden with coal. The famous London buses rattled past him, and further downstream he could see and hear the occasional train rumbling across the Southern Railway bridge outside Charing Cross. After a while he got up and joined the stream of people walking on the wide path which ran alongside the river. Most of them seemed to be women, quite a few of them were pretty, and several gave him an unsolicited smile as they walked by. Megan wasn't the only girl in the world, he told himself.

By the time he'd recrossed the river on the Hungerford footbridge hunger was beginning to gnaw at his stomach, and just up the Strand from Charing Cross Station he found one of the 'British Restaurants' the papers had been so full of. The place was far from full but the food didn't seem half-bad to Tobin, probably, he thought, because he was so used to the crap the Army served up. Here too the women seemed to outnumber the men, and a pretty sophisticated-looking bunch they were, with jaunty little hats over their Veronica Lake hairstyles. Some of them were even wearing lipstick, which was almost impossible to find in Swansea. For more than an hour Tobin just sat watching them come and go, revelling in the fact that he was actually there, in the heart of London, which everyone knew was the centre of the world.

Trafalgar Square was bigger than he'd imagined, Piccadilly Circus smaller. A pub in Shaftesbury Avenue offered a rest for his feet and a pint of beer, and he sat sipping it slowly, wondering what the people around him would say if they knew he was about to be dropped on a dangerous mission behind enemy lines. The men would all try and buy him a drink, he thought. The women would be interested in him.

He bought himself another pint, wishing he was back in Swansea with people he knew.

Around ten o'clock he realized that it had grown dark outside, and that he'd left it rather late to find the hotel in Bayswater. He stumbled out into the blackout, grateful that there was a moon to help him see his way. Farnham had said the nearest tube station was Queensway, and a passer-by pointed him in the direction of the nearest Central Line station, Tottenham Court Road. He was pretty sure he'd only had four pints, and it had to be the blackout which was making it so difficult for him to stay on the pavement.

He also seemed to be hearing voices, but these, he soon realized, were real. Women were standing like sentries in almost every doorway of the road he was walking down, and as he passed each one a vividly painted pair of lips would part to make him an offer. His mute refusals were met by a mixture of laughter, derisory snorting and anger.

There were so many of them, and they were a lot better-looking than the pros who worked the Swansea docks. The summer clothes were revealing, and some of the women helped his imagination along by caressing their own breasts as he walked by. 'Just ten bob,' one girl whispered, and she looked so pretty that he hesitated in his step.

She was beside him in an instant, putting an arm through his, and urging him across the street. He started to protest but his eyes were hooked by the glistening trace of sweat in her cleavage and the jiggling of her unseen breasts. 'Where are we going?' he asked stupidly.

'Just in here,' she said. They were now about ten yards down an alley, and the darkness hid everything but her face. 'Ten bob,' she said again. 'Or five bob for a suck,' she added when he didn't reply.

Tobin didn't know what she meant. 'A fuck,' he said, knowing what that was.

'Ten bob,' she repeated.

'OK,' he said.

He bent to kiss the painted mouth, but she shrugged him aside and reached for his trouser buttons. The trousers dropped to his feet, and she almost delicately lifted his cock from his underpants. 'I'm not wearing anything under the skirt,' she said, leaning back against the wall.

A fleeting feeling of utter foolishness was overridden by the urgency of his desire, and he pressed forward against her, uncertain of exactly how he had to do it. She seemed to realize this, and with a small snort of impatience used one hand on his shoulder to push him down and the other on his cock to push him up inside her. It felt drier than he expected, and the pain of entry momentarily lessened his desire, but he started pumping up and down the way he knew it was done, and the pain quickly gave way to mounting excitement. He groaned as he spouted inside her, and stood there, his knees bent, until she shook herself off him.

'Ten bob,' she said again, and after he'd pulled up his trousers he took a note out of his tunic pocket. 'Ta,' she said, and turned away to go.

'Hold on,' he said, and she stopped, her face just visible in the gloom.

'Ready for another, Taff?' she asked with a smile.

'No . . . nothing,' he said. As she walked away he leant back against the wall, feeling suddenly sick to his stomach. He had a mental picture of himself pumping away at her like his uncle's dog trying to fuck his mother's leg, and felt half ashamed, half angry. Fuck Megan, he thought. Fuck her. At least he wasn't going to die a virgin.

Rafferty took the streaming plate from McCaigh, waited till most of the water had dripped off, and applied the drying-up cloth. It had been one of the best meals he could remember for a long time, and not just because Mickie's mum was a good cook. There had been about eight friends and relations around the table, with ages ranging from ten to eighty, and every one of them had contributed to a conversation that had been not only interesting but downright entertaining. The McCaighs and their neighbours knew how to laugh.

He had obviously made the right decision in accepting Mickie's invitation. There was less time to brood than there would have been in Cambridge, and he'd taken an instant liking to McCaigh's mum. He'd only had to entertain himself for about half an hour, and in that time he'd managed to write to Mary Slater at last. She'd written three letters, after all, and now that they were bound for France he didn't want her wasting her time writing to someone who wasn't there. He hadn't really known what to say to her, and the letter was only about half a page long, but at least he'd written something. She was a nice kid. A nice woman, even. She'd make someone a really good wife.

Mickie's brother Patrick was just a kid, but he seemed nice enough. He'd spent about ten minutes explaining to Rafferty how much he wanted to do his bit in the war, and how near he'd come to fiddling his way in. Eventually Mickie had just told him to put a sock in it. 'Dad was in the last war, I'm in this one and you're welcome to the next. This family only offers up one sacrifice per war.'

For some reason that had seemed to boost Patrick's spirits. Rafferty's own had been boosted by McCaigh's friend Jimmy Cullen, who seemed to know even more about the car business than Tommy, and was just as certain what a gold mine it was going to be after the war. 'Think about it,' he said. 'Who's going to use a train or a bus when they can drive from their own front doors to exactly where they want to go, without a crowd of people digging them in the ribs or showering them with germs. Have you ever seen a television? It's like having your own cinema in your living room. That's what the future's going to be, Neil. Things that people used to do in crowds they'll be doing on their own, or just with their family.'

'It's sad, if you ask me,' Susan McCaigh had interjected.

'Maybe, but that's progress.'

The only member of the family that Rafferty hadn't met was Mickie's Uncle Eamonn, who was on duty down at the fire station. The plan was to call in and say hello to him on their way to a favourite pub in Church Street, but as Rafferty, Jimmy Cullen and the two McCaigh brothers strolled down the High Road fate took a hand. The whine of the doodlebug had only just established itself in their consciousness when it cut out, and after looking at each other like idiots for a few seconds, the four of them made a run for the inadequate shelter of a shop doorway. Only seconds later the street ahead of them erupted in a shower of brickwork and a vast cloud of smoke and dust. The roar of the explosion seemed to roll past them in the direction of central London.

In its wake they could hear the screams of the trapped or injured, and all four men instinctively started forward into the billowing smoke. McCaigh stumbled across an old man lying on the pavement, blood running down his face from a gash just above his eye, his arm stretching out hopefully in the direction of an old woman who was lying a few yards away. Her eyes were staring blankly at the sky.

'She's dead, isn't she?' the old man whispered.

'Yeah,' McCaigh said softly, and the old man's arm went limp. He sighed once, in the manner of someone experiencing a minor inconvenience, closed his eyes and died.

As the smoke cleared the damage done by the V-1 became visible. Three three-storey buildings had been effectively destroyed, their roofs and top floors blown to kingdom come, their second floors broken and flung down into the three shops that lay beneath. On both sides of the wide road windows had been blown in, and as McCaigh looked round he saw a woman stagger out of one door with blood pouring down her face.

Behind him there was a child's cry for help from inside one of the shops, and then, as if in reply, the sound of something shifting on the floor above, followed by a series of thunderous crashes as things fell through. McCaigh strained his ears but there was no further sound from the child, and a few seconds later all he could hear was the sound of the approaching fire engines.

'Saved us the trouble of visiting,' he murmured, as the first engine disgorged his uncle and a team of firemen. Eamonn McCaigh looked momentarily surprised to find his nephews there before him, but was soon fully occupied in trying to reach an agreement with the head of the salvage-rescue team as to how they should best approach the business of reaching those trapped in the wreckage. This agreement once reached, firemen, salvage-rescue people and members of other volunteer services were soon at work on a cautious shifting of the rubble. The McCaigh boys, Rafferty and Jimmy Cullen all pitched in without being asked, and no one told them to leave it to the professionals.

It took just over half an hour to recover two adult bodies from the grocer's, and about the same again to reach the young girl at the back of the shop. She was about six years old, McCaigh reckoned, and her dust-caked face peered blankly round the corner of the wardrobe which had crushed the life from her body. As the firemen carried her out his uncle pulled him aside. 'Go and get your drink, Mickie,' he said. 'There's nothing more to do here.'

They walked on towards the pub, not talking, not feeling much like doing anything, and were about a hundred yards

143

short of their destination when the two MPs stepped out of the shadows and barred their way. From the smart red caps to the mirror-like surface of their boots they looked like they'd just stepped off the parade ground.

'And where do you think you're going, Sergeant?' one of them sneeringly addressed Rafferty.

'For a drink,' he told them shortly.

The MP pointedly studied the two dust-covered uniforms in front of him, and poked Rafferty gently in the chest with his truncheon. 'Not like this you're not.'

In that moment it all came to a head for Rafferty – Beth's betrayal, the loss of his son, the endless frustrating wait in Gloucestershire, the dust-caked face of the girl in the bombed shop – and almost before he knew it his fist was crashing into the MP's nose, blood was spurting, more blows were flying and something very hard was coming down on his own head. The last things he remembered were the sounds of whistles blowing and boots on stone.

Farnham had managed to borrow a car for the Saturday morning, and he and Eileen took a picnic out to Epping Forest. As they walked through the summer trees the war seemed unusually far away, and when he told her he'd soon be leaving she seemed less worried than usual. 'I know you can't tell me where you're going,' she said, 'but will you be seeing her? Madeleine, I mean, or whatever her real name is?'

'I don't know,' he told her. 'I hope so. It just seems almost too theatrical – dropping in behind enemy lines to see my lady friend.'

'Like the Scarlet Pimpernel,' she said.

He'd dropped her back at the Shelter on the Isle of Dogs, returned the car to his friend in Knightsbridge and walked back across Kensington Gardens to the hotel, where he found Tobin nursing a hangover and a most unwelcome telephone message from Rafferty.

He and Tobin took a taxi to the barracks in Camden Town, where his men were being held, listened to their story, and satisfied himself that their actions, though stupid, had hardly been criminal. He then set to the task of talking the two men out of their predicament. Several times he nearly lost his own temper, but eventually, after issuing just about every veiled threat he could think of, he managed to persuade the oaf in charge that the two men would be more use to their country risking their lives in France than consuming rations in an English jail.

The taxi deposited the four men alongside the platform at Paddington with what they thought was seconds to spare, but it turned out their train had been delayed for at least an hour. While the other three wandered off in search of a drink, Tobin, feeling guilty about not seeing his parents that weekend, ensconced himself in a telephone kiosk and called them.

His father answered.

'I'll be going away for a few weeks,' Tobin told him.

'Anywhere exciting?' his father asked with an almost-visible wink.

'I'll tell you when I get back.'

His mother took over at the other end, told him to look after himself and wished him luck. She kept up a good front but Tobin could almost hear the tears in her voice, and was about to claim someone else wanted the phone when she dropped the bombshell. 'Your Megan came round,' she said. 'Asked me to give you a message if you rang. She said she's sorry, she still loves you and she hopes you'll forgive her.'

'That's nice,' Tobin said neutrally, as if he expected that the forgiveness part would take some time. And so it should, he reminded himself, but there was a wave of relief sweeping through his body and his feet seemed to want to dance on the kiosk's concrete floor.

5

France, August–September 1944

The banter and the laughter slowly died away as the Halifax approached the drop zone in the Vosges. Sixteen men were crammed in on either side of the plane's belly, and the floor between them was piled high with their supplies, leaving no room for the stretching of cramped limbs. Looking down the rows of faces, Farnham was struck by the similarity of expression they wore – a sort of artificial stillness, a tightly controlled anxiety.

With only one plane at the squadron's disposal, the original plan had been to fly in half the men and half the jeeps on two successive nights, but Farnham had insisted on the whole squadron dropping together. The jeeps would not be needed for several days, and the more he thought about it, the less he liked the idea of bringing them down from the high meadow. Once the men were down he and Yves could find a more convenient place to receive the drop.

Always assuming that Yves was still alive. Since leaving the area in May Farnham had received fairly regular updates on the Maquis group's record of successes and failures, but he had heard nothing of a personal nature. There were bound to have been some casualties. Yves might be dead. So might she.

'Five minutes,' the dispatcher yelled as he came through the cockpit door. He clambered across the equipment containers and wrenched open the bomb bay doors, letting in the wind and revealing a moving square of moonlit France. 'Lovely night for it,' he shouted above the roar of their passage, and a couple of the men made faces at him behind his back.

They all got to their feet, fixed their static lines to the fuselage and waited in line behind Farnham for the order to jump. It wasn't usual for the CO to lead off, but as his was the only face familiar to the Frenchmen below, it seemed like the diplomatic thing to do.

'Go,' the dispatcher yelled in his ear, and he stepped out into the void. The plane's engines roared briefly in his ears, then abruptly faded. The slipstream tried to tip him, but the opening parachute jerked him upright and suddenly the landscape made sense again. Beneath him the L-shaped pattern of red lights was visible at one end of the huge meadow. Above him a line of open chutes was strung across the sky, palely reflecting the moon.

He could see figures in the meadow now, and hoped to God they weren't Germans. As the ground rushed up to meet him he braced himself for the impact, bending his knees as his feet touched the grass and executing a perfect roll. A swift glance was enough to confirm that the men running towards him were French, and he concentrated on reeling in the billowing silk.

'Robert!' a familiar voice cried out, and a garlic-breathing Henri embraced him like a long-lost friend. 'And this time you're in uniform,' the Frenchman said, examining him. 'That must mean the war's getting serious, no?'

Farnham grinned, and shook hands with two more smiling Maquisards. On the far side of the vast meadow the last of his men were drifting to earth – the pilot and his French contact on the ground had done a perfect job. The Halifax was now flying a wide circle, giving the men time to clear the field before dropping the supply canisters.

Farnham was about to ask Henri where Yves was when the Maquis leader limped up to him, hand outstretched. 'A fall,' he explained, noticing Farnham glance at his leg. 'It is good to see you again,' he said, 'though whether you should be here is another matter. But we will talk when we reach the site we have picked out for your camp. It is about two miles north-east of ours, in the hills above Sadey.'

'I know where you mean,' Farnham said, feeling pleased. By this time the supply containers had all been recovered, and were being carted by mixed teams of SAS and Maquisards to the edge of the meadow. A few minutes later everyone was gathered in the same spot, the two groups smiling at each other with their mouths, sizing each other up with their eyes.

They started down the mountain, leaving the relative brightness of the meadow for the less comforting darkness of the silent forest. About ten men back in the forty-strong column Rafferty found himself hoping the locals knew what they were doing, because this seemed as good a spot for a German ambush as any he'd ever seen. Behind him McCaigh was having a spot of trouble with the knee which the fucking MP had slugged with his truncheon. But as he limped downhill he could still see that look of utter disbelief on the face which Rafferty had bloodied, and he knew it had been more than worth it.

They walked on through the endless trees, making little more noise than the breeze in the branches above, and despite Rafferty's anxieties no German fire erupted out of the darkness on either side. The occasional logger's track offered the only sign of another human presence. There were no houses, no lights, no fields – only trees and more trees.

After about two hours of walking they reached the site chosen for the SAS camp-site. At first sight this particular section of forest didn't look any different from any of the others they had passed through, but it soon became apparent that their hosts had chosen well. The soil was dry yet water was only a short descent away; no existing paths crossed the area but access remained easy; the lie of the land offered good perimeter defences and lookout positions.

As the men set up camp, digging latrines and putting up the camouflaged tents, Farnham and Yves sat on a hamper full of Sten guns and talked. In the last couple of weeks, it seemed, the situation in this part of France had radically changed. 'Of course we can't see the whole picture from here,' Yves said, 'but it looks to me as if the Germans have given up any hope of holding any line west of the Moselle, and that they're considering withdrawing all the way to the Saar and the Vosges. Whichever it is, the whole of eastern Lorraine is crawling with them, and I'm afraid your chances of carrying out the sort of raids we talked about before have worsened considerably. It's not just a matter of avoiding the main roads any more – there's a chance of running into the bastards almost anywhere.'

'It couldn't just be that your exploits in June have caught their attention?' Farnham asked hopefully.

Yves smiled. 'Oh, we caught someone's attention all right, but it wasn't the Wehrmacht's. The Gestapo's anti-partisan units in Strasbourg and Nancy received big reinforcements, and in the second half of July they swept through a couple of areas to the north of us, but they didn't do much damage. They're still a problem, but what I'm talking about is regular troops swarming all over the place. They won't be looking for you – not until you make them, anyway – but the chances of just running into a troop convoy are too high for comfort, and once you've been seen, well, it's not hard to bottle up a motorized force in these mountains – there are so few roads.'

Farnham was thinking. 'I see what you mean,' he said eventually, 'but if the Germans are planning to make a stand in this area then all the more reason for us to find out just how they intend to do so, and with what. After all, creating mayhem is only one of the reasons we're here; the other is to gather intelligence. We'll just have to put the emphasis on the latter, at least until we have a clearer picture of what's going on, both around here and on the main front. Like you said, it's easy for a motorized unit to get bottled up, but if the worst comes to the worst we can always abandon our jeeps – the Americans seem to be making more than enough for everyone on the planet.'

Yves grinned. 'So where are these famous jeeps?'

'They're coming. I need to find a drop zone with better access. I took another look tonight – the path down from the meadow is too narrow in too many places.'

It was the Frenchman's turn to look thoughtful. 'How about the meadow above La Truche – do you remember? The track which goes across it eventually intersects with the road down the valley to Sadey. But first we must check that the Germans haven't set up shop in that area. I'll get Henri on to it.'

Henri seemed to be Yves' second in command these days. 'I haven't seen Jules,' Farnham said pointedly.

Yves sighed. 'He was killed in June, only a week or so after you left. Four of them had just wired a bridge when they heard a train in the distance – they'd used half-hour pencils to give them a good start – and Jules went back to exchange them for the ten-minute kind. He just couldn't resist the idea of getting the train too.' Yves shrugged. 'He must have done something wrong – the bridge went up and him with it.'

'I'm sorry,' Farnham said, thinking of Jools Morgan and Morrie Beckwith under the bridge at San Severino.

'Jean-Paul was killed too,' Yves added. 'He walked into a German patrol down in the valley and panicked for some reason. They just shot him in the back.'

Farnham didn't want to ask, but the look on his face must have given him away.

'She's all right,' Yves said.

By first light the SAS camp was fully operational; lookouts had been posted and most of the men invited to catch up on lost sleep. The Maquisards had long since departed for their own camp, happily carrying the new shipment of weapons with them. Twenty new recruits had come forward in the past week, Yves had told Farnham, and he was considering setting up a second camp a few miles to the south.

Farnham was still sitting on the hamper, which looked set to become an unofficial seat of command. In a circle around him sat Captain Hoyland, his number two, and the unit's two sergeants, Rafferty and Wycherley.

Phil Hoyland was a career soldier who had joined the SAS late in 1942. Tall, gangly and extremely bald for someone in his late twenties, he had a reputation for over-icing the cake in times of calm and clarity of thought in times of crisis. Which, Farnham reminded himself, was certainly preferable to the other way round. He had never really taken to Hoyland – the man was too 'public school rugby club' – but the men who'd served under him didn't seem to have any complaints. Steve Wycherley was one of these. Also a two-year veteran of the SAS, he was a dour Scouser with crinkly fair hair and the face of a pugilist with a lot of pyrrhic victories to his credit.

Farnham gave them a rundown of what Yves had told him, taking care not to sound as deflated as he felt by the news of the growing German presence.

'Can we trust what these Resistance chaps tell us?' Hoyland asked. 'I mean, I assume they believe what they're saying, but how good is their information? When you're stuck up here in the woods it must be hard to come by that sort of hard intelligence.'

'And after being stuck like that for a while, you can start exaggerating enemy strength just to justify the fact that you're doing sweet fuck all,' Wycherley suggested.

Farnham shook his head. 'I know we've had mixed results in our dealings with the Maquis, but I'd stake my life on this group being reliable. The fighters may spend most of their time in the woods, but they've got excellent contacts in the nearby towns' – a picture of her sprang into his mind – 'and the intelligence, as far as it goes, will be good. Yves didn't claim to know exactly what was happening, only that the area's filling up with Germans. Now we don't have to let that little fact cramp our style too much, but I don't think we can afford to ignore it either.'

'Right,' Hoyland agreed.

'So what I suggest is this – that while we're waiting for Yves to check the drop zone for the re-sup, we set up OPs overlooking all the major roads within a ten-mile radius. That'll not only give us a good idea of just what we're dealing with – it'll also give the men a chance to familiarize themselves with the area. In fact, before they go anywhere I want them all to know the immediate area of the camp – say within a mile radius – like the back of their hands. Neil, Steve, if you could get on to that straight away. Nothing on paper though, just in case. Mental maps only.' He looked round at the others. 'Any questions?'

'What about cooking, boss?' Wycherley asked.

'I don't see any problem with using the hexamine stoves,' Farnham decided, 'provided the usual precautions are taken. In fact I could do with a hot cup of tea right now.'

Two days later Tobin was counting the lorries of the German troop convoy which was slowly winding its way along the road below. There were seventeen in all, and he dutifully recorded the figure in his logbook.

'Say about twenty-five per lorry,' McCaigh murmured by his side. 'That's more than four hundred men.'

Rafferty sighed. 'The Maquis bloke was right – the place is crawling with them. I mean, I don't mind the odds being a bit on the chancy side, but this is ridiculous. We're just going to end up hiding in the woods for a month.'

'Makes you feel nostalgic for Fairford, doesn't it?' said McCaigh. 'At least we caught sight of a woman every now and then.'

The three of them were peering through the observation slit of a rectangular scrape high above the road from Colmar to St Dié. They had arrived a couple of hours before dawn to excavate the OP, and it was now mid-afternoon on a hot summer day. Five troop convoys had so far passed below them, one of them accompanied by two motorbike dispatch riders and a solitary staff car carrying what looked like a high-ranking officer. McCaigh had taken a photograph, but the distance was probably too great for identification.

All their sightings had been entered in the logbook and conveyed via the 'biscuit-tin' MCR radio to the SAS camp, where someone was collating the information from this and the other six OPs before passing it on to Allied Command headquarters. It was vital work, but that didn't stop it from being deadly boring.

'What do you think's going to happen after the war?' Tobin asked, as the last lorry in this particular convoy disappeared from view.

'I expect we'll all go home,' Rafferty said helpfully.

'No, I mean . . . I was talking with this bloke in London, and he was saying that the peace after the last war didn't work because we were too hard on the Germans, and they didn't have any choice but to try and get their revenge. So he reckoned this time we should be easier on them . . .'

'What, slap their wrists and tell them to go home?' McCaigh asked sarcastically. 'Tell them we understand how difficult it must be for them, bearing all that responsibility for starting the bloody thing?'

'I think we should be harder,' Rafferty said. 'Make damn sure they can't do it again.'

'How?' McCaigh asked. 'What exactly would you do?'

Rafferty thought about it for a minute. 'I don't know,' he said eventually. 'Not let 'em have an army for a start.'

'They tried that after the last war.'

'Oh, well, I don't know then. Break Germany up into small countries, like it used to be.'

'When?' Tobin asked, interested.

'About a hundred years ago,' Rafferty said airily, not at all sure.

'I don't know either,' McCaigh said, bringing them back to the subject in hand. 'Makes you think though, doesn't it? We've been trying to beat the bastards for five years, and we still don't have a clue what we're going to do when it happens.'

'The government must know,' Rafferty protested.

McCaigh snorted. 'Like they did last time? If they knew, don't you think they'd tell us? I tell you what my dad says: he says the trouble is, this war isn't really *for* anything at all. It's like someone hits you in the face and you hit him back and he hits you back and it just goes on and on until someone can't hit any more. It's like a fight to the death – only you can't kill a country.'

'I'm sure Bomber Command are doing their best,' Rafferty murmured.

'You can kill the people who started it,' Tobin suggested.

'Yeah, but that's the whole point. The First War was about ending wars – or at least that's what they said it was about – but this one's just about winning. I mean, shooting Hitler's not much of a war aim, is it? It's like going somewhere just so you can go home again.'

'There must be more to it than that,' Rafferty said.

'All right, but what? Do you think the world's going to be a better place when it's over?'

'It will be for the Poles,' Rafferty said, without much conviction.

'If the Russians don't roll all over them. But if you want a happy ending, my dad's got another theory.'

'Only one?'

'He reads a lot. And he says being a parkie gives him a lot of time to think.'

'So does this, but you don't see Ian here thinking.'

'Hey,' Tobin said indignantly.

'He calls it his accidentally-on-purpose theory. You remember what the boss said about that concentration camp north of here? Well, I told my dad about that and he wasn't at all surprised. Apparently there's been hints in the papers for a couple of years that the Germans are killing people in droves, and that the only half-decent reason for this war is to stop them.'

'But how could we have known about that in 1939?'

'We couldn't, but that's his theory. The politicians never have good motives, but if you look hard enough you can usually pick up one as you go along. That's the accidentally-on-purpose bit – despite their worst intentions, something good usually comes out of it. The trick is to recognize what it is, and not let the bastards claim credit for it.'

'Hmm,' Rafferty said. 'Your old man hasn't applied to join the Brains Trust, has he?'

'Not yet.'

'Tell him not to bother.'

'I think he's got a point,' Tobin said. He was thinking about how the war had changed Megan and her friends, something which couldn't have been uppermost in the government's mind when they set the whole thing in motion.

'Yeah, maybe,' Rafferty agreed. 'But I still think we should carve Germany up into little bits.'

'They'd still all be Germans,' Tobin argued.

'Just like this lot,' McCaigh said, putting the black binoculars to his eyes as the first lorry of another convoy appeared round the bend in the road below. This time there were twenty-one lorries in the column heading west.

'Do you think they know the war's lost?' Rafferty murmured, watching a Wehrmacht trooper in the last lorry flick a spent cigarette out on to the road.

'They might know it,' McCaigh said, 'but I don't suppose there's too much the poor bastards can do about it.'

* * *

Soon after dusk that evening Farnham started out alone to cover the two miles which separated the SAS and Maquis camps. It was fully dark by the time he arrived, but Yves was still sitting outside his tent, almost invisible but for the glowing tip of his cigarette. The Frenchman's greeting was friendly enough, but his face, lit up by the glow as he dragged on the cigarette, seemed drained and worn.

'Sometimes I just don't know,' the Maquis leader said, as if they were already halfway into a conversation. 'I've just had some bad news,' he went on. 'The Gestapo have just executed a couple of sixteen-year-old boys in Corcieux.'

Farnham gave a sympathetic sigh. 'Were they with a Maquis unit?'

Yves' snort blended amusement and disgust. 'No.'

'So why . . .?'

'Oh, one of them threw a rock at a Gestapo car. He hit it too, broke the window. One of the bastards in the back seat got his face cut by the glass. Not badly, but badly enough that nothing short of torturing two children to death would satisfy him.' He took another drag on the cigarette and looked across at Farnham. 'Did you ever hear of the see-saw?'

'You mean the children's thing?'

'No, the Gestapo thing. You hang two people from the opposite ends of a suspended beam, making sure that both of them have their toes just off the ground. Of course they both struggle to get their feet down, and when one succeeds the other starts choking to death. Desperation makes that one stronger, and he in turn hoists the other man into the air. And so on, for a long time, until they are both dead. The Germans stand around joking that they haven't killed anyone – the two poor sods have killed each other.'

The dispassionate words seemed to hang in the darkness, and like light burned on to a retina they seemed slow to fade.

'It was Ziegler again,' Yves added. 'By our tally he's now been responsible for thirty-three murders since he took over the Gestapo operation in St Dié.' He crushed the cigarette out beneath his boot. 'I can't understand people like that. I don't mean the cruelty – I mean the stupidity. Doesn't he know the war is lost? Doesn't he realize this will all catch up with him? He surely can't believe that once the war's over everyone's going to shake hands and forget what's happened? I tell you, Robert, there's enough Frenchmen with good reasons for fearing the peace, let alone Germans.'

Farnham shook his head. 'It's a mystery to me,' he said.

Yves laughed suddenly. 'I just hope none of them live to explain themselves in their memoirs,' he said. 'Now, tell me what your surveillance teams have discovered over the last couple of days.'

'Lots of Germans. Most of them moving west, though. It doesn't look like they've completely given up the idea of holding a line somewhere between here and Paris.'

'Maybe not,' Yves agreed. 'I don't think they really know what they're doing.'

'You could be right. I heard in London that a lot of the prisoners taken recently have been claiming that it's next to impossible to get the Wehrmacht High Command to OK any sort of tactical retreat. Everyone's being told to stand and fight where they are, and that if they really want to win then they can . . .'

'Ah, the power of the will,' Yves interjected. 'Nietzsche and all that rubbish. You know, I studied that at university twenty years ago, and even at the time I thought it was a joke.'

'Yes, well, as long as they're confused it's our job to keep them that way.'

'You still think the motorized raiding columns are feasible?'

'I think they're worth a shot.'

'I hope you're right, my friend. We've taken the decision to just watch and wait for a couple of weeks until we're certain which way the wind's blowing. Your air forces haven't left us much to do in any case, and now that Ziegler's killing at least ten hostages every time we make a move, we're not going to give him an excuse just for the sake of it.' He extracted half a cigarette from a pocket and lit up. 'The war is almost over, and people are more reluctant to take risks. No one wants to die on the last day.' He grinned suddenly. 'And Maquis leaders don't want to risk their men on that day either.'

'I think we're still quite a long way away from the last day.'

'Maybe. Like I said, we're taking a two-week holiday. Now, about your drop zone. It looks fine – the nearest Germans are in St Dié.'

'Good. I'll get on to London when I get back, and try and arrange the drop for tomorrow night. I'll let you know . . .'

Someone was coming towards them through the trees, someone with light footsteps and a graceful walk. All Farnham could do was sit there, his heart blocking his throat.

She was less inhibited. As she made out the two figures in the gloom she seemed to hesitate for an instant, then broke into a run, flinging her arms around his neck and pulling him close. 'I'm so glad you're here,' she whispered after a while.

Yves had disappeared into his tent. 'I have things for him,' she said, 'and then we can . . .' She finished the sentence with a kiss.

Inside the tent Yves smiled up at them, and Farnham had the feeling that for some reason the Maquis leader was genuinely pleased to see the two of them so in love. Perhaps it was just that the war had brought them together, the disease creating its own anti-bodies. Love was an antidote to horror. To see-saws.

Madeleine delivered her report, but Farnham only half listened to the news of German movements, the upcoming rail schedule, the bombing reports, all of which would soon be on their way to London. Every now and then she would glance round at him, as if to make sure he was still there. Why me? he wondered. What had he done to deserve someone like this?

Once she had finished they both took their leave of Yves, and started back down the path to Le Chipal, frequently stopping to kiss and hold each other. They managed to get about two hundred yards beyond the camp sentries before desire overwhelmed them, and in a glade some fifty yards from the path they tore off each other's clothes, searched each other's eyes and clung naked to each other in a long, hungry kiss, before tumbling to the soft ground and entwining their bodies in the wonderful throes of passionate love.

Twenty-fours later Farnham was standing in the meadow chosen for the re-supply drop. Half of the SAS unit were present, as were Yves, Henri and several other Maquisards. The SAS men were spread out round the field, eyes turned outward in search of possible German interference, but the Frenchmen were standing in a group nearby. They had only come, Farnham suspected, for the novel experience of seeing motor vehicles dropped by parachute.

The planes – the RAF had found a second at the last moment – would be due in a few minutes. For the moment the silence of the night and the stillness of the vast forested slopes was broken only by the murmur of the Frenchmen and the shuffle of his own feet.

'What sort of range do these jeeps have?' Yves asked at his shoulder.

'They used to have a basic range of 250 miles,' Farnham answered him, 'but now they've squeezed in several extra tanks, and more than doubled that.'

'I can hear them, boss,' McCaigh said at his side, and a few seconds later so could Farnham. By this time the Londoner had plugged in the directional aerial on the S-phone and was aiming it in the general direction of the distant drone. Farnham gave the signal for the red triangulation lights to be turned on and scoured the north-western sky for the dark silhouettes of the approaching planes.

After a while he had them – two specks flying out of the low-slung Plough towards the Eureka-Rebecca's homing beacon. He began flashing a Morse confirmation with his white light, continuing until McCaigh had established radio-telephone contact with the pilots. Soon the leading Halifax was overhead. The first four parachutes bloomed on the corners of the first crated jeep and the whole package drifted down, landing on its underside airbag with a noise like a deflating rubber cushion. More followed, and Farnham had a mind's-eye picture of the men in the planes above dragging the crates across the floor and heaving them out into the night.

Six large crates came out of each plane, and several smaller ones. As the roar of the engines faded the SAS men were already splitting open the crates and putting together the armoured jeeps like a bunch of fanatical hobbyists. A pair of twin Vickers K guns and a half-inch Browning heavy machine-gun were mounted on each of the four-wheel-drive jeeps, in-built radios and fuel tanks quickly checked for damage and spare fuel canisters loaded aboard. Other modifications had obviously been made recently, and Farnham was pleased to see both an armour-plated bumper guard and a bulletproof windscreen. The designers had even added a single K gun for the driver to use with his non-driving hand. The whole thing might look like an eight-year-old's dream, but it was hard to fault as a tool of men.

While most of the men had been getting the jeeps ready for travel some had been carting off and burying the pieces of wooden crate in pre-dug holes just inside the trees. Once this was done, and all the various equipment had been loaded aboard the jeeps, Farnham invited Yves into the lead vehicle and the column set off, sounding alarmingly noisy in the open meadow. Once inside the trees it followed an already-scouted path for about half a mile before debouching on to a little-used farm track, which it then followed west.

Each bend in this forest track offered the chance of running, quite literally, into a German patrol, but the possibility was too remote to dampen the enormous sense of exhilaration which Farnham experienced in the lead jeep. It was partly the success of the drop, the beauty of the night, even the lingering joy of his evening with Madeleine, but there was also something else at play, something new, and eventually he realized what it was. They were no longer skulking around on an enemy-occupied continent – they were driving down the bastards' roads as if they owned them.

Early the next morning Farnham briefed the unit on what came next. The first light of dawn was filtering down through the trees, and as his eyes scanned the men gathered round him – some sitting cross-legged, some with their backs to trees, some squatting on their haunches – he remembered the Robin Hood stories of his childhood, and a particular illustration of the outlaw leader addressing his Merrie Men in a forest glade like this one.

'The jeeps have all passed inspection,' he began, 'so we'll be leaving tonight. We're going to split up into two equal groups, six jeeps and sixteen men to each. Group B, under Captain Hoyland, will head south. That group's primary objective will be the railway which runs through the Belfort Gap between Belfort itself and Mulhouse. As far as London can tell, all the German units who were stationed south and east of Paris will have to withdraw along this line, so it's vital for them to keep it open. As a consequence, it will probably be heavily patrolled. Unfortunately, this railway does not run through a convenient forest, so several days' observation may be necessary before a suitable plan of action can be drawn up. Once the railway has been put out of commission then the unit will be free to patrol on a more aggressive basis.

'Group A will head north. There are three east-west railway routes north of the St Dié–Strasbourg line – one double-track line through the Saverne Gap and two smaller-capacity lines through the northern Vosges – and we shall attempt to inter-rupt traffic on all three for as long as possible. The northern-most of the three is about sixty miles away as the crow flies, a lot further by the roads we shall be using, but I'm assured that each jeep has fuel for six hundred miles.'

'We could drive straight to Berlin,' a voice said.

'We could drive home,' someone else suggested.

'We'll probably end up doing both before we're through,' Farnham told them. 'But first you all have this adventure holiday in France. The current plan is for the two groups to meet back here in eighteen days' time, but circumstances may change, some irresistible opportunity may present itself . . .'

'We might even catch sight of a woman,' someone said mournfully.

'Not one that'd give you an opportunity.'

164

Farnham grinned. 'The two groups will be in radio contact with each other, so the rendezvous can always be brought forward or put back. OK, any questions?'

'Are we travelling by day or night?' a trooper asked.

'Good question. We're going to start off by night, but there are good arguments for both. We'll obviously be less visible in the dark, but the Germans may be doing most of their driving at night to avoid air attacks, and if so we'll be more likely to run into them. But of course if we travel by day then we run more risk of being seen, not to mention the possibility of being attacked by our own planes. It's a bit of a toss-up. One thing we'll have in our favour is a decent moon – it'll be full in six days' time. So we'll be able to drive without lights.'

'Just how hard are we trying to stay out of the Germans' way?' another man wanted to know.

'Our aim is to put those railways out of business, and since that'll be easier if the Germans aren't actively looking for us, then the longer they remain in ignorance of our existence the better. So we definitely won't be seeking confrontation with them. Then again, there's always the chance we'll just run into them, in which case we'll obviously do as much damage as we can.'

'How about the Froggies?' someone else asked.

'What about them?' Farnham asked. The British nickname for the French had lost much of its appeal since he'd met Madeleine.

'Are we trying to stay out of their way too?'

'We're not going to be advertising our presence to anyone, but sometimes a bit of help from the locals will be damn useful. For one thing, they'll have a better idea of where the Germans are than we will. And that reminds me – a couple of the Maquisards have volunteered to ride along with us, and their presence should reassure any of the locals who have doubts about us.' He looked round the faces. 'Anything else? Good. We've got the rest of the day to get some sleep, pack up camp and remove all traces of our stay. We'll be moving out at 2200 hours.'

The men slowly got to their feet. There were a couple of jokes, but the faces were mostly thoughtful. They knew full well what they were in for.

At the appointed hour the engines of a dozen jeeps spluttered into life and the column started wending its way up through the trees to the track which hugged the side of the ridge above their camp. Turning right, they followed it for a mile or so before reaching a fork, and here the two groups separated, waving mute farewells to each other in the dark.

Group A's road plunged down a narrow valley towards Fraize, and a few scattered lights in the small town were visible when they reached the turn-off they were looking for. This road would carry them through several small villages, Le Chipal and Sadey among them, before reaching the main St Dié–Strasbourg road at Raves, where Farnham had caught his bus to Schirmeck three months before. Here it was hoped that they could cross the main road unobserved and start climbing into the densely forested hills beyond.

The moon was not yet up but once out of the forest they found they could drive without lights at a reasonable speed. Rafferty, Tobin and the ginger-haired Pogo Young – a talkative steelworker's son from Rotherham – were on point duty in the front jeep, and they were now running a good two hundred yards ahead of the rest of the column. Young was driving, Rafferty beside him, the barely visible map on his knees and both hands on the grips of the half-inch Browning as he scanned the road ahead. Behind him Tobin was grasping the twin Vickers Ks, his eyes scouring the darkness to either side.

Second in line was the command jeep, with McCaigh driving, Farnham checking a second map and the young Maquisard François perched happily in the back. He'd come along for the ride in more ways than one – the foreigners and their heavily armed jeeps had clearly caught his imagination, and the expression on his face as they motored down the winding lane was that of a young boy having his first taste of a roller-coaster. François' youth had almost disqualified him from the trip, but the boy had more than enthusiasm to offer – after Yves, he had the quickest mind of all the Maquisards whom Farnham had met.

The third jeep contained the taciturn Albert Lowe, Jimmy 'Wallis' Simpson and the witty Lancastrian Pete McLaglan; the fourth Sean Mayles, Brendan Armstrong and the mortar; the fifth Brian Shearer, John Downey and Eric Lennon. The sixth and last jeep, performing the 'Tail-end Charlie' role, contained the unit's second sergeant, Andy Lynton, and both of its corporals, the baby-faced Gerry Chadwick and the saturnine Ronnie Hill. Their attention was mostly concentrated on the road behind, which they grimly watched for any sign of pursuit, or any indication that the column's passage had been noted by unfriendly eyes.

They were now more than halfway to Raves, and had met no other vehicles. The houses of the intermittent villages were mostly in darkness, though a couple of curtains twitched in lighted windows as the column drove by. In the command jeep Farnham tried to keep track of their position on his map, and wondered again if he should have put François in the front jeep, at least for the early part of the journey. He could navigate without a map, but he didn't have the military experience that would be needed in the lead jeep if they ran into trouble.

So far it hadn't mattered, for Rafferty had encountered no difficulty in finding and following their chosen route.

The light of the moon was now suffusing the sky above, though the satellite itself was still hidden by the dark bulk of the Vosges to their right. The road twisted this way and that like a pale snake, squirming towards the shadowy massif to the north, whose forested humps were crowned with silver.

Just south of Raves they crossed the road to Ste Marie aux Mines, and a couple of minutes later all six jeeps drew up in the shadow of a high hedge some fifty yards short of the main road from St Dié to Schirmeck. Two cars went by in the direction of the latter, and then, just as it seemed that the road was clear, a long convoy appeared from the opposite direction. It passed slowly by, and the SAS men could see the faces of the German soldiers sitting in the backs of the lorries. Though Farnham's mind assured him that his own unit was invisible in the shadows, it felt all too visible, and he sat there half expecting the shout, the pointing finger, the squealing brakes.

But the convoy kept rumbling on towards St Dié, and he found he could breathe again. The road, what's more, was now clear.

The six jeeps raced across like guilty schoolboys, and roared up the narrow road which the map claimed would lead them right up into the hills. Two more sleeping villages presented themselves, and then they were back in the forest, and having to slow down for fear of missing a turn in the dark. The next half-hour was difficult, the roads refusing to conform to what the map expected of them, and after the whole column had twice been forced to double back, Farnham began to feel a touch of apprehension. But their luck changed almost immediately, an attempted short cut proving just that, and they found themselves on an almost straight road for several miles.

It was now past midnight, and they were getting close to the village of Ranrupt, where the Maquis had a sympathetic contact. 'Half these village names sound German to me,' McCaigh told Farnham. 'Are you sure we're in the right country?'

'This area's more like Germany than France in most ways,' Farnham told him, 'but the people are really anti-German.' He grinned in the dark. 'It's like you Tottenham supporters,' he said, recalling something McCaigh had once said. 'The enemy you hate most is the one just down the road.'

'Ah, Arsenal,' McCaigh said. 'I see what you mean.'

In the seat behind them, François suddenly put his arm between them, pointing ahead. 'Ranrupt,' he said, and they could see the roofs of a village a little further down the valley. 'It will be better if we go in on foot,' he told Farnham in French. 'That way we will wake the village when we leave rather than when we arrive.'

Farnham agreed, and was about to radio the lead jeep accordingly when he saw that Rafferty had already pulled it up just ahead. Drawing level, he explained that he and François would go in on their own.

'We can get a lot nearer than this just rolling downhill with the engines off,' Rafferty suggested, and they did just that, the line of jeeps, now both lightless and virtually silent, descending the hill like a column of ghosts. About a hundred yards short of the first building, Farnham and François clambered out on to the road and, with Tobin and Pogo Young watching their backs, walked into the village.

Lines of stone cottages crowded either side of the road and others clung to the sides of the widening valley. The Maquisard's contact, a heavily built farmer in his forties with a mop of dark wavy hair and a luxuriant moustache, lived in one of the latter, and once he realized who it was had come to call, seemed eager to be helpful. Farnham and François were treated to glasses of red wine and invited to toast France, De Gaulle and the King before he would get down to business, but the information he had was more than worth the wait. After patiently studying Farnham's map of the area to the north he confidently picked out three small towns as hosting German soldiers and one section of road along the spine of the Vosges on which foreign workers were constructing defensive positions under German supervision. 'My son is somewhere in Germany,' he added. 'He thought he was safe as a medical student, but he was caught by the forced labour drive.'

Farnham was just wondering where the man's wife was, always assuming he still had one, when he heard the sound of creaking bedsprings overhead.

'My wife is a heavy sleeper,' the man explained, after seeing Farnham's eyes look up.

Mine was too, Farnham thought, surprising himself. Since meeting Madeleine his thoughts of Catherine had been few and far between.

They took their leave and walked back through the village to the waiting jeeps. The gibbous moon was now riding high above the hills, but the western sky was beginning to fill with clouds. Farnham gave Rafferty a brief rundown on what the farmer had told them, then climbed back in beside McCaigh. The column moved silently forward, only engaging its engines once the trailing jeep was a hundred yards beyond the village.

They drove on through the maze of mountain lanes and tracks, occasionally retracing their steps when a road petered out at the head of a valley, and no doubt provoking whispered conversations of the 'who the fuck was that?' variety in several conjugal beds. The strain of keeping a constant lookout was a telling one, particularly after several hours of seeing nothing but trees, but if the standards of watchfulness slipped during the last part of the journey they did so with impunity. The war might have been over for years, the Germans long gone home, for all the evidence of their occupation on display that night.

By two-thirty in the morning the column was within a few miles of its first target – the Bettborn Tunnel, which carried the railway for a mile and a half under a spur of the Vosges – and the search began for somewhere to lie up during the day. This proved more difficult than expected, and Farnham was beginning to feel a slight twinge of panic when they finally found a track which offered disguisable access to the woods above. The tunnel recce teams were sent out immediately, so as to give them plenty of time to dig themselves in before dawn, and the rest of the unit set to work camouflaging the jeeps, digging scrapes and disguising any tell-tale tyre tracks on the dry ground.

Farnham felt content – they had driven well over fifty miles across enemy territory without raising a single alarm. Things would no doubt get more difficult – once they attacked the railway the Germans would certainly know someone was out there – but he thought they had more than a sporting chance of staying one step ahead. Like Yves had said, no one wanted to die on the last day of a war, and it was hard to believe that the Germans wouldn't rapidly be losing their stomach for a fight.

* * *

Rafferty and McCaigh, who had been assigned the western end of the tunnel, took about an hour to reach the wooded slopes above the entrance, and about another twenty minutes to work themselves cautiously into a position almost parallel to the entrance. About a hundred feet beneath them several German soldiers were sitting round a glowing brazier beside a platelayers' hut.

Since the slightest noise or the dislodgement of a single stone might invite discovery the observation scrape took longer to dig than usual, and it was not until both men were securely ensconced in the finished article that they had time to take a thorough look at the scene below. The small hut, which was set back in a bay carved out of the cutting slope, was about ten yards from the mouth of the single-track tunnel, and there were now four helmeted soldiers gathered round the brazier. They were all wearing long coats, and two had their Schmeisser sub-machine-guns across their shoulders. The hut door seemed to be open but there was no way of knowing if there was anyone inside until one of the brazier men turned and shouted something in that direction. The sound of laughter came from within, maybe from one man, more likely from two.

About forty yards from the mouth of the tunnel, away to the SAS men's right, the track divided, and just beyond the points, on the other side of the tracks, there was a wooden signal box. The windows were blacked-out, but thin lines of light seeped out around the edges, and they could detect the movement of at least one person inside. Beyond the signal box the cutting slowly widened and the twin tracks disappeared in a long curve towards what looked, in the gloom, like open farming country.

The two men had been taking in the scene for a few minutes when they became conscious of a rumbling inside the earth and realized that a westbound train was coming through the tunnel. There was a momentary flash of light away to the right as the signalman widened one of the blackout slits in his windows, the roar of the oncoming train seemed to surge in volume and a great plume of smoke poured skyward as the locomotive emerged from the tunnel. Twenty-three closed goods wagons followed, their wheels beating out a foreign rhythm on the rails. The French presumably used different length rails, Rafferty thought, as he noted the time and type of train in his logbook.

That done, he made the mime for sleep and pointed enquiringly at McCaigh. There was a breeze in the branches above them, and the vanished train was still audible, but it was hard to know how much noise would carry to the Germans below.

McCaigh nodded, yawned, and laid himself out with his head furthest from the observation slit.

Rafferty looked at the boots twitching a foot from his face and sighed.

In the last hour of darkness three more trains passed through – two more composed entirely of closed wagons, one of flat wagons carrying eighteen Tiger tanks. This latter was defended by anti-aircraft guns mounted on sandbagged flat wagons fore and aft, and seemed worth a brief radio message to the camp, for transmission on to Bomber Command in England.

Dawn finally broke, and two of the Germans started strolling to and fro along the track between the tunnel mouth and the signal box, yawning mightily as they did so. Another, disappearing inside the signal box for several minutes, proved the first of several in search of a morning crap.

As the light improved, Rafferty was able to get a better look at the slopes of the cutting on either side of the line. These were both high and steep, but a man could easily slide down to track level in a matter of seconds. The problem would be managing it in silence, and not giving any of the Germans time to alert either HQ or their opposite numbers at the other end of the tunnel. A well-aimed grenade might take out all of them in one go, but the bang might echo down the tunnel.

It was a solvable problem, Rafferty thought, and he found himself feeling a twinge of sympathy for the Germans below. They were presumably only there to deter any local Resistance units, because there was no way they could hope to survive a determined attack by well-armed regulars.

He began working on a diagram of the area, realizing as he drew that the signal box could be utilized to mask an approach from the men around the hut. There would still be the problem of getting up the steps before the signalman had a chance to alert the next box down the line . . .

The sound of a train approaching from the west rose above the early-morning birdsong and McCaigh's faint whistling snores. The locomotive appeared round the curve and the signalman emerged from his box to watch it, giving Rafferty his first good look at the man. There was no way of telling, of course, but he looked French.

The locomotive swept by, leaving its trail of smoke above the cutting as it was swallowed by the tunnel, and the goods wagons rattled after it. Rafferty wasn't sure why – perhaps he detected some movement through a broken slat – but he had the strong feeling that these wagons were loaded with people. Prisoners of war or slave labour for German factories. Or maybe something worse. He didn't like the thought that the train was travelling by day, in full view of the Allied air forces, because the Germans didn't really care what happened to its occupants.

Another hour went by and the sun slowly clambered above the hill behind the tunnel. Shortly after seven o'clock Rafferty heard the sound of a lorry on the road which ran down through the trees to the south, and not long after that a party of six German soldiers came into view beyond the signal box, walking along beside the tracks. They exchanged a few words with the six they were relieving, who then shuffled tiredly off down the track in the direction of the invisible vehicle.

A few minutes later a new signalman arrived, wheeling his bicycle alongside the tracks, and the incumbent departed, having collected his own bike from behind the box.

No more trains appeared, and Rafferty's tired brain started drifting in unwelcome directions. Whenever his mind was blank she seemed to be there, filling it with anger and resentment and hurt. He tried to think about something else – films he'd seen, the car business he was going to start, even Tommy's sister – but nothing had the power to shift Beth for more than a few seconds. All those years, and she couldn't have ever really loved him. It had all been unreal and he hadn't had a clue. So how would he know next time if he was making the same mistake? Well, that was easy – there wouldn't be a next time.

Another train saved him, a hospital train, emblazoned with red crosses on each coach roof, and he thought about the men inside it and felt a little ashamed of feeling so sorry for himself.

'I'm awake,' McCaigh murmured above the rumbling of the train in the tunnel. He reversed himself rather like a racing swimmer at the end of a pool, pulled the logbook over to his side of the observation slit and gestured for Rafferty to take his turn in the land of nod.

The sergeant needed no second encouragement, and it soon became apparent to McCaigh why that was – this was undoubtedly the most boring observation detail either of them had ever been cursed with. The rest of the morning passed without a single train appearing, and the Germans below looked as bored as he felt. 'The war we watched,' McCaigh murmured to himself.

Since arriving in France they'd basically played hide-and-seek with the Germans. He knew the information they had gathered was valuable, that it might well save Allied lives over the next few weeks and months, but it wasn't action. Eight months had passed since the night in San Severino, and he was beginning to wonder whether he'd ever find himself in a fire-fight again. If he wasn't going to, then he'd just as soon know now, so that he could start dismantling the mental defences he'd built up and get back to living.

It had been trains at San Severino, he thought. What did you do in the war, Dad? I was a train-spotter, son.

In the forest camp the day went by no faster. Farnham set sentries on the perimeter and let the rest of the men sleep while he considered the problem of the tunnel. They didn't have enough explosive to collapse it, but there were several ways to create a serious blockage without using any of their limited supplies. The choice of which would have to wait on the reports of the recce teams, so there wasn't much point in thinking about them.

He closed his eyes and found Madeleine's face in his mind. They were in the forest, which wasn't surprising – the two of them had only been under one roof together, Marcel's in Schirmeck. He wondered what her house in St Dié looked like, if indeed she lived in a house. He didn't even know whether she lived alone, with her parents or with friends.

After changing the sentries at noon he went to sleep himself, leaving orders that he be woken the moment the recce teams returned. Pogo Young and Sergeant Lynton were back soon after dark, but they had to wait another half-hour for Rafferty and McCaigh. 'We thought it was worth waiting to see if the day signalman was relieved by the one who was on last night,' the former explained. 'And he was.'

Farnham listened to the two teams' reports, studied their logs and glanced at the maps they had drawn. 'Was there any sign of contact between the two lots of Germans?' he asked.

Both Lynton and Rafferty shook their heads.

'But there must be between the two signal boxes,' McCaigh said. 'Stands to reason with a single-track tunnel.'

Farnham thought for a moment. 'The signalmen are French, you think? How friendly with the Germans were they?'

'I don't think ours said a word to them, unless he sat on their laps in the bog,' Rafferty said, turning to McCaigh for confirmation.

'He never came down the stairs all day,' the Londoner added.

'Ours was more pally than that,' Lynton said. 'I mean, there weren't any long conversations, but there were a few nods and smiles and stuff like that.'

Farnham examined the maps again. 'OK,' he said at last, 'the eastern end offers less in the way of cover, the signalman seems more likely to be a problem, and at least eighty per cent of the trains are coming from that direction. So I say we leave that end to Jerry.'

'Why not take both?' Lynton wanted to know.

'Because I want to be certain we get a train into the tunnel,' Farnham told him.

Shortly after one in the morning the eight men advanced stealthily through the trees above the mouth of the cutting and slid as quietly as possible down the bank, taking care to keep the signal box between themselves and the German soldiers on duty outside the platelayers' hut. At the same time McCaigh was guiding two other men to a point on the edge of the trees immediately above the enemy. The other six SAS men had drawn the proverbial short straw, and were with the jeeps a couple of miles away.

Having reached the back wall of the signal box, Farnham and the others crouched in the shadows and waited for a train. If the last twenty-four hours had been typical, the odds were on a westbound train, but as far as he could tell it would only make a difference if the train in question was travelling at an unheard-of speed. Five minutes went by, and ten, and twenty, and the first small signs of physical restlessness were becoming evident in the men around him when the sound of a train in the distance edged its way into his consciousness. In the signal box above he heard footsteps and the clank of a lever being pulled. An answering noise from the left had to be the signal arm descending.

As the train grew nearer the men got to their feet, both hands grasping the Sten guns which were slung across their chests. At the corner of the box Rafferty had his service revolver out, and next to him François was looking so excited that Farnham was afraid he might burst.

The train swept into view. It was only moving at about thirty miles an hour, Farnham thought, and was probably slowing marginally to take the trailing point before plunging into the tunnel. More important, it was a train of covered wagons, so there weren't likely to be any prying eyes behind the locomotive. He gave his sergeant the nod, and as the locomotive surged by, pistons pumping and smoke pouring, Rafferty and François made a run for the signal box stairway. With the thunder of the train in their ears they didn't hear their own feet on the steps, and the first the signalman knew of their approach was when the door flew open and he looked up to see Rafferty's revolver pointing at his heart.

Farnham, meanwhile, was leading the other five men at a steady lope down the side of the track, no more than a couple of yards from the rattling wheels of the passing wagons. The lack of light made running treacherous, but at least it would prevent the Germans from seeing them through the wheels, and as long as no one slipped and fell to their left . . .

The last wagon abruptly slid past, exposing the four Germans on the other side of the track. Two were sitting, two standing, and one of the latter managed a brief exclamation of surprise before the six Stens opened up, throwing him back across the brazier, which collapsed in a shower of sparks. The guns sounded louder in the narrow cutting than Farnham had hoped, but he still felt certain that the train in the tunnel would have masked the noise from those at the other end.

Andy Lynton was already at the door of the hut, firing another short burst, when a wail of despair came from within. He disappeared inside, to re-emerge a moment later, prodding what looked like a very young German with the butt of his Sten. 'One prisoner,' he said disgustedly.

McCaigh and his two companions, who had been waiting with grenades on the bank above in case something went wrong, slithered down to join the rest of the party. 'All right,' Farnham said, 'let's get the bodies behind the hut. Ronnie, you get inside with the prisoner. Pogo, Ian, get coats and helmets on and look like you're ready to die for Adolf. I'm going to see what's happening in the signal box.'

A bell rang inside as he ran up the steps, and he opened the door just in time to hear Rafferty asking the signalman what it meant in understandable if awkward French.

The signalman took his pipe out of his mouth and told him.

'It's the box at the other end of the tunnel,' François confirmed.

'Does it need a reply?' Farnham asked.

'No,' the signalman said flatly.

Farnham looked enquiringly at François, who shrugged. 'I think he's telling the truth,' the Maquisard said.

'Of course I am,' the signalman said calmly.

'Are you for France, monsieur?' Farnham asked him with a thin smile.

'Of course. But I am also for my wife and children.'

'Would you like us to tie you up once we've finished our business here?'

The man smiled. 'That would seem to be a good idea.'

'OK. When's the next train due?' Farnham asked.

'I don't know. The Germans . . .' He shrugged.

'How much warning will you get?'

'About ten minutes for an eastbound, five for a westbound.'

Farnham turned to Rafferty. 'You and François stay here. If a train's on the way give us a signal from the mouth of the tunnel – two flashes for an eastbound, four for a westbound.'

'Right, boss,' Rafferty said, but Farnham was already on his way. He arrived back at the hut just as McCaigh triumphantly emerged with two armfuls of track-laying wrenches and hammers. Explosives would have done the intended job, but not as quietly or as neatly, and Farnham felt relieved to see the tools. He grabbed a platelayer's wrench and led the five available men into the tunnel at a brisk walk, leaving Tobin and Young to do their Wehrmacht impersonations and McLaglan to guard the prisoner.

'How far, boss?' McCaigh asked, and his voice seemed to echo in the enclosed space.

'Keep it down,' Farnham advised. The tunnel might be a mile and a half long but for all he knew it worked as a sound amplifier. A memory from his childhood surfaced, of telephones made from two tins and a long piece of string. 'At least a hundred yards,' he murmured, as much to himself as McCaigh. 'We want to make damn sure it doesn't just shoot out of the tunnel.'

'I hope we don't meet a train coming the other way,' one of the other men muttered.

'There are places you can stand,' Farnham said, shining his torch on one of the embrasures built into the tunnel wall. He didn't bother to add that if the oncoming train was carrying troops, and they were seen, then they would be trapped between two groups of Germans.

Looking back at the pale circle of the tunnel mouth, he reckoned they'd come far enough, and stepped across the track to the outer curve. After searching out the rail joints with his torch he settled on the two lengths they would loosen, positioned the other five men accordingly and applied his long wrench to the first bolted spike. It unscrewed more easily than he'd expected, and a few seconds later he was able to lift it out, insert the folded piece of cloth as a muffler and use the other end of the wrench to knock out the rail anchor. He moved on to the next bolt.

The six of them laboured on in the dim light, trying not to let haste make them clumsy, the sound of their breathing making common cause with the soft thud of the hammers and the reluctant grating of the bolts coming free.

They were about three-quarters done when the light flashed four times in the mouth of the tunnel, and as the darkness reasserted itself a low rumble could be heard in the distance. 'Shit!' Farnham muttered. How long had they got? Five minutes minus one . . . four at most. 'Keep at it,' he shouted, realizing the others had stopped. At least there was no longer any need for silence.

For the next couple of minutes the clanging reverberated through the tunnel, but it was fighting a losing battle with the approaching train. By Farnham's reckoning they still had two minutes but the evidence of his ears was suggesting otherwise, and at least one full length of rail had been comprehensively loosened. 'Let's go,' he screamed at the others, who dropped their tools and started running towards the tunnel mouth.

The noise behind them was almost deafening, the rails beside them seemed to be vibrating, and Farnham could have sworn that orange light was dancing on the tunnel ceiling, but as they raced out into the open air the oncoming locomotive was still about a hundred and fifty yards behind them. There was time to turn and watch the train's signal lights falter and dip as the length of rail gave way, and the wheels plunged into the gap it left. There was an almighty noise of grinding as the locomotive slewed forward in a hail of ballast, and for one horrible moment Farnham thought he'd miscalculated, and it would slide right out of the tunnel. But it didn't. Showering blue sparks and screeching like a banshee, the engine finally came to a halt some twenty yards inside the mouth, where only a magician could bring a crane to bear.

The next moment smoke had engulfed it, and Farnham sent a burst of fire from his Sten into the tunnel ceiling to discourage anyone from venturing out. Behind him the helmets and coats were being discarded, the prisoner offered a cheery goodbye, the signalman tied up. On the road beyond the signal box the jeeps would now be waiting, and as the unit ran back up the tracks to board them, Farnham ticked off a mental finger. One down, two to go.

An early sighting would give away the direction they had taken after blocking the tunnel, and for the next thirty-six hours the unit hid out in a secluded section of the forests which lay to the north of the line. On the third night Farnham set the jeeps in motion once more, and through that and the following night they moved slowly but steadily north, keeping to the smallest roads and doubling back to choose another route whenever the threat of discovery seemed imminent. They crossed one of the two railway lines through the northern Vosges a few miles west of Wingen-sur-Moder, and made camp a few miles south of the Bitche–Lemberg section of the other. From here reconnaissance patrols were sent out to explore the line, and a couple of nights later three separate teams took out three bridges several miles apart, while a fourth team ostentatiously drove north through the un-garrisoned town of Bitche before doubling back to rejoin the others.

They lay low for another couple of nights and then headed south once more to explore the Wingen-sur-Moder line. There was more traffic now, and more Germans to protect it, but nothing like enough of the latter to cover ten miles of winding track through wooded hills. Farnham had his men on surveillance duties for several days before picking his spots and sending the same men back as demolition squads. Three more bridges were brought down, and the SAS unit once more melted away into the forest. In ten days they had severely disrupted three major supply routes across the Vosges and given the enemy a succession of logistical headaches he could ill afford, all without losing a man.

Not surprisingly, the mood in the unit was little short of euphoric. The tensions which accompanied the constant fear of discovery didn't just evaporate, and living by night in such conditions took a gradually mounting toll, but when push came to shove most of Farnham's men knew how lucky they were. On the radio they heard news of the Russian and Allied advances, the fall of Bucharest in distant Romania and the triumphant march into Paris, Monty's surge through Picardy and Patton's drive towards the Vosges and themselves. In the sky above they saw the bomber formations heading for the cities of the Reich. And here they were camped out in the forest, occasionally venturing out to blow up railway bridges, while others suffered artillery bombardment, tank and mortar fire, the visceral nightmares of close combat and the cold horror of bombs raining from the sky. It occurred to Farnham that here behind enemy lines they were in the military equivalent of the hurricane's eye, the calm at the heart of the storm.

Home felt far away, but as the days went by absence made the heart fonder, the memory kinder. Tobin decided that he had forgiven Megan for not trusting him, Rafferty found himself rereading the letters from Mary which he had accidentally brought with him, and McCaigh, thinking about Billy Sangster one night, almost felt sorry for the bastard. As commanding officer, Farnham had less time for introspection, and when he did think about England it was usually to imagine the first meeting between Eileen and Madeleine. He found that worrying about how that might go gave him less time to worry about what was actually happening in London and St Dié.

They kept moving south, and by midnight on the last day of August were only a long night's journey from their original camp, where the rendezvous with Hoyland's group had been fixed for three nights hence. *En route* they would have to cross the valley which carried the railway and road between St Dié and Schirmeck, and since it was likely that this would be heavily patrolled Farnham decided to use one of their nights in hand for some extra surveillance. At worst this would increase their chances of crossing the valley unseen; at best it might offer the chance to cause more chaos in the enemy's travel arrangements.

With the jeeps drawn off the mountain track some two miles north of the valley, Rafferty, McCaigh, Tobin and Pogo Young were dispatched to check out the favoured crossing-point and the possibilities for mayhem. Tobin and Young returned two hours later with mixed news. The track down into the valley was safe, but the mile of main road which the unit would need to traverse lay in full view of a German-guarded railway bridge across the river. And since there was nothing special about this bridge it seemed safe to assume that units of enemy troops were guarding all the railway bridges.

That was the bad news, and it was another two hours before Rafferty and McCaigh returned with some corrective medicine. The next bridge across the river was also under guard, but the three miles of track between them were not. In the middle of this stretch a second dirt road crossed the river and climbed into the mountains beyond, and almost opposite its intersection with the main road another wide path descended the northern slopes of the valley. They only had to find the top of this path and their way was clear, for both the crossing of the valley and another night of sabotage.

Farnham checked his maps and sent them back out with a jeep to search. An hour later, with the first hint of light appearing in the eastern sky, they returned wreathed in smiles.

The path could be reached from where they were without any trouble, and the way down was clear.

They broke camp soon after dark, loaded up the jeeps, and set off. The tracks through the trees were narrow tunnels, the thin light on offer from the waning crescent moon was better than nothing but not much more, and it was almost midnight before they reached a spot some half a mile away from, and a couple of hundred feet above, the intersection with the main road. There they sat in their jeeps for over an hour waiting for the moon to set, the boring vigil only occasionally interrupted by the sound of a train or lorry convoy passing through the valley below.

Finally Farnham gave the word and Rafferty's lead jeep rolled silently down towards the main road, Tobin and Young ready behind the twin Vickers and Browning, eyes scanning the valley for approaching headlights.

There were none. Rafferty flicked his lights once, and the other five jeeps rolled down after their leader, swinging right on to the main road and only engaging their engines when they were almost at the turn-off to the left. There were headlights in the distance now, but too far off to worry about. After rattling over the river bridge and a crude sleeper-made level crossing the jeeps followed the dirt road up into the trees and there came to a halt. The non-drivers all climbed out, taking with them the tools which had been stolen from the Bettborn Tunnel platelayers' hut, and while the jeeps roared off out of sight they crouched in the darkness waiting for the traffic on the main road to pass.

Once the column of four lorries had eventually trailed by on the far side of the river Farnham sent someone down to the river bridge to check out the road, and having received the signal that it was empty led the men down to the railway tracks. The line to the left, in the direction of St Dié, looked the better bet. The tracks were channelled between the river and a shallow, grassy slope which soon vanished into the trees. The latter could easily be reached if a hiding-place was needed, and the river, which here tumbled itself through a cataract of large rocks, was noisy enough to mask their efforts with wrench and hammer. The only disadvantage Farnham could see – one that was also true of the other direction – was that the outer curve of the track, the one which they would need to loosen, was furthest from the river. If the train tipped over it would be on to the grassy slope, not into the water.

The eleven men spread out up the track and started working at the now familiar task, unscrewing the heavy spikes and knocking out the rail anchors. Twice in the next twenty minutes approaching traffic on the road forced them to scurry up into the shelter of the trees, but by the end of that time some sixty yards of rail had been deprived of everything which held it to the track, and Farnham was about to declare their work complete when the first sounds of an approaching locomotive carried down the valley. It was coming from the west, and he found himself hoping that it wasn't a hospital train carrying wounded enemy troops back to Germany.

He ordered the men back up into the trees, and spread them out in a line above the expected position of the derailed train. It would probably have been more correct to simply run for the jeeps, but Farnham told himself there was always the possibility that the train might be carrying Allied prisoners. Deep down, he knew full well that the child within just wanted to see the train crash. But there was no risk attached – even if the train was full of armed troops they wouldn't be able to pursue a motorized SAS unit into the hills.

The noise of the locomotive grew steadily louder, but the wait still seemed endless. And then suddenly it was in view, a moving black shadow against the darkness of the valley, its crew silhouetted against the orange glow which suffused the cab. Farnham had a brief glimpse of a guard seated on the roof of the first covered wagon, and then the rail abruptly gave way, and the locomotive was ploughing through sleepers and ballast. One of the two crewmen was flung out into the darkness, leaving his partner holding on for dear life.

The two leading wagons concertinaed as the heavier locomotive ground its way to a reluctant halt. All stayed upright, but the doors of the first wagon broke open, and in the dark interior Farnham thought he could detect movement. Several seconds later two shadows jumped down from the doorway, and suddenly the SAS men became aware of voices, many voices, rising above the tumult of the river and the hissing engine. Inside the covered wagons people were asking each other, asking the world outside, what had happened to the train.

Men with lights were now walking along the side of the track towards the locomotive, and in the criss-cross of the beams the SAS men could make out uniforms and boots and guns. Orders were being shouted in German, and then one torch beam caught the two who had climbed down from the gaping doors, and behind them a sea of faces staring down. The two were both no more than children, and like the adults crowding in the wagon doorway, they wore yellow stars on their chests.

As Farnham realized who these people were and where the train was going, the younger of the two broke out of the imprisoning torch beam and began scurrying up the grassy slope towards him. The torches whirled after him and caught him in flight, and in that moment several irrefutable truths flashed through Farnham's mind.

It would be the height of foolishness to start a battle with an unknown number of Germans.

He had no right to risk his men or the mission for a group of foreign civilians.

And even if he did save these people now, there was no way he could keep them safe tomorrow.

All the same, his finger squeezed down on the Sten's trigger, scattering the torch-bearers, bringing forth shrieks of concern from the people on the train. And all along the line, as if they'd been waiting for the cue, his men opened fire with their own guns, engulfing the sounds of human distress in a mechanical storm.

From his position at the other end of the SAS line Ian Tobin had watched the two illuminated coaches at the rear of the train shudder to a halt. One was a brake coach, the other a saloon of some sort, and through the lighted windows of the latter he had a clear view of men struggling to keep their balance as the train faltered and inertia threw them forward. There were about six or seven of them in the coach, and his eyes just had time to register the fact that only a few of them were in uniform before the lights blinked out.

A few seconds later he heard rather than saw a coach door open, and then picked out a shadowy figure cautiously descending the steps. Another man followed, then there was a clatter of feet as several men descended from the brake coach. Torches winked on, and a party started forward up the side of the train.

A few seconds later two more men descended from the saloon, and as one capped his hand to light a match Tobin could make out the black uniforms, the zig-zag SS logo on their collars. One of them said something in German, causing the other to turn and look up the train, and then gunfire erupted away to Tobin's right. As if suddenly aware of his presence, the two SS men's faces jerked in his direction, just as his finger tightened on the trigger.

He felt rather than saw them go down, and lifted the barrel to rake the black mirrors of the coach windows. They exploded inwards in a succession of loud snaps, leaving in their wake cries of pain and a tapering tinkle of falling glass.

From the brake van next door a gun opened up, and Tobin fired a burst in the direction of its muzzle flash. There was a crash as a body tumbled off the train and the sound of a door slamming, presumably on the other side of the train. He heard boots splashing through ballast but could see nothing, and realized that the guns had fallen silent.

The sound of a motor vehicle coming up the valley seemed to seep out of the sudden silence. The guards on the bridge, Farnham realized. They were coming to see what had happened.

'Neil! Mickie!' he yelled out. 'Cover the road.'

They raced past him and the still-hissing locomotive, clattered across the river bridge and threw themselves into the long grass beside the road. Two headlights were now visible in the distance, and the vehicle behind them seemed to be slowing down as it grew nearer, which suggested an unfortunate level of common sense on the part of the driver.

'Keep coming,' Rafferty murmured, urging the unknown enemy forward, but to no avail. The vehicle stopped a couple of hundred yards short of their position, well beyond range of the Stens, and extinguished its light. For about half a minute it just sat where it was, and the two SAS men could imagine the conversation as the Germans looked at the stricken train and wondered where the gunfire had come from. 'None of our business,' McCaigh murmured on the enemy's behalf, and the vehicle's driver obviously agreed, abruptly reversing into a three-point turn and roaring off back down the valley.

'The better part of valour,' Rafferty muttered as he got back to his feet.

'They must like living,' McCaigh decided.

Back at the train the lull had settled into a lasting silence. It seemed as if the Germans had all died or run away, but some might still be hiding in the darkness nearby – it was impossible to tell. The whole business was a nightmare in more ways than one, Farnham thought as he walked down the train, instructing his men to let out the prisoners. At the rear he listened to Tobin's description of the men in the last coach and looked at the bodies of the two SS officers lying beneath the open door. A cigarette end was still smouldering between one of the men's fingers, blackening the dead skin to match the uniform.

Farnham stood there trying to think. They couldn't have much time, but there was no way of knowing how much. Another train could appear at any minute, as could a troop convoy on the road. He had to assume that the guards on the bridge two miles down the valley had heard the gunfire and reported in to their local HQ, which was probably in Schirmeck. Ten miles away. A small unit could already be on the road.

The train was emptying, and the sound of the river was now mingling with hundreds of voices, most of them subdued, a few nervously strident. They sounded like people who had just survived a disaster, Farnham thought, but in reality they had only postponed it. The crematorium at Struthof was still awaiting them.

He turned to Tobin. 'Tell Andy Lynton to get the men together up by the engine,' he told him. 'We'll be pulling out in a few minutes.'

As the Welshman scurried away Farnham walked towards the nearest group of prisoners, and the faces turned towards him seemed pathetically hopeful. 'Have you got a leader?' he asked in French, directing his question to the oldest-looking man. It felt like a stupid question, but he couldn't address them all.

'No,' the man said helplessly. 'We are just prisoners. We . . .'

'I understand,' Farnham cut him off. 'But I cannot talk to everyone, so if I tell you . . .'

'Tell us what?'

Farnham took a deep breath. 'The Germans will be here soon. I don't know where they were taking you, but there is a concentration camp further down this valley, and Jews are being killed there.'

There were gasps of horror all around him. 'So what should we do?' the old man asked him calmly.

'I think you should head into the forest and try to hide there until the war is over, or at least until the Americans reach this area. They could be here in a couple of weeks.'

The old man looked at him. 'All of us?' he asked. 'There are old people and small children. How will they survive? What will we eat?'

Farnham shrugged. 'Anything must be better than certain death.'

'Surely the Germans will come after us?'

'Probably, though maybe they'll be too busy saving their own skins. Take the guns from their dead soldiers . . .'

'Won't you take us with you?'

Farnham had dreaded this question. He felt like saying that there was no way to save them all, that the only result of trying would be to get his own men killed as well, but such honesty was too brutal. 'If we all stayed together we would be caught,' he said. 'You should split up into small groups. That will give at least some of you a chance.'

'Robert,' François said quietly, and Farnham realized for the first time that the young Maquisard was standing at his shoulder. 'I do not think you will need me for the next few days,' the Frenchman went on.

'No, I . . .'

'I will stay with these people,' François said. 'I know the country around here. I know which villages will take people in.'

Farnham looked at him and found that the eager boy had grown into a man. He offered his hand to both François and the old man, wished them both luck and walked away up the train, conscious of all the eyes following him, feeling more helpless than at any time in his life.

The eleven men jogged up the dirt road to where the jeeps were waiting, engines spluttered into life, and soon they were back in the familiar world of the mountain forest, surging up slopes and coasting back down again, mostly tunnelling through the endless trees but occasionally catching glimpses of dark hills rolling away to a far horizon. There was enough time before dawn for them to reach their original camp, but with the scheduled rendezvous still almost forty-eight hours away there was no need to hurry, and with the local Germans probably running around like headless chickens Farnham reckoned that the sooner they got off the roads the better. About six miles south of the railway Rafferty noticed a barely discernible path to their left, and following it up through the trees, discovered an ideal site for the day's camp.

By this time a light rain was falling, which did nothing to lighten the sombre mood of the SAS men as they dug scrapes and camouflaged the jeeps. Most of them couldn't help wondering what had happened to the Jews on the train, and some of those given the first shift in the scrapes had an unusually hard time getting to sleep.

On watch with Rafferty, McCaigh asked the other man if he could see anything different about his face.

'What the fuck are you on about?' Rafferty asked.

'Time before last that I went home,' McCaigh explained, 'I went for a drink with my old man, and in the pub we looked at each other and he just kept looking, you know, like a real long stare. And I asked him what he was looking at, and he said that in the last war a few men got it but most men didn't, and he could always tell from the look in their eyes.'

'Got what?' Rafferty asked.

'What it's all about. And he said he'd never worked out who was better off – those who got it or those who didn't. But he was pretty sure I hadn't. Not yet, anyway.'

'Well, your face looks as ugly as ever to me,' Rafferty told him.

The rain stopped soon after dawn, but the dense grey clouds hung almost motionless in the sky for the rest of the day, a fitting accompaniment to the mood of the unit. Several times during the morning gunfire was faintly audible in the far distance, and a German spotter plane was seen by one of the sentries circling the hills to the north. In the afternoon that sentry's replacement noticed a dense cloud of dark smoke on the horizon, but there was no way of knowing what was being burnt.

The clouds rolled away with surprising rapidity after dark, revealing a thin sliver of a moon which hardly seemed bright enough to delay their night's journey. They advanced with more than the usual caution nevertheless, with Rafferty's lead jeep often ranging far ahead of the main column. Farnham would have liked to stop in one of the sleeping villages for any news the locals might have of German movements, but François was no longer with them and he wasn't sure enough of his own ability to accurately gauge the villagers' reactions.

What he'd told the old man – that the Germans would be too busy losing the war to worry about one train-load of Jews – might be true, but somehow he doubted it. He remembered things Yves had said about the Gestapo chief in St Dié, who didn't sound like the sort of man to take such an insult in his stride. At the very least there would be more executions of hostages.

They had warned the SAS officers about this in England. The taking and killing of hostages was nothing more, and nothing less, than a form of blackmail, and the teams working behind enemy lines would have to steel their hearts against the knowledge that the Germans were making others pay for their actions. All of which had sounded very sensible in a briefing room in deepest Gloucestershire. The briefer, after all, had probably never taken a decision which he knew would probably condemn innocent people to death.

Farnham found himself wondering whether there was a God up there making the necessary calculations. In one column the Allied lives supposedly saved by their bridge-blowing and tunnel-blocking; in the other the hostages shot, the boys on Ziegler's obscene see-saw. Throw in a few Jews on the plus side – at least some of them must have got away – and a few French railwaymen on the minus side . . .

Farnham stopped himself. There was no point in thinking about all that now. Later perhaps, but not now.

He consciously steered his mind back to the world around him – the rattle and hum of the jeeps, the silence of the trees. They had climbed high into the mountains, and he was just thinking that this must have been an old military road when the silhouette of a ruined tower appeared briefly on a crag above the trees. The remains of an earlier war, he thought, and once again the absurdity of it all seemed almost overwhelming.

He remembered the conversation he'd had with Yves soon after arriving for his first stay in May, and the Frenchman's comment that wars were mostly fought by men who'd rather have stayed at home. It might have been true, but it hadn't applied to him, or not then anyway. But now . . . now at least he could imagine wanting to stay at home, and the realization that this was so he found extraordinarily pleasing.

It was about one in the morning when the column of jeeps coasted down the familiar stretch of road and turned off on to the partly man-made track which led down through the forest to their original camp. The moon had long since set but the stars seemed preternaturally bright and the trees seemed to glow with silver light. It occurred to Farnham that after three weeks of night prowling he was beginning to see with a cat's eyes.

The area of trees which had been their home for the better part of a week looked as though it had never seen humans before, but maybe the light of day wouldn't be so flattering. Farnham picked out Tobin, McLaglan, Young and Lowe to check the perimeter and stand the first watch, and the rest of the men got down to the business of unloading and camouflaging the jeeps. After seventeen days of sleeping in scrapes the popular demand for tents was irresistible, and Farnham could see no reason to resist it. 'I'm going to walk over to the Maquis camp,' he told Rafferty, 'and find out what they know about German movements. I'll take McCaigh with me.'

'OK, boss.'

'We'll be back well before dawn.'

McCaigh was pleased – a walk was better than work at any time – and the two men set off in silence, Farnham indulging himself with the possibility that Madeleine might be there. They had only just passed Pogo Young's sentry position when they heard the sound of movement further down the path. Both men stopped dead in their tracks and listened. It was more than one man, more than five. Coming closer.

And then a burst of gunfire sounded from another direction altogether, away to their right. A new silence seemed to fall across the forest, but only for a moment – the sounds on the path below seemed to double in intensity and more gunfire erupted from a third point of the compass.

Tobin had been given the western perimeter to check, the sector encompassing the receding brow of the hill which looked out across the open countryside towards St Dié. He was pleased to be back in their first camp – it felt like coming home, and that was a feeling he had always cherished. In the Landore shop it would soon be time for his parents to get up and sort out the morning papers for the delivery boys.

As he reached the edge of the clearing his eyes were drawn upwards to the star-filled sky, and for several seconds he stood there, trying to remember which constellation was which. There was a breeze ruffling the branches of the trees and perhaps this was what prevented him from hearing the approaching

Germans. He did catch a glimpse of movement on the other side of the clearing as he lowered his eyes, but far too late to do anything about it. The pain was as sudden as a heart attack, the clatter of the gun almost an afterthought.

The Sten slid out of his grasp, and the next thing he knew he was kneeling on the ground. His chest seemed to be on fire and a dreadful pain was rising in his groin. He tried reaching out a hand but nothing seemed to be working.

Oh Megan, he thought.

Gravity was pressing down on his head like a ten-ton weight and he finally bowed to it, dropping face first into the damp earth of the forest floor.

On hearing the first burst of gunfire, Neil Rafferty started off at a run in Tobin's direction, yelling at Ronnie Hill to come with him and Andy Lynton to get the jeeps ready to go. He had covered about twenty yards when the second burst exploded to his right, from the rough direction of the path where Albert Lowe was standing sentry. Rafferty's step faltered, but only for a moment – Farnham would be on his way back up the hill to take charge, and Tobin obviously needed help.

Farnham had left McCaigh and Pogo Young to cover the western path, and they were now squatting down behind two thick-trunked beeches some twenty feet apart. In the dark forest below they could hear a lot of feet and see a lot of vague shadows moving slowly towards them. 'Time for some discouragement?' McCaigh called softly, and Pogo's white teeth flashed in the gloom. 'Why not?'

Both men stepped out, aimed the snouts of the Stens downwards, and raked the general area below, stepping back smartly before the enemy returned fire. Bullets zipped through the branches above, and a couple even thudded into the trunks in front of them. On the path below one man was mewling with pain, and another two seemed to be talking in angry whispers. McCaigh took a hand-grenade from his belt, did his best to pinpoint a gap through the trees in front of him, unclipped the pin and launched it out and down. There was a faint 'phish' sound as it landed, then a burst of yellow light as it exploded among the suddenly silhouetted Germans.

There were more than a few of the bastards, McCaigh realized. And since the sound of gunfire now seemed to be coming from just about every fucking corner of the compass they had presumably surrounded the hill.

Farnham was now back in the centre of the camp, trying to make sense of what his ears were taking in. There was gunfire to the south, west and north, but not, so far, to the east. The Germans had sent parties up the three known paths, he realized, but they hadn't known about the track his men had made for the jeeps. Which offered the SAS at least the chance of a way out. Any German officer worth his salt would have backed up his assault groups with a cordon of encirclement, but the SAS's chances of breaking through one of those had to be better than sitting out a siege by superior forces. Especially with daylight only a couple of hours away.

He thought of sending someone up to check with the southern sentry position, but there was no time. The jeeps were ready to go, and they might as well use them. He turned to the men waiting beside him. 'Andy, you take the north, Gerry, the west, Brian, the south. Give the order to pull out. Quietly, if possible.' As those three raced away he rounded on Lennon and Downey. 'You two head back up the track and keep Pete company. We'll be picking you all up in a couple of minutes.'

These two disappeared into the trees, leaving Farnham standing beside the jeeps, Mayles, Armstrong and Simpson waiting behind three of the driving wheels.

McCaigh and Young needed no second bidding to fall back – the shadows in front of them were slowly turning into the shadows all round them as the Germans worked their way up the slopes to either side of the path. The two men made a parting gift of two more grenades and slipped back up the hill, running the last hundred yards in about twelve seconds flat.

'Mickie, I want you in front,' Farnham told McCaigh, pointing towards the jeep which already contained Lynton and Lowe. 'Pogo, take the last,' he added, his eyes scouring the darkness for Rafferty, Hill, Tobin and Chadwick. 'Where the fuck are they?' he murmured.

Rafferty had spent the last couple of minutes crawling forward through the grass on the forest's edge while Hill offered sporadic covering fire from behind a large oak tree. Eventually he got close enough to satisfy himself that Tobin really was as dead as he looked, and he was still squirming back, German bullets scything through the air inches above his back, when the order to pull out arrived. 'Not a minute too soon,' he murmured to himself, getting to his feet behind a suitable tree. 'Get going,' he told Hill and the recently arrived Chadwick. 'I'll be right behind you,' he added, firing a burst round the trunk in the general direction of the enemy. Take that, you miserable fuckers, he thought, and took off in a crouching run after the others.

As he approached the jeeps all six engines burst simultaneously into life, giving the impression they had all been wired to the same ignition. McCaigh's swung out in the lead, and the others jerked into motion one by one. Rafferty jumped aboard the back of the already moving last jeep and swung the mounted Browning round to cover the column's rear.

Now that they were all moving forward in line the drivers followed Farnham's order to turn on their headlights. The noise of the engines was giving them away in any case, and a speedy ascent of the winding track seemed essential. The jeeps roared along, shaking and jolting their occupants, who clung grimly to gun grips and steering wheels, and then suddenly the headlights picked out the backs of the three men holding the eastern path – each of whom was standing behind a tree – and beyond them a scattering of Germans in the forest. In the seat next to McCaigh, Lynton opened up with a fusillade from the Vickers, causing the Germans to dive for cover. Once past the SAS men on the ground he took the left side of the track, leaving the right to Hill on the Browning behind him, and both men raked the forest with continuous fire. A similar division of labour was enacted in the jeeps behind them and the column roared on uphill like a line of miniature battleships delivering broadsides.

The last two jeeps slowed slightly to pick up the sentries, allowing Downey and Lennon to jump aboard the fifth in line and McLaglan to unceremoniously throw in his lot with Rafferty and Pogo. He was still muttering 'Jesus Christ' and rubbing his shins when the front of the column debouched on to the dirt track half a mile from the camp, to find their chosen route to the left blocked by a small troop carrier. The two Germans in evidence bolted from sight, but there was no time to move the carrier, and several seconds were wasted while McCaigh turned the lead jeep round. 'Lights off,' Farnham yelled, and the order was shouted back down the waiting column.

The lead jeep took off again, quickly gathered speed round a long curve in the narrow track, and almost ran over a group of Germans who had innocently stepped out of the trees to flag it down, presumably in the belief that it was one of theirs. Lynton's Vickers opened up, knocking at least one man to the ground and causing the others to scatter, and as the other jeeps roared by the mounted guns swivelled to rake the surrounding undergrowth.

The track in front of them was now empty, but in a mile or so they would reach the small road down to Fraize, which the enemy would probably have blocked. The next couple of minutes were anxious ones, but the intersection was empty, and Farnham was still breathing a sigh of relief when an armoured car appeared round the first bend in the road below. The jeeps accelerated away up the hill, and it looked as though the Germans had neither seen nor heard them.

That was the good news. The bad news was that the sixth jeep in line, the one containing Rafferty, Pogo and McLaglan, was no longer riding shotgun at the rear of the column. And with the armoured car now sitting astride the intersection below, there was no chance of going back to look for them.

It had happened at the point where the forest track emerged on to the dirt road. As the five jeeps in front of them accelerated away one of the Germans with the troop carrier had opened fire with his rifle, and either great skill or cruel fortune had driven the single bullet straight through the back of Pogo's head, splashing blood and brains across the armoured windscreen and killing him instantly. Bereft of control, the jeep had veered violently right, miraculously finding several gaps in the trees before crashing down a short bank and jolting skywards over a fallen trunk, at which point both Rafferty and McLaglan had been lucky enough to lose their grip on the careering vehicle. No sooner had they taken flight than the ground rose to hit them, and neither of them had heard the jeep's swan song as it crunched head-on into a large beech. Nor had they been conscious of the boots crashing down through the trees towards them, or the hands which had grabbed their own feet and started dragging them back up to the dirt road.

About three miles south of their last contact with the enemy the five jeeps burrowed into the forest once more and set up a defensive laager. The Germans couldn't have enough men to mount more than selective sweeps, and Farnham wanted to stay within reach of his missing men and the Maquis camp. It was possible that the latter had also been attacked, but all the gunfire they'd heard that night had been distressingly close to home, and he was betting that Yves and his men were still there.

A brief radio call confirmed as much – brief because a longer conversation would have given the German D/F operators time to fix their locations. Farnham desperately wanted information from Yves, not least about his missing men, but a visit to the Maquis camp in the hours before dawn, while the woods were no doubt crawling with Germans, seemed far too risky. He told the French radio operator that he would make the journey after dark that evening, and cut the connection.

The next step was to contact Group B and let Phil Hoyland know that the Germans had invaded their camp. A fall-back location for their rendezvous had already been arranged, and the time was now put back seventy-two hours – Farnham wanted to at least investigate the possibility of rescuing his three missing men. Two of Hoyland's men had already been killed in a fire-fight with a German patrol, and Tobin's death had raised the squadron's toll to three. Farnham was damned if he'd let it rise to six.

The day went by slowly, but no sign of the enemy disturbed the men in their forest lair, and soon after dusk Farnham set off alone for the Maquis camp. The usual practice would have been to take at least one companion, but he knew the area so much better than anyone else, and two men made twice as much noise.

The journey took about an hour and a half, and in that time he saw neither hide nor hair of the Germans, who had apparently returned to the low ground. His most dangerous moment came at the approaches to the Maquis camp, where a recruit he had never seen before gave them both a shock and seemed perilously close to pulling the trigger of his British-donated Sten. He wasn't the only one who looked jumpy, and several familiar faces seemed perilously worn by anxiety and lack of sleep.

Even Yves looked more serious than usual, and Farnham soon found out why. After his unit's attack on the prison train two nights earlier the SS in both St Dié and Schirmeck had executed twenty hostages, seized another twenty and taken about eighty people into custody for questioning. It was suspected that one of the latter had been tortured into giving the location of the SAS camp. 'He probably chose yours rather than ours for patriotic reasons,' Yves added with a faint trace of a smile. 'Though for all we know he may have given up both, and the Germans are heading towards us at this very moment.'

That explained the jumpiness. 'What happened to the Jews?' Farnham asked.

Another faint smile. 'The Germans are having more trouble than they expected rounding them up. As of this morning there's still a couple of hundred unaccounted for.'

'Thank God for François,' Farnham said, and explained what had happened.

Yves was obviously pleased. 'But two of your own men were captured last night,' he went on.

'Two? I hoped it was three.'

'Two men were killed, according to the Germans. And the other two are to be executed tomorrow morning. At precisely nine o'clock.'

Farnham's heart sank. 'Where? In St Dié?'

'No. In Fraize. The Germans want to teach the town nearest to your camp a lesson in humility. They also have two of our people whom they picked up without papers. We don't know who they are – probably just a couple of kids who hopped a train into the country to join us.'

Farnham was hardly listening. 'Tell me about the town,' he said.

Yves looked at him. 'There'll be at least a hundred Germans down there,' he said. 'More likely two hundred.'

'I know, it's probably out of the question. But tell me about the town.'

Yves sent for a Maquisard named Charles whom Farnham hadn't met before. He had lived all but the last two months of his life in Fraize, where his father was the postmaster, and at Farnham's instigation he managed to produce a painstakingly detailed map of the small town.

'And all these roads run downhill into Fraize?' Farnham asked him, pointing them out on the map.

'Yes.'

'Which is the steepest?'

'This one,' Charles said without hesitation. 'In winter that is the one we use for our sleds.'

'You have a plan?' Yves asked Farnham.

'That's rather a grand word for it,' the SAS man replied. He explained what it was, and what role a chosen few of the Maquisards could play if they so wished.

Yves smiled and shook his head in wonderment. 'Now I know they are right when they say the English are mad,' he said. 'And yes, some of us will be there.'

'Thank you,' Farnham said, getting to his feet. He hesitated for a moment, then smiled to himself. 'Have you seen Madeleine?' he asked.

'Yes, she is fine. But at the moment it is safer for her to stay in St Dié.'

'Of course,' Farnham agreed, half of him wishing that she was right there beside him at that moment, the other half wishing she was as far from the war as someone could possibly be. In Timbuktu perhaps, or on the moon.

'Until tomorrow morning,' Yves said with a smile.

Farnham nodded, returned the smile and started off on his return journey. By midnight he was back in his own camp, with all but the sentries gathered in a circle around him to hear the information which Yves had passed on.

'Do we know which two they've got?' Lynton asked.

'No,' Farnham admitted. 'But it seems that the third man is definitely dead.' He outlined his plan, thinking as he did so how reckless it sounded. He had no idea how many Germans would be in Fraize, and any advantage they gained from surprise would only last for a short while. It might be a death-trap for all of them. He knew the men would follow him, but he wasn't at all sure he had any right to ask them.

'I don't like people who come visiting at night without an invitation,' someone was saying.

'Aye, it's time we saw the bastards in the daylight,' Hill agreed.

'Let them see how beautiful we all are,' McCaigh said lightly. He supposed it was unkind to the other two, but he was hoping that Rafferty was still alive. He'd grown quite fond of the big oaf over the past few months.

As basements went it wasn't particularly damp, and the single bare light-bulb offered more than enough illumination. Rafferty could make out every strand of the cobwebs which covered the empty wine rack, so he had no trouble making out the bruises and contusions on Pete McLaglan's sleeping face.

Both men had been questioned, but to say they'd been tortured would have been something of an exaggeration. Beaten up perhaps, but not much more than that – the Milice man who'd stubbed out his cigarette on Rafferty's arm had seemed more interested in impressing his Gestapo counterparts than eliciting information. The latter had seemed peculiarly apathetic, for reasons that Rafferty could only guess at. It was possible that the presence of regular French police, SS and Wehrmacht officers had cramped their style, or maybe the realization had finally struck home that retribution would be waiting at the war's end. If so, it had struck only as regards torture – the execution of uniformed prisoners was apparently still considered ultimately pardonable. 'You have one night to make your peace with God,' one of the SS officers had told Rafferty in passable English.

Or to make peace with himself. It was a strange thing, knowing you were going to die. Rafferty's brain found it hard to believe, but the knot of panic in his stomach was a measure of his body's conviction. Just one of millions, he told himself, but that didn't make the prospect any more inviting. He had never believed in God, and there was no fear of hell inside him, so what was he worrying about? It wasn't as if life had been that wonderful lately, and no one would really miss him. It would solve Beth's problem for her, and as for his son . . . well, Dad could be a dead hero. Nothing upsetting in that, nothing awkward.

But there was no sense pretending he wanted to die – he didn't. All his anger with Beth seemed so beside the point. People did what they had to, and sometimes that included breaking someone else's heart. She hadn't wanted to – he knew that. It had just happened, and for the first time he found himself hoping that her new life would work for her. He wanted one of his own, to see the war ended, to build up his car business with Tommy. He wanted – he realized for the first time – to kiss Mary Slater.

But it didn't look likely. He had double-checked all the possibilities of escape and come up empty – their only hope was the others. He wondered if Corrigan and Imrie had come to the same conclusion in San Severino, and had nursed that hope through their last night. If so, it had been in vain. No one had come for them.

And he didn't suppose they'd come for him and McLaglan. With so many Germans about it seemed pretty certain that a rescue force would lose more men than they could possibly rescue, and that didn't seem the sort of bargain a responsible commanding officer would find appealing.

He hoped it would be a firing squad – there was something so degrading about being hanged.

Rafferty felt tears in his ears, and brushed them away angrily. Better to cry now, an inner voice told him, because you won't want to give them the satisfaction tomorrow. Which sounded like something out of Hollywood. In the films the heroes always went to their deaths with such dignity, but then the writers presumably weren't writing from experience.

But I can try, he told himself.

McLaglan stirred, opened an eye and groaned. 'Christ, did I fall asleep?' he said, pushing himself into a sitting position and gingerly feeling his split lip. 'I can't believe it. I've got about ten hours left on earth and I sleep through them. Why didn't you wake me up?'

'I thought you'd be happier asleep.'

McLaglan grimaced. 'I think I was.' He pulled his back up against the wall, and searched through his pockets for a cigarette.

'They took them,' Rafferty told him.

'Christ. You know, I'm hoping there really is a God, just so those bastards roast in hell.'

Eight and a half hours later four of the unit's six jeeps were waiting in the trees about a mile north of Fraize, and Farnham was busy sorting out their order of attack. McCaigh and Lynton would take the lead, with Brian Shearer driving Farnham himself in the second, Eric Lennon and John Downey in the third, Sean Mayles and Brendan Armstrong bringing up the rear. Looking round the faces, he saw seven men in the process of coming to terms with one more throw of the war's dice. Grim or joking, they all looked anxious, as well they might. There were somewhere between eighty and a hundred Germans in the town below, not to mention several hundred innocent locals, any of whom might make the SAS's job that much more difficult by wandering into the line of fire.

It was a quarter to nine. Farnham covered his mouth with the S-phone mike and spoke to Albert Lowe and Jimmy Simpson, who were sitting just inside the edge of a wood about three-quarters of a mile to the south-east, with a view which took in at least two-thirds of the town square below. 'Any developments?' Farnham asked rhetorically. If the German positions had changed Lowe would already have told him.

'None,' came the predictable reply.

'The mortar's ready?'

'Yes, boss.'

This with a faintly reproachful tone. Farnham realized he was as nervous as his men. 'Three minutes,' he confirmed, and turned to point the S-phone's antenna in the opposite direction.

'Ready to go?' he asked Hill and Chadwick, who were waiting with the other two jeeps about half a mile above the town.

'Ready as we'll ever be, boss,' Hill told him.

Farnham smiled and looked at his watch again. Two minutes to go.

In the cobbled square below, Yves watched and waited. There were about three hundred townspeople gathered in the centre of the square, a road's width separating them from the three German troop carriers. The troops were still sitting aboard the two parked on the eastern side, while a machine-gun had been mounted on the empty rear of the one to the south. Not surprisingly, this disposition had made the north-facing crowd somewhat nervous, and people kept turning their heads in search of reassurance, as if they believed the Germans would be unable to open fire while anyone was looking.

The swastika flag which some zealot had raised above the entrance to the small town hall was so large that it hung across the doors like a curtain. A line of ornate lampposts stood in front of the building, and four of these now supported nooses. Ordinary-looking office chairs were waiting underneath them, and beside these stood the four townspeople who'd been given the honour of yanking them away. All four looked pale and distraught, and none of them was making eye contact with those in front of them.

The mood of the crowd was harder to judge. There was a sort of numbed resignation in many of the faces, but Yves could also detect strong undercurrents of anger and, more disturbingly, excitement. Many of the young people seemed more curious than outraged, which seemed no more excusable for being easy to understand.

There was movement behind the flag. Yves took out his pocket watch and checked it, just as the four prisoners were brought out through the doors. The Germans seemed to be running early for once, which didn't bode well. He took a last glance around at the machine-gun, and sought out Henri's beret in the crowd to his left. Where were the SAS?

The captured men were being led across to their chairs, the two English soldiers expressing their defiance, and masking their fear, with an almost jaunty stride. The two French boys looked as scared as they were.

Yves thought he heard a faint whistle, and there was a dull 'whumpf' from somewhere behind him. Like everyone else in the square, he turned to see a cloud of smoke rising above the building behind the machine-gun. There was another 'whumpf', and more smoke. It was at least a quarter of a mile away, beyond the railway station, and Yves found himself wondering if Farnham had made an error of judgement.

But a squad of soldiers – a dozen at least – was already leaving the square to investigate when heads were turned in another direction by the sound of approaching vehicles. These were descending the road which entered the square from the north-east, their guns already firing on some unseen enemy. As the Germans in that corner of the square were being organized to face this new threat Yves gripped the two grenades in his pocket a little more tightly, and tried not to look too obviously at the entrance to his right.

A quarter of a mile away the four jeeps were still gathering speed as they rolled downhill, their engines silent. The road was empty of people, and only a couple of surprised-looking cats and dogs watched the vehicles with their grim-faced foreigners rattling down towards the still-invisible square. The nine men could hear the racket Hill and Chadwick were making with the other two jeeps, and could see the smoke effects which Lowe and Simpson had conjured up beyond the town, but they had no idea how the Germans in the square below were reacting.

The last bend was only fifty yards in front of them, and the drivers all applied a little pressure to their brakes – a dramatic entrance was all very well, but arriving upside down would verge on showing off. In the lead jeep McCaigh swept into the bend and suddenly there was the square in front of him, the troop carriers almost directly ahead, the edge of the French crowd visible to his right. A couple of faces turned his way, then twenty more, and a German officer on foot by the carrier was pointing straight at him, shouting as he fumbled at the holster on his belt. Behind the officer a squad of troops was milling in the roadway, apparently waiting for the rest of their unit to get off the first troop carrier.

As McCaigh aimed the jeep straight at them, Lynton opened up with the twin Vickers, scything down the officer and several of his men. To their right the more quick-witted of the townspeople were already halfway to the ground, and it took only a split second for the example to spread. Up ahead, McCaigh saw the two Germans on the lorry-mounted machine-gun swinging the barrel in their direction, and shouted as much to Lynton, who was still concentrating all his fire on the men around the troop carriers. McCaigh swerved the jeep to the left almost within scratching distance of the carrier, hoping that the machine-gunner would hold fire for fear of killing his own comrades, and was rewarded by a fatal moment of hesitation on the Germans' part.

Two dark objects arced towards the machine-gun position from the centre of the square, one landing beneath the cab, the other right in the truck. The two explosions seemed to ripple together, and as the two men on the lorry's open back were thrown skywards the vehicle's petrol tank went up, shattering every window in the building behind.

The third SAS jeep followed the first, but the second and fourth swung sharply right along the northern side of the square, where Rafferty and McLaglan, hands tied behind their backs, had sunk into a watchful crouch beside the chairs arranged for their executions. The two French boys had followed the example of their intended audience and thrown themselves to the ground.

In front of the town hall a motley crew of uniformed French police and SS officers, leather-coated Milice and Gestapo men was now staring aghast at the jeeps bearing down on them. Farnham's finger tightened on the Browning's trigger, and three men collapsed on the cobbles. Another two were caught in the doorway by a burst from Armstrong in the jeep behind, a leather-clad arm reached out to grab the drooping swastika, and with a tearing noise that seemed to echo round the square the giant flag came billowing down.

Shearer skidded the jeep to a halt in front of Rafferty and McLaglan, and as he leapt out to cut their hands free with his commando knife Farnham swung the Browning in search of new targets. Bullets suddenly pinged off the reinforced-glass screen in front of Shearer's empty seat. The Germans were recovering from their surprise, and both the troop carrier survivors of Lynton's onslaught and the squad which had been on its way to investigate Hill and Chadwick's fake attack were now firing on them. Farnham opened up on the latter just as two grenades landed among them, and felt the jeep rock as Rafferty, Shearer and McLaglan leapt aboard. He looked back to check that Mayles and Armstrong had picked up the two French boys, and saw one of them cut down by a burst from across the square. The other hesitated at the side of the jeep, and Armstrong pulled him aboard roughly.

The two jeeps jerked into motion. In the first Rafferty had seized control of the other twin Vickers and was pouring fire at the German soldiers around the troop carriers. In front of him Farnham was still trying to sweep their escape road clear of the enemy.

By this time the other two jeeps had almost completed their swing round three sides of the square. Yves and Henri had been picked up by McCaigh and Lynton, and this jeep was now offering covering fire as the one behind them slowed to collect the other two Maquisards. As Farnham waved them on a burst of German fire knocked Lynton back in his seat, but McCaigh didn't hesitate, accelerating the jeep away as Henri opened up with the rear Vickers. All four jeeps were now converging on the north-eastern exit to the square, and as the fourth slowed to avoid hitting the third a last fusillade from the German troop carriers blew a small but bloody chunk from the side of Armstrong's head. He slumped back into the arms of the disbelieving French boy as the jeep roared on up the hill.

* * *

The previous summer Yves' Maquis group had searched the higher reaches of the mountains for a fall-back sanctuary – somewhere to go to ground should their camp above Le Chipal ever be betrayed or overrun. They had found a suitable spot in a remote stretch of forest several miles south of the meadow used for supply drops, and it was to this which the SAS unit now retreated.

Yves and the other Maquisards had been dropped off in the forest a couple of miles west of Fraize, intent on returning to their usual home, but Farnham doubted whether they'd be safe there for long. He wasn't at all sure the SAS unit was safe in the back-up camp, four thousand feet up and sheltered by two thousand square miles of forest. Two many people had seen the column of jeeps during its daylight journey, and it only needed one of them to point the Germans in the right direction.

Farnham knew his men were fully aware of the dangers. The adrenalin rush of the Fraize rescue had subsided, but these men had become too professional to allow any slide into complacency, and their resolution would only have been bolstered by the fate which had befallen their two comrades. Lynton and Armstrong were in a bad way, the latter especially so, and both needed proper medical attention.

To get it they would need to be taken west. Around noon that day, with the wind blowing from that direction, Farnham had heard the rumble of big guns in the far distance, and briefly entertained the hope that the Americans would soon be with them. His superiors at Moor Park had swiftly disabused him of this notion. Patton's advance had apparently stalled some forty miles short of the Vosges, and there was no immediate resumption on the cards. Fortunately, it was lack of petrol rather than German resistance which was holding the Americans up, so it seemed unlikely that the SAS unit would have much trouble traversing the forty miles which separated them from the Allied front line.

Farnham contacted Hoyland, and the two men agreed that the two groups should rendezvous and make their break for the west in two nights' time. The delay wouldn't help Armstrong and Lynton, but it might give the Germans time to tire of the search, and there were the other men to consider.

He was re-dressing Lynton's wound late that afternoon when more sounds of distant gunfire filtered through the trees. The vagaries of the wind made such things hard to judge in these mountains, but his best guess put the fire-fight about five miles to the north-west, uncomfortably close to the Maquis camp. The sound was fairly continuous for about twenty minutes, and thereafter became increasingly sporadic, but it didn't subside completely until some time after darkness had fallen. Attempts to reach the Maquis camp on the radio met with no response.

Farnham slept badly that night, waking at dawn with a dry taste in his mouth and a sinking feeling in his heart. Hill, who had just come off guard duty, reported that a huge cloud of smoke was smudging the north-western sky, and Farnham went to see it for himself. There was no doubting the direction this time, and he found himself fearing the worst.

The morning brought no good news. The radio offered only silence, and Armstrong died soon after ten o'clock. Lynton, though, looked like he would pull through.

And then, in mid-afternoon, Yves, Henri and another twenty or so Maquisards walked into the camp. Several were wounded, and those that weren't seemed more than simply exhausted. There was hopelessness in their eyes, even despair.

'They attacked our camp,' Yves told Farnham. 'And they burned Le Chipal – the whole village.' He looked at Farnham, his eyes full of pity. 'She is dead, my friend. I am sorry.'

Farnham closed his eyes and felt a sudden emptying, as if someone was pouring away the contents of his soul.

Yves put both hands on the Englishman's shoulders and gently enfolded him in an embrace. He had decided during the long walk through the forest that he wouldn't tell Farnham how Madeleine had died. Sometimes the truth was worse than one's direst imaginings.

6

McCaigh put the binoculars down on the window-sill, rubbed his eyes and looked at his watch. It was three in the afternoon on 9 May, which meant the war had been over for fifteen hours, at least insofar as north-western Europe was concerned. The Russians were still fighting in Prague, and stubborn bands of Germans were still holding out, for reasons best known to themselves, in scattered enclaves across the continent, but the Americans' proverbial fat lady was busting a gut to sing. It was over.

Looking out across the north German port city of Lübeck, McCaigh reckoned that peace could hardly have come a moment too soon. Driving into the city a week earlier, the men of the 11th Armoured Division had found ample evidence of previous visits by the RAF and USAF – a third of the buildings levelled and a harbour littered with half-submerged ships. Now, staring out from the third-floor window of a relatively unscathed block of flats, McCaigh thought the German city's skyline looked like a row of broken teeth.

In the street below people were moving, but mostly with that listlessness which the SAS men had come to identify with a defeated nation. This near-universal torpor was doubtless part and parcel of the hangover which followed defeat, but it also had a simple physical cause – the people of Lübeck were hungry. And as more and more boats inched into the crowded harbour, packed with people in flight from those areas to the east which were now under Russian control, the food situation continued to deteriorate and the hordes of hungry children who dogged the steps of the occupiers seemed to proliferate.

It was easy to feel pity for the children, but the adults were a different matter. A couple of weeks earlier McCaigh and Rafferty had been part of a unit which entered the concentration camp at Neuengamme, and the sight which had greeted their eyes would be with them to their dying day. Lines of bodies stretching away into the distance, laid out like a trophy collection; bodies of men and women and children who had simply been allowed to wither away. The intention had no doubt been to bury them, and some had indeed been tipped into large open pits, but either time or energy had run short, and those responsible had headed for the nearest horizon, pausing only to burn or bury their uniforms.

McCaigh sighed at the memory. Neuengamme, where he'd seen the evil which justified his war. Neuengamme, where he'd met Rachel.

'It looks like him,' Rafferty said, passing him the binoculars.

McCaigh trained them on the man walking past on the opposite pavement. His jacket collar was turned up, a workman's cap pulled down over his forehead, but what McCaigh could see of the face was consistent with their photograph of Kuntz. He certainly looked furtive enough, but then who didn't.

The man stopped by the front door of one of the old houses, and paused to glance up and down down the street before turning a key and disappearing inside.

'It's number thirty-three,' McCaigh murmured. Their informant had known the street, but had been unable to remember the number.

Rafferty was on the radio, telling the two MPs who were stationed at the other end of the street to cover the alley which ran behind the houses opposite. Once he'd signed off, the two SAS men made their way down the stairs, running the now-familiar gauntlet of stares – resentful on the part of the adults, hopeful on the part of the children. The street outside was almost empty, and they strode across it, feeling the chill of the wind whipping in from the Baltic as they took the Webleys from their holsters. Rafferty banged on the door with his fist.

There was no answer, and no sound from inside. He banged again, and this time they could hear someone running downstairs. Another door slammed, there was a shout from somewhere at the back, and a few moments later an unsmiling MP opened the door for them.

Rafferty and McCaigh walked in. The German had been taken into the back room and was now sitting on the only piece of furniture, a badly worn sofa. Rafferty removed the man's cap. 'Wolfgang Kuntz, I presume,' he said.

The German said nothing.

'Look after him, lads,' Rafferty told the MPs. 'We're going to take a look around.'

He and McCaigh went through the house, starting at the bottom and working their way up. The rooms were virtually empty – in some there was nothing more than a frayed carpet and a few bare nails in the walls – and their search proved as simple as it was fruitless. There were no valuable paintings here.

The two men walked slowly back down the stairs, wondering if their informant had made up the whole story. According to him, Kuntz had seven paintings in his possession, all of which had previously been on display in the Berlin home of a prominent SS general. The latter, who had stolen the paintings from an unknown European gallery, had since been killed, but the steps he had taken to get the paintings out of the country had supposedly involved, in one capacity or another, the man on the sofa downstairs.

Kuntz was picking at the few days' growth of beard which clung to his chin, and looking none too happy.

'Where are they?' Rafferty asked him in German.

The man grimaced, as if the news that he shared a language with his persecutors was decidedly unwelcome. Which somehow made the endless language lessons they'd suffered since the return from France worthwhile, McCaigh thought.

'Where are what?' Kuntz asked hopefully.

Rafferty looked at the papers which the MPs had removed from the man's pocket. 'You are from Stettin,' he said. 'Would you like to be sent home?'

Kuntz looked at him. 'If I tell you where they are, will you let me stay here?'

'I expect that can be arranged.'

The two SAS men's German wasn't that good, so it took about fifteen minutes to extract the full story. Kuntz had thought himself part of a brave plot to foil the Russians and save the seven paintings for Western civilization, but his partners had blackmailed him into accepting a different plan. The paintings were to be smuggled across the Baltic into Sweden, where they would be hidden until such time as the postwar dust settled, and private buyers could be found. At this moment they were on board a boat in Travemünde harbour, about ten miles to the north-east.

'How many people are there on this boat?' Rafferty asked.

'Two.'

'And why are they still there?' McCaigh asked.

The German just looked at him.

'What are they waiting for?' Rafferty asked.

Kuntz smiled for the first time. 'No one is allowed to leave. And even if they were, there is no fuel for the engines.'

Rafferty looked at McCaigh. 'It shouldn't take more than the four of us,' he said, and turned back to Kuntz. 'OK, up you get. Point out the boat for us and we'll see you get your papers.'

The German looked less than eager for the trip. 'They have guns,' he said.

'So do we,' McCaigh assured him.

The SAS men recovered their jeep from behind the flats on the other side of the street, rendezvoused with the MPs in theirs, and drove out of the city down mostly empty streets. Kuntz, sitting in the front next to McCaigh, held the threadbare jacket tight across his chest to keep out the wind. It was much too small for him, Rafferty thought – it had probably been all that was available when the time came to throw away his uniform.

They left the suburbs behind, arrowing across the flat farm country which lay north of the Trave estuary. There was an air of peace about the people working in the fields, but in the broad river behind them a small cargo boat was limping slowly upstream, its decks packed solid with refugees from the east. Too many sad stories, McCaigh thought, as he swerved the jeep to avoid a mangy-looking ginger cat.

It took them about twenty minutes to reach the outskirts of the village, where they abandoned the jeeps, and another five to reach the harbour office on foot. It was empty. Someone had obviously decided the fuel drought was enough to keep the boats in port, because there was no sign of a police or military presence.

'I suppose Sweden's too far to row,' McCaigh murmured.

There were about forty boats in the harbour, and from the window of the office Kuntz pointed out a sad-looking motor launch tied to one of the wooden jetties. A thin plume of smoke was issuing from a pipe on the roof.

'I bet they're cosy,' McCaigh said.

'Let's hope they're not burning the paintings,' Rafferty replied.

Neither man felt like waiting several hours for darkness to cloak their approach, and neither felt any enthusiasm for a dip in the Baltic, so they simply ambled out into the late-afternoon sunshine and casually strolled down the jetty in question, looking for all the world as if the only thing on their minds was to contemplate the beauty of sea and sky.

They did step softly, though, and there was no twitch of the curtains on the suspect launch. Rafferty stepped across the gap, gently rocking the boat as he did so, but there was still no sign of activity on board. McCaigh also stepped across, and, Webley in hand, Rafferty slipped down the steps and eased open the door to the cabin quarters. A loud snore emerged from within.

Fifteen minutes later the two Germans were being escorted away by the MPs, and McCaigh had returned with their jeep to load up the paintings. According to the scrawled writing on the newspaper-swathed rectangles, there were two by Klee, two by Nolde, and one each by Rouault, Heckel and Kirchner. Catching the rueful expression on Kuntz's face, McCaigh felt obliged to congratulate the German on saving them for the West.

While Rafferty and McCaigh were driving back into Lübeck with several hundred thousand pounds' worth of art in the back of their jeep, Farnham was standing in a meadow some four hundred miles to the south-west, staring at a grassy mound and a newly erected plaque. 'We thought it would be better to bury your men here with ours, and with those who died in the village,' Yves was telling him.

'You were right,' Farnham said. If any of Ian Tobin's or Pogo Young's loved ones ever came to this meadow above Le Chipal they would be pleased with what they found.

'I'll leave you to your thoughts,' Yves said awkwardly. 'I'll wait for you in the car.'

Farnham watched the Frenchman walk away down the hill, and turned his eyes upward to the forests which had once hidden their respective camps. Only eight months had passed since the Germans had overrun them, eight months since the fifty-six bodies in the ground behind him had breathed their last. The war had brought him and Madeleine together; the war had pulled them apart. Like God, Farnham thought. Like a playful, heartless God.

There were no thoughts to think, only the abiding emptiness. He took one last look at the grassy mound and followed Yves back down the hill to the waiting Renault. The Frenchman was sitting on the running board, smoking a cigarette, and for a moment Farnham was reminded of all those evenings they had spent talking together in the dark forest. There were few times he had enjoyed more.

Yves got to his feet and stubbed out the cigarette with his foot. 'I don't suppose there's any news of Ziegler,' he said once they were both in the car.

'Not yet,' Farnham said. There had been no reported sighting of the St Dié Gestapo chief since the Germans' eviction from France, and Farnham was beginning to fear that the man had somehow slipped through the Allied net. 'If someone finds him, I'll let you know,' he promised.

'But what if no one tells you?' Yves asked with his usual directness.

'I keep checking the lists,' Farnham told him.

They drove north along the road which the Maquis had followed on the night of the great uniform robbery in Ste Marguerite. It looked different in the daylight, but then so did everything else. He was used to living by night here, to looking down from the safety of the forest at the vulnerability of the open countryside, and here he was, blithely driving down an open road, looking up at forests which seemed remote and impenetrable. Meeting Yves at his house in St Dié had been another such experience – he had never seen the Maquis leader under a roof before.

'How are things in Germany?' Yves asked.

'Pretty dire for the Germans in our half, and much worse than that in the Russian half. Life in the cities is more difficult – they're mostly in ruins and food's hard to come by. Of course, not a single German admits to ever liking the Nazis, let alone being one.'

Yves snorted. 'It's like that here – now that it's over it seems everyone but Pétain was in the Resistance. It's amazing the war lasted so long.'

Farnham smiled.

'But they are going to try these bastards, aren't they? None of this "now it's over let's all shake hands and go home" nonsense.'

'Looks like it. Churchill was apparently in favour of shooting all the bastards they could catch in the first six weeks and then calling it a day – the British legal establishment didn't like the idea of making up retrospective laws – but the Russians refused to go along. The story is that Stalin told Churchill that in Russia they never shoot anyone without a trial.'

Yves laughed. 'And the Americans?'

'Most of them are only interested in going home.'

'What are you going to do when you finally go home?' Yves asked.

'I don't know,' Farnham said lightly, but his companion must have heard something else in his voice.

'You must go on,' Yves said quietly.

Farnham felt his muscles tense, and he wanted to yell at the man in the seat next to him: 'What fucking business is it of yours? How the fuck would you know what I ought to do with my life?' But he didn't. He just closed his eyes for a moment, and willed the rage in his body to die down. 'I know,' he said eventually.

'Sometimes it takes a long time,' Yves said.

'How about you?' Farnham countered. 'What are you doing?'

'Ah, I'm back at work already. My school was bombed by your people or the Americans – on a Sunday, I'm glad to say – but the rebuilding has already been completed. I have been regaling students with the sins of Louis XIV for several weeks now.'

They were turning left at the junction where he had waited for the bus to Schirmeck, and for a moment he could see her looking up at him from her seat by the window, smell the lily of the valley as he sat down beside her. As they accelerated down the road towards St Dié a train passed by in the opposite direction on the nearby railway line. 'How many of the Jews escaped?' he asked.

'From the train you attacked? A hundred and thirty-seven. About four hundred and fifty were recaptured – only the Germans know the exact figure – and they were all gassed in Schirmeck. But the hundred and thirty-seven were sheltered right through the winter in about twenty different villages.' He sighed. 'I think I'm beyond being surprised by how badly

227

people can treat each other, but I can still be shocked by how well they can behave. Twenty villages,' he repeated, 'and not a word to the Germans from any of them.' He smiled suddenly. 'And François is going to marry one of the girls from the train,' he added.

They drove through Ste Marguerite and into St Dié. Farnham's jeep was still standing outside Yves' house, but there were now four young boys sitting in it, all armed with make-believe weapons. As Yves shooed them away, Farnham could see the hero-worship in their eyes, and he doubted whether the Maquis leader would ever have much trouble enforcing discipline in his classroom.

'Are you sure you won't stay the night?' Yves asked him.

'Thanks, but no. I'm supposed to be back first thing on Friday, and I've no idea how easy it's going to be to get a flight from Luxemburg.'

'I'd have thought Strasbourg would be a better bet.'

Farnham shrugged. 'I have to get the jeep back to the people I borrowed it from,' he explained, not bothering to add that he'd ended up in Luxemburg in the first place because he hadn't wanted to drive the road from Strasbourg to St Dié, the road of their bus journey together.

But Yves wasn't stupid. 'If Ziegler is caught I want to know,' he said.

'You will,' Farnham told him, and the two men embraced. 'I'll be back,' he said, climbing aboard the jeep. 'And say hello to the others for me. Especially François.'

In the temporary Field Security HQ at Lüneburg, some forty-five miles south of Lübeck, Sergeant Stuart Willoughby rose stiffly from his chair and carried his cup of tea across to the single office window. The darkening sky above the flat flood plain of the Elbe perfectly mirrored his mood. He had interviewed another thirty men since breakfast, listened to another thirty stories of misfortune and cruelty, and felt emotionally drained by the cumulative wretchedness of it all.

He walked back to the table for the second biscuit, broke it neatly in two, and popped one half in his mouth. He had been interrogating people for over eighteen months, ever since his transfer to Port Security late in 1943. There had been four months in Scotland questioning arrivals on neutral boats, a short period of waiting for the Allied advance in France to gather speed, and then another four months in Ostend doing similar work. Early in 1945 he had been transferred to Field Security, whose main brief was to interview captured German security policemen and local Nazi politicians. He had ended up here in Lüneburg, interrogating the flotsam of the war, people found in camps, people picked up on city streets or simply wandering the countryside, people who had no means of identifying themselves, who could be victims or victimizers in disguise.

Corporal Bunn stuck his head round the door. 'Ready for more?' he asked with a grin.

'How many more are there?'

'Only seven.'

Willoughby thought about asking them all to come back tomorrow, or maybe next year, but he didn't. 'Send the next one in,' he said, and bit down on the other half of his biscuit. It tasted stale, but then he doubted whether any of the men he was questioning had seen anything as exotic as a digestive for quite a while.

Both the next two interviewees claimed to be Slovaks, and their partial grip on the German language was either wonderfully judged or that of genuine foreigners. They claimed they had been brought from Bratislava in 1942 to work in a Hamburg munitions factory, and that during one of the huge night raids they had escaped into the countryside, where a German farmer had fed them in exchange for working his fields. He had been killed by some British soldiers – they didn't know why – and now they wanted to return home.

Willoughby questioned the two men separately, and judged that their story was true. It wasn't so much the tallying of the facts each told him – they'd had plenty of time to rehearse – as the look of utter weariness which he saw in their eyes. It was always possible that they had killed the German farmer themselves, but if so the whys and wherefores would be impossible to establish. He bestowed official approval on the identities they had claimed, and handed over the special ration cards which went with such approval.

The next man had been found wandering near the Esterwegen concentration camp, which he claimed had been his home for the past three years. A tall German with dark hair, blue eyes and prominent cheek-bones, he said that his name was Josef Balck, and that he had been imprisoned when someone overheard him call the Nazi regime unchristian.

Willoughby didn't believe him – the man didn't look like he'd been in a concentration camp for three weeks, let alone three years. But proving as much was something else again. He listened to Balck's story, asking the occasional question, but there were no obvious inconsistencies, just a growing conviction on Willoughby's part that he was listening to a well-concocted piece of fiction.

It was fully dark outside now, and he couldn't face an hour and more of futile verbal sparring. Just take one shot, he told himself recklessly, and if it misses then the bastard gets away scot-free. He certainly wouldn't be the first, and it seemed extremely unlikely that he'd be the last.

'That's a very well thought-out story,' he said suddenly, stopping Balck in mid-flow. 'But I'm afraid I know who you really are.'

The German's face turned suddenly white, and Willoughby felt a surge of elation. 'All right,' Balck said. 'But I was only the administrator – I didn't decide policy.'

Willoughby risked a guess. 'But you held the rank of commandant.'

'Yes,' Balck admitted reluctantly, and for a long time neither man spoke. Then the German leaned forward in his chair. 'I will give you names, tell you where others are hiding, if you promise not to hand me over to the Russians.'

'I think I can promise that,' Willoughby said. He always handed prisoners over to the British Army HQ, and what they did with them was none of his business. 'So give me some names,' he said calmly, pen poised above a clean sheet of paper.

McCaigh woke up feeling happy. Today was Friday and tomorrow he would be driving down to Neuengamme to see Rachel. He supposed it would have been better if she could come north to see him – a concentration camp, even a liberated one, wasn't the most romantic of venues – but the new administrators couldn't spare her, even for a couple of days. McCaigh had found out why in his first hour there – as far as the emaciated men and women who crowded the huts were concerned she was the camp's resident angel.

He remembered his first sight of her in the makeshift nurse's uniform, the beautiful eyes burning in her haggard face. He even remembered the first words she'd ever spoken to him – 'Please, you're in my way.'

He smiled at the memory and levered himself off the narrow bed. Rafferty was singing in the shower, which was invariably a sign that hot water was available. Life was good.

Ablutions complete, the two SAS men made their way to the canteen, where things took a predictable turn for the worse. Even knowing that most of Lübeck's population was half-starved couldn't make the food taste any better, and the tea had obviously been stewing for at least a week. Rafferty sipped glumly at the turgid brew, and wondered what on earth his partner had to smile about. 'You're looking cheerful,' he said accusingly.

'I'm in love,' McCaigh told him.

'So am I, but it hasn't turned me into a simpering idiot.'

'Oh, I don't know.'

Rafferty laughed. 'Come on, we're late. Just for a change.'

They threaded their way through the chaotic base area to the hut which housed the headquarters of 54 Field Security, the unit to which they were seconded. The previous day's blue sky had disappeared overnight, and now an almost featureless grey blanket of cloud hung over the city.

'Late as usual,' Sergeant Cunliffe moaned as McCaigh closed the door behind them.

'We thought we deserved a lie-in after yesterday's triumph,' the Londoner said.

'Triumph!' Cunliffe snorted. 'Have you seen those paintings?' he asked as he rummaged round the crowded table in front of him. 'My daughter could do better than that, and she's only seven!' Several clipped-together pieces of paper emerged in a beefy hand. 'Here you are – new stuff from Lüneburg. Some Kraut commandant has been baring his soul.' He handed over the list. 'Take your pick – anyone but Ziegler.'

Rafferty and McCaigh exchanged surprised glances.

'Ziegler?' Rafferty asked.

'Hans-Magnus himself,' McCaigh said, looking up from the neatly typed list. 'He seems to be in Schwerin.'

'Which isn't our territory,' Cunliffe told him.

'Whose is it?'

Cunliffe shrugged. 'They're still arguing about it as far as I know. The Russians and the Americans are both on the spot, and after what happened in Wismar I expect there's a bit of tension in the air.' The previous Thursday a drunken dispute over a couple of *Fräulein* had left several contending Russian and British soldiers dead in the small Baltic town. 'Why, what's your interest?' Cunliffe asked the two of them. 'Have you run across this Ziegler before?'

'In France,' Rafferty said.

'When's the boss get back?' McCaigh asked him.

'Tonight, I suppose.'

'So who's the lucky fugitive going to be?' Cunliffe asked, bringing them back to the day at hand.

'Oh, whoever's top of the list.'

'That'll be Herr Berndt Hassinger. Late of the Hamburg Gestapo, currently passing himself off as Corporal Dietrich Brunner in the POW camp at Grömitz.'

'We'll fetch him for you,' McCaigh said.

'Take a couple of MPs.'

'We won't need them . . .'

'And they clutter up the jeep . . .'

'Take them.'

Fifteen minutes later their jeep was speeding out of Lübeck on the north road, the two MPs their usual silent selves in the seats behind. As McCaigh drove, Rafferty stared out at the flat and peaceful countryside, mulling over the matter of Ziegler's reappearance.

So much had happened since those incredible days in France, since he himself had been grabbed from under a waiting noose. The hair-raising night ride through the German lines had been followed by a crazy week with the Americans, long months in England preparing for the invasion of Germany, the kiss he had promised himself with Mary. And then the invasion itself, with the SAS jeeps roaming ahead of the Allied armies, graciously taking the surrender of units ten times as large as their own. Even McCaigh had found someone to fall in love with, in a concentration camp of all places. Things just kept getting better, and then one day the war had finally ended, and they were still alive and whole.

But for Farnham – the man who had saved him from the noose – it had not been like that. Since the death of the woman in France he had been like someone going through the motions of life, not someone truly living. Perhaps the fact that her murderer had resurfaced would help. Once the bastard had an appointment with the hangman maybe Farnham would feel able to put a line under the past and start living again.

Rafferty wasn't optimistic, but there was no harm in hoping. Losing Beth had seemed like the end of the world, and now here he was expecting to marry Mary before the year was out.

It took them an hour to reach Grömitz. The POW camp had been built by the sea, and the Allied prisoners who had previously been incarcerated there would have felt the full force of the winter winds which swept across the Baltic. Today, though, there was hardly a breeze, and the steel-coloured sea was as flat as a pond under the blank grey sky.

The twenty thousand Germans in the camp were held prisoner more by self-interest than guns. There were no guards to be seen, but there was a regular delivery of food and other

essential supplies. Rafferty and McCaigh introduced themselves to the Wehrmacht reception committee, explained the
reason for their visit, and were immediately escorted to the
barrack where Brunner-Hassinger had his bunk. The man's
denials were so lacking in conviction that even his barrack
mates quickly disavowed him, and the two SAS men marched
him off to the jeep, where the two MPs still seemed to be
scouring the horizon for non-existent guards.

Farnham arrived back in the city early that afternoon. He
had shared a dawn flight from Luxemburg to Osnabrück
with several tons of food, and thereafter hitched lifts to
Bremen, Hamburg and finally Lübeck. Feeling exhausted, he
laid himself out on the bumpy barrack bed with sleep in
mind, but his brain refused to turn itself off, and after about
fifteen minutes he sat down at the wooden table and wrote
to the parents of Tobin and Young. Their sons shared a
resting-place of honour, he told them, and if any family
members wished to visit the grave they could write to Yves
Langevin, who would be happy to show them where it was.

This chore done, Farnham thought about going in search
of a drink, something he'd been doing rather a lot in recent
days. It was too early, he told himself, and he sat down again
to write another letter, this one to his sister. But the words
wouldn't come, and he found himself dreading his imminent
leave in London. The last one had been awful – she had been
so happy, so full of life, and try as he had, he couldn't seem
to respond to her in the way he always had.

She was part of the new world, and all he wanted was the
old one back.

And nothing had changed since then. He wouldn't go, he
decided. He would tell her there was too much work to do.

Work, he thought. It was still only five o'clock – he'd go and check up on what had been happening over the past few days.

He walked over to the Field Security hut, where Sergeant Cunliffe was busy typing. Rafferty and McCaigh had apparently brought a wanted Gestapo chief back from Grömitz that morning, and were now looking for an SS Hauptsturmführer in Bad Segeberg. Lynton and McLaglan had gone to arrest a concentration camp doctor in Hamburg.

Farnham glanced idly down the new list from Lüneburg and the name Hans-Magnus Ziegler seemed to leap off the page. He stared at it for several seconds, just to make sure his brain wasn't playing tricks on him. 'So no one's gone after Ziegler?' he asked, managing with a conscious effort to keep his voice steady.

'McCaigh said you lot had run into him in France. But no, he's outside our jurisdiction. Either the Americans or the Russians will be getting the pleasure of the bastard's company.'

'Right,' Farnham said, memorizing the address which went with the name. 'OK, I'll see you in the morning,' he told Cunliffe.

Once outside the door he stood still for a few moments, staring blankly into the distance. Schwerin was only about thirty miles to the east, and if the Americans and Russians were still disputing control of the town then the situation on the ground was probably confused.

He walked across to the garage, signed out his usual jeep and drove it slowly out of the base. A couple of hundred yards down the road he stopped and sat there, oblivious to the curious stares of passers-by. He told himself that what he was about to do could land him in a court martial, but the threat didn't seem to have any bite to it. Justice for Ziegler's victims was more important, justice for her. After all, if he didn't go after Ziegler, then the chances were that no one would. The Russians would have no interest in trying anyone for crimes committed in France, and the Americans – to Farnham's utter disgust – were too busy pulling Nazis aboard their anti-communist bandwagon to punish them. The thought of Ziegler ending up as part of the Western Allies' intelligence apparatus was too sickening for words.

But he knew he mustn't kid himself. He wouldn't be doing this for God or morality. King or country. This was personal. This was for her, and for himself.

He exhaled noisily, turned the ignition back on and accelerated away down the street. To the west the clouds seemed to be breaking, but to the east they remained an impenetrable mass, hanging over the flat landscape like a heavy ceiling, and for a moment Farnham imagined himself trapped between heaven and earth, like a rat in a generous maze.

Rafferty and McCaigh dropped off the MPs and Hauptsturmführer at the Lübeck detention centre and drove back to their base. In the Field Security office Cunliffe was just packing up for the day.

'Your boss is back,' he told the two SAS men.

'Did he see the new list?' Rafferty asked.

'He took a gander at it.'

'And how did he take it?' McCaigh asked.

Cunliffe shrugged. 'He didn't seem that bothered.'

Rafferty and McCaigh shared a knowing look.

'You think he's gone after the bastard?' Cunliffe asked disbelievingly.

'Off the record,' Rafferty said, 'I wouldn't be surprised.' He turned to McCaigh. 'Let's see if he's taken a jeep out.'

'Don't forget Schwerin's off limits,' Cunliffe muttered as they disappeared through the door.

At a crossroads ten miles to the east Farnham sat in the stationary jeep and studied the map. It was still only about six o'clock but the thick clouds overhead cast such a pall of gloom over the north German plain that it was difficult to read. There seemed to be several ways of approaching Schwerin, and he tried putting himself in the position of the local American commander – perhaps a roadblock here, perhaps a roadblock there. Of course, the Yanks would be more worried about the Russians to the east of the town, but he expected that the main road to the west would be watched. He folded up the map, set the jeep in motion and took the small road to the left, thinking that it was somewhat ironic to be using avoidance skills learned fighting the Germans against his supposed allies.

For most of the next hour he zig-zagged his way eastwards across the plain. Twice dead ends forced him to double back, and he was beginning to wonder whether he had misread the map when the flat expanse of the Schwerinsee suddenly loomed into view at the end of a poplar-lined lane. It looked like a wide river, but he knew from the map that the lake stretched for about fifteen miles from north to south, with a width ranging from one to three miles. The medium-sized town of Schwerin was about six miles south of his current position on the western shore.

He drove in that direction, down a road which sometimes bordered the lake, sometimes veered inland around large houses and their lakeside grounds. There were a few walkers on the road but no other traffic, and none of the windows seemed lit against the early-evening gloom. Two houses in a row were in ruins, and then he was entering what remained of the town's industrial outskirts, with empty shells of factories rising on both sides of the cratered road.

He was almost past the old man when he saw him, sitting on a broken wall with an unlit pipe in his mouth. Farnham pulled the jeep to a halt, leapt out and walked back. A scrawny-looking dog at the man's feet growled but didn't move, and the man eyed his uniform without much interest.

'I'm looking for a house,' Farnham said. 'It's called the Bärslager.'

The man laughed, displaying a near-toothless mouth. 'Talk about idiots,' he said. 'Hitler called his homes after animals, so they had to too. Bärslager,' he repeated, almost spitting out the word, 'we haven't seen a bear in these parts for about five hundred years.'

'Do you know where it is?'

'Of course. It's where the idiots used to gather for their parties. It used to belong to a Jew named Feinstein, but he got out in '38, and they just moved in. No one lives there now.'

'But where is it?' Farnham asked patiently.

The old man pointed up the road Farnham had just come down. 'It's the first house on the lake after the big bend in the road.' He cackled. 'They used to have a big flag outside – you'll probably find it somewhere in the bushes.'

Farnham thanked him, reversed the jeep and headed north. Minutes later he drove past the big house, and noticed with a thrill that a faint light was now visible in one of the downstairs windows. After about a quarter of a mile he pulled the jeep off into the grass, checked the ammunition in his Webley, and clambered up on to the six-foot wall which bordered the road. There was an orchard on the other side, and beyond that the shore of the Schwerinsee. He dropped lightly to the ground, squelching a rotten apple with his right boot, and began walking towards the water.

The roadblock had been visible a mile away, but Rafferty and McCaigh knew they didn't have time to fuck around on back roads. 'Any ideas?' Rafferty asked as he stuffed the Sten guns under his seat.

'I'll think of something,' McCaigh said confidently.

One figure detached himself from the group by the side of the road, and walked over to meet them, arm upraised. He was wearing sergeant's stripes. 'And where might a couple of Limeys be heading on such a beautiful evening?' he asked.

'We're going to a party in Schwerin,' McCaigh told him. 'One of your boys invited us. Lots of *Fräulein*, we were told.'

The sergeant looked at him suspiciously.

'His name was Max,' McCaigh insisted, throwing in the first name that came into his head. 'He's in supply.'

'These days, who isn't?' the sergeant said cynically.

McCaigh grinned at him. 'Give us a break, mate, it's been a long war.'

The sergeant shook his head in sympathy. 'Just don't shoot any Russians,' he said. 'I want to be home for the summer.'

'We'll try,' McCaigh promised him.

Ten minutes later they were entering the town. There was plenty of bomb damage in the outskirts but most of the town centre, including the medieval cathedral, was still standing. Small groups of Americans and Russians were both roaming the streets, presumably in search of wine, women and song.

'So how the fuck do we find this place?' McCaigh asked, flashing a victory sign at a couple of Americans who had obviously found some wine.

'When you want to know the way, ask a policeman,' Rafferty quoted. 'And we've just passed a police station.'

'It's the time, not the way,' McCaigh argued. 'And you've got to be joking.'

'Have you got a better idea?'

'No,' McCaigh admitted. He U-turned the jeep and pulled up outside the empty-looking German cop shop.

'You'd better stay with the jeep,' Rafferty told him. 'I don't fancy walking back to Lübeck.'

He was gone about ten minutes, emerging just as a group of friendly Red Army soldiers turned up to admire the jeep. So friendly, in fact, that they wanted to take a ride in it with the two Englishmen. One was already trying to clamber into the back seat when McCaigh took off, hurling him out on to the cobbled street. The two SAS men crouched low in their seats, half expecting bullets to come their way, but only laughter was audible in the street behind them.

'Did you get it?' McCaigh asked.

'Of course,' Rafferty told him.

It began to rain as Farnham worked his way along the shoreline, a persistent drizzle-like rain which swirled in the breeze above the placid surface of the lake. The sky above now seemed almost black, and he could feel the tension in the air. It occurred to him for the first time that he had no idea what he intended to do.

Take the man in, he supposed. In the absence of any help he could have done with some handcuffs, but he'd manage somehow. He could always just knock the bastard out and throw him into the back seat.

About a hundred yards ahead he could see a wooden jetty jutting out into the lake. A small motor boat and several wooden rowing boats were tied up beside it – fishing for the Party faithful, he supposed.

He walked towards them, keeping an eye on the house, which could now be seen to his right through a thin curtain of bushes and trees. The rain was coming down a little heavier now, further dimming the premature dusk.

McCaigh and Rafferty found no trace of Farnham's jeep in the road outside, which meant one of three things – he hadn't yet arrived, he wasn't coming at all or he had hidden it somewhere. The first possibility suggested a wait in the rain, the second that they turn round and go home, the third that they take a closer look.

'Now that we've come all this way . . .' Rafferty said with a shrug.

They cautiously approached the front of the house, Sten guns at the ready. There was some sort of light in the large room to the left, and Rafferty risked a swift glance round the edge of a window. A candle was burning on the mantelpiece, a woman sitting in a large chair, two young girls playing on the floor.

Was it possible that a monster like Ziegler had a family? Or had they come to the wrong house?

He took another look, ducking back just as someone entered the room. But not quickly enough. A boy's voice shouted out something in German, a door slammed, a female chorus of alarm erupted.

Farnham was about halfway across the untended gardens which lay between lake and house when he heard the door slam. Stopping to peer through the curtain of rain, he could just make out the dark shadow of a male figure hurrying down the path which led to the jetty. The boat was not just a relic, he suddenly realized. It was Ziegler's escape hatch, his ticket to the other side of the lake. And with the Russians in control, the other side of the lake might just as well be the other side of the world.

He moved to cut the German off, a sense of triumph welling up in his throat. Twice Ziegler looked back towards the house, but the two men were only about twenty yards apart when he caught sight of Farnham. 'Halt,' the SAS man yelled, noticing the gun in the German's hand for the first time.

Ziegler seemed to hesitate, the gun hanging loose in his right hand, and for a moment Farnham thought he was going to surrender. But the German had apparently made a realistic assessment of his life expectancy in Allied captivity, for he suddenly accelerated down the path, firing off a shot as he did so.

Farnham instinctively ducked, and his foot slipped in the wet grass, sending him sprawling. He scrambled back to his feet and went after Ziegler. In the distance another door slammed.

On the jetty the German was desperately working at the knotted mooring rope. As Farnham walked calmly towards him he looked up, desperation in his eyes, and wildly opened fire with his revolver. The SAS man braced his legs, raised the Webley into the firing position with both hands and pulled the trigger. Ziegler spun with the impact, and collapsed with a dull thud on to his knees, the gun still in his hand. There was probably no need for a second bullet, but Farnham fired one anyway, a surge of terrible satisfaction blazing in his mind. The body collapsed into a foetal crouch on the edge of the jetty, and then slowly slid off, entering the water below with a dull, plopping sound.

On the path he could hear running feet.

'Boss,' a familiar voice yelled.

Farnham was smiling to himself when the first bullet hit him. Once, twice, he felt the agony of something ripping through his chest, and a cloud of pain seemed to expand inside him, red to purple, purple to black.

Rafferty and McCaigh opened up with the Stens, raking the bushes where the muzzle flashes had come from. There was no returning fire, and they found the boy lying face down, half his head blown away. He couldn't have been more than twelve.

There were footsteps behind them, and a woman walked into view, rain streaming down her face. She said nothing, just bent down and cradled her son's bloody head in her hands.

Rafferty picked up the boy's gun and walked back down the path to where Farnham was lying, his eyes closed, his lips slightly curled in a smile of satisfaction. McCaigh walked up to stand beside him, and in the dim light his face was the one his father had described.